A GIRL WITH A KNIFE

HEARTS AND SAILS, BOOK 1

ALINA RUBIN

Alina Rubin
Copyright © 2022

All rights reserved.
Printed in the United States. No part of this book may be used or reproduced
in any manner whatsoever without written permission from the author. Brief
passages may be quoted for the purpose of interviews, reviews, or press
with permission and must be credited.
Every effort has been made to ensure this book is free from errors or
omissions. This is a work of fiction. Characters, names, businesses, places,
events, and incidents are either the products of the author's imagination or
have been used in a fictitious manner.

Publisher: Alina Rubin

ISBN: Hardback 979-8-9855378-1-9
ISBN: Paperback 979-8-9855378-2-6
Cover Design: GetCovers

Editor: Kirsten Rees | Book Editor & Author Coach
Proofreaders: Kirsten Rees, Alice Millar-Thompson, Dominic Pattison
Formatter: Claire Jennison

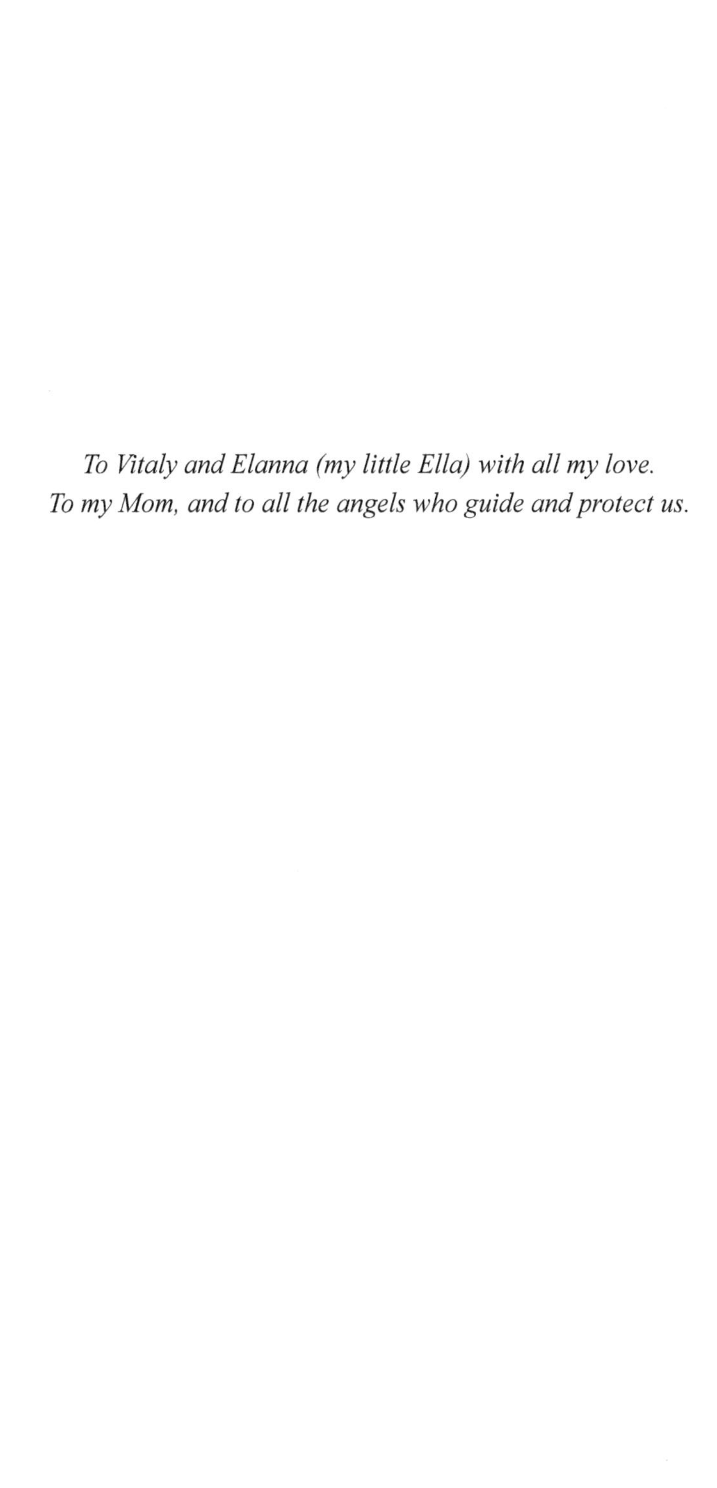

To Vitaly and Elanna (my little Ella) with all my love.
To my Mom, and to all the angels who guide and protect us.

CONTENTS

CHAPTER 1

ENGLAND, NEAR NEWCASTLE, EARLY 1800S

T he doctor's carriage had arrived more than eight hours ago, according to the clock above the fireplace. The pendulum, in a wavelike motion, dismissed each second without a care.

Eloise paced the length of her chamber as if she were a prisoner in a cell. Her maid, Ivy, and her governess, Miss Samson, checked on her from time to time, and had already brought her breakfast and dinner. They reminded her to be patient and to stay out of the way.

She obediently remained in her room and did not pester anyone with her questions. A few times she thought of throwing something at that clock to make it tick faster. An hour ago, two midwives rushed past her room, carrying basins with water, their faces strained with tension. Mother's wails chilled her body. To calm herself, Eloise imagined rocking the baby in her arms, like the caring fourteen-year-old big sister she would soon be.

The screams ceased for several minutes, *hallelujah*! With her pulse beating in her ears, she listened for a baby's whimpering. When a quarter of an hour had passed, and with no discernable cry from her mother or the baby reaching her ears, her stomach lurched. Unable to wait any longer, she bunched her skirts and crept towards her mother's bedroom.

She passed through the corridors, by maids washing floors and the midwives with their heads bent together, whispering to each other. When she reached the door, and got a glimpse of the scene inside, a bloodcurdling scream left her lips. Her mind registered the blood on the linens and her mother's ghostlike face. *And the doctor, what was he going to do with that knife?*

The hand of their valet, Mr. Lewis, circled her arm, dragging her away. "You don't want to see this, Miss." His voice was gentle, but firm.

She struggled from his steel grip. "Why was there all that blood? What's happening?"

Instead of an answer, he called to her maid. "Ivy, please stay with your mistress in her bedroom."

Guarded by Ivy, a feisty woman in her thirties, Eloise stared at the clock and counted to herself every minute that passed. Ten minutes, eleven minutes, thirteen minutes… Ivy tried to distract her with chatter, but she ignored the woman. Another carriage came to the door; Reverend Father Fletcher descended and was ushered in by the butler. *Please, God, no,* she prayed silently. Until someone confirmed her fears, they would not be a reality.

Miss Samson shuffled in; her eyeglasses were wet with tears. "Miss, please take courage. It was God's will to take your mother and your baby brother into heaven."

She shook herself, hoping against hope that she would wake from this nightmare. Her tongue failed her. Nothing seemed adequate to put her pain into words. Her mother, who drew landscapes with her, who comforted her through the nights she was ill, who desired to give her a sibling at last.

Her mother's face glowed like a tea rose, and her olive-green eyes sparkled with joy, looking deep within as if she could see the soul she would soon birth. Someone who was Eloise's universe could not leave this life with such abruptness. Not even an embrace or a goodbye for her daughter.

Her baby brother would never play in the nursery all prepared for his arrival; never see the toys she made for him, wear the shirts she embroidered. She had even imagined the fairytales she would tell him before sleep and the lullabies she would sing. Ivy was weeping into her apron, and Eloise wondered where her own tears were.

"What was the doctor doing? It looked like he was going to slice into Mum's stomach." She wished she could erase what she saw from her mind, but the thought was cutting at her chest like the scalpel the doctor held.

Ivy shrieked, and Miss Samson covered her mouth with her palm. "You should not have peeked," she answered with sternness when she had composed herself. "I am sure it was some medical operation to save the baby, but it's nothing for you to dwell on. Ivy, would you please bring us some lavender tea? We need to calm our nerves."

The maid hurried out, and Eloise turned her gaze to the view of the yard from her window, where her father was dismounting his horse. *Did he go riding while Mother was in labor?* She inhaled sharply, fearing what he would do when he heard the news.

Reverend Father Fletcher's kind face appeared at the door, and he asked Miss Samson if it was alright to speak to Eloise alone. "My dear child," he addressed her when the governess left. "Take comfort that your mother and brother will be angels in Heaven."

She nodded with submission, while wondering why the thought should soothe her when she needed them alive.

"You will need to be steadfast and obedient to your father. The loss will devastate him, but your patience and kindness will be an anchor to him. The earl has not always seen eye to eye with me, but lately he seems to have started on the right path."

"He frightens me, Reverend Father. He will start drinking again and say strange things. Do you remember the time you came for dinner, and he was yelling at his parents, who are long dead, as if they were there in the room? He scared my mother as well; he locked her in the cellar last week." She hugged herself, chilled to the bone from her memories.

The reverend shook his head. "Oh, child, our minds are mysterious and fragile. If such things occur again, please persuade him to see the doctor and to speak to me. Now, let us pray together for your mother and brother's souls."

Eloise kneeled and put her head down, but the prayer froze on her lips. Her father, Earl of Greenwoods, barged into the room, his face red with rage and eyes that could throw lightning. He pointed his finger at the reverend. "You, get out of my house!"

The reverend father shuddered. "Sir, I am terribly sorry for your loss, but I don't see what I've done to provoke your anger. Why don't you join us in prayer? It would ease your pain."

"I listened to you. I prayed for a son every day. I stopped drinking and was kind to my wife, so she would not lose this baby like all the others, except for this useless girl. After everything you said, look how it turned out!" He took a step towards the reverend.

The holy man raised his hands in a gesture of peace. "It's all the Lord's will. Please, sir, calm yourself. The doctor said you should not get agitated, it's bad for your condition."

"Enough of you. Go, before I drag you out of here by your cassock."

The reverend raised his chin and made a move towards the door.

Eloise, still kneeling, wept into her hands. Tears of fear and shame took place of those of grief.

"Why are you on your knees?" her father bellowed. "You are not to see the reverend anymore or attend church to listen to his lies."

Eloise rose, staring at the floor and wishing a sinkhole would open underneath her feet and swallow her.

The reverend, who had almost reached the threshold, turned. "Worship and community would bring comfort for the young woman. The churchgoing ladies would be happy to take her under their wings in this difficult time."

"If I see any of those busybodies with their baskets, they will severely regret coming here." The earl crossed his arms.

The reverend opened his mouth to answer, but Ivy hobbled in, balancing the tray with the china tea set. "Would you like some tea, sir? And you, Reverend Father?" the maid asked, walking towards the table.

"What's this? Who asked you to bring tea for the reverend?" The earl pulled the tray from Ivy and knocked it to the floor. The fine china cups broke into pieces, and the burning liquid splashed onto his leg. He yelped, and Ivy rushed to help him, as he cussed.

In the commotion, the reverend approached Eloise. His sky blue eyes looked at her with pity. "I appreciate the difficulty of the test the Lord is sending you. I think it would be better if I and my flock pray for you and your father from afar, and not come here anymore. Is there a relative or a neighbor who may help you take care of your father? I am afraid he will only grow worse."

No trustworthy relations resided in England, and their gossipy neighbors would only irritate her father, doing no good. She already knew that his illness was a family matter; something to be hidden and not discussed with outsiders. The reverend stared at her expectantly, and Eloise mustered all the confidence she could find in such a moment.

"You need not worry, Reverend Father. My father and I will be fine."

* * *

Eloise took her seat in one of the chairs, smoothed her black skirts, and watched the ladies of the embroidery circle sigh and regard her with saintly sympathy. Their voices dripping with honeysweet kindness, they asked how she was holding up.

Four months into her mourning, the initial shock worn off, and she rarely spent a night without weeping into her pillow, missing her mother. She had already learned that candor did no good.

The one time she said that she was doing terribly, everyone stared with awkwardness, and then proceeded to tell her she must find strength and courage, as if she were weak and cowardly for admitting how she felt. It was better to pretend to be fine; that's what everyone wanted to hear. After reassurance that she was well, and receival of pitying smiles, the conversation went into the usual trivialities, and the ladies dove into their needlework.

"Eloise, do you still prefer the church at Newcastle? I can't believe you enjoy going that far," said the hostess, Lady Fillips. She and her two daughters, Marietta and Henrietta, embroidered nightshirts for the trousseau.

"Yes, it's quite nice," she answered, hoping the woman

would ask nothing else of her imaginary new place of worship.

Miss Samson kept her head down, pretending to be engrossed in her handiwork. The governess herself announced that Eloise patronized a new church when both grew tired of being asked about their absence at the pew.

"My sister-in-law and her children worship there. I shall arrange to introduce you," Lady Allen said. "Veronica, don't you think Eloise would enjoy the company of your cousins?"

The girl, Eloise's closest friend Veronica Allen, yelped as she stabbed her finger. Realizing her mother was staring at her, she nodded and mumbled that they would get along splendidly.

Eloise thanked the women with a smile that hurt her lips. *Terrific, soon I will have to say that I go to Westminster Abbey to worship.*

While the mothers and Miss Samson complained about the hot weather and the lack of rain, Eloise, seated on the edge of the chair with ease, worked on a handkerchief with a design of flowers in the corner. Repetitive handicraft calmed her and she was thankful for the company. In the past few months, the embroidery circle meetings had become her only outlet into the world outside her home.

Henrietta showed her the flower pattern she was making. The young woman wore a salmon pink dress, and Eloise admired the color. Her own black gown, appropriate for mourning, did not suit her much. Her raven black hair, which touched her waist, faded into the fabric of her dress. Her skin paled in contrast, and even her green eyes, that her mother called her emeralds, dulled.

"Thank you for lending me *Hamlet*," Henrietta said. "I read it all in one night and loved it. Mother would disapprove of the violence, but it was fantastically moving."

Eloise smiled brightly. "Isn't it incredible? Did you have a favorite part or line?"

"Yes. The speech Polonius gives to Laertes, who goes off to the university, 'To thine own self be true.' So ironic, coming from him!"

"Interesting. I prefer Hamlet's soliloquies, especially "To be or not to be". You can keep the book if you like." Somber thoughts of death, such as in Hamlet's speech, suited her mood these days.

While Henrietta thanked her, Eloise's mind wandered into memories of reading Shakespeare with her mother. Even though they read only for themselves, they changed their voices for every part, and even made hats and capes for the main characters.

Brightening with an idea, Eloise spoke up to the whole group. "What if we put on a Shakespeare play, one of the comedies, like *Twelfth Night*? We could sew costumes."

Henrietta perked up with interest, but the mothers frowned, and Miss Samson gave a scandalized gape. "Miss Eloise, you forget you are in mourning! Such frivolity would hardly be appropriate."

Lady Fillips shook her head, her double-chin shaking with it. "Much of Shakespeare is quite lewd and improper for a girl your age. Your governess should monitor your reading better."

"Yes, Madam," Miss Samson said, lowering her eyes.

Eloise's mouth tightened, suppressing a groan. Since her mother's passing, she never received support to try anything new, to apply herself in ways outside of a handful of approved activities. One could die from such boredom.

"Well, I have some splendid news!" Lady Fillips announced, and her eyes sparkled. "The matter of Marietta's engagement is practically settled. We received a most promising letter from Baron Monroe. He will grace us with a visit on Sunday."

The ladies offered congratulations, but Marietta's shoulders slumped.

"Mother, please give me a little more time. I can still meet someone… closer to my age, and… with fewer war injuries."

Lady Fillips reddened. "That's enough, Marietta! The baron is a decorated hero and an important man. No reason for you to fear unhappiness just because he is seventy and lost an eye and a leg."

The girl wiped a tear running down her cheek and excused herself. The conversation changed to eligible bachelors as potential matches for Henrietta. Eloise jumped in to change the subject before anyone produced any ideas that would concern her. She was too young for marriage, but these ladies strategized years ahead. If such maneuvering minds applied themselves to battles, they would have won the war already.

The subject of war weighed on her mind, and Eloise asked, "Has anyone heard any news from the front? Is Spain joining forces with France against our troops?"

The ladies gave side glances, and Miss Samson declared politics an unladylike subject, chiding Eloise again. Living here, one could hardly believe Britain was at war.

Veronica shrieked as she poked her finger with a needle again. Eloise turned to her friend. "Are you all right, dear? You seem distracted, and your fingers are suffering for it."

The girl gave a quiet sob. "I received a letter from Earnest. He has been wounded and brought to the hospital at Plymouth." Earnest was Veronica's sweetheart, a midshipman. They could not marry yet, for Earnest lacked funds to support a wife, but their parents allowed them to correspond.

Taking her friend's hand, Eloise asked, "How was he wounded? Bullet, cannon, shrapnel? And to what body part?"

Veronica blanched and broke into tears.

Miss Samson gave Eloise a stern stare. "Miss, you had better console your friend and wish the young man a smooth recovery, not question her like a doctor."

"Why can't I ask?" Eloise rebutted. "An injury to an arm is quite different from a chest wound. It does not take a doctor to see why."

The ladies glared with disapproval, and she stopped her protest. Instead, she gently patted Veronica's shoulder and assured her Earnest would be fine. Noticing drops of blood on the girl's fingers from the pricks, Ella pressed a handkerchief to her hand.

With her tears paused, the girl whispered back. "I wish I knew more of his injury. He said nothing in the letter, not even if the wound was light or serious, which makes me think the worst." She looked ready to start crying again.

"Why don't you travel to the hospital and speak to him or his doctor?"

Veronica shook her head. "Father and Mother forbade it. They are taking me to the seaside instead to distract me from my nerves, but it will be awful without your company. And I will be beside myself worried about Earnest, even on holiday. The only thing Mother allowed was to embroider a pillow for him." After ensuring that her mother was not listening, Veronica mouthed, "Do you think if I make a little red heart right here, he would see it as my admission of love?"

Eloise reassured her that Earnest would grasp the subtle message. Inside, she despaired that Veronica would travel to the seaside without her this year. Swimming and walks on the beach were enjoyable but incompatible with mourning.

A servant brought a tray of eclairs, and Eloise could barely hold her delight, reaching for the pastries.

She all but inhaled the dessert, ignoring the governess's reproachful gaze. Still chewing the first one, she reached for another.

Miss Samson stopped her hand before it found its target. "Only one pastry, Miss."

"I have not eaten eclairs in a while. These are delicious."

"You are a young lady, not a starving urchin. Besides, do you remember your tenth birthday, when you ate too much cake, and how sick you were afterwards? Do you want that to happen again?"

What Eloise remembered was how her mother comforted her, massaging her belly till it stopped aching. Last week, when their cook experimented with a new recipe, her stomach rebelled, but Miss Samson and Ivy shrugged and said that the discomfort would go away on its own. She spent the night moaning and groaning in her room alone.

After some more light conversation, the party broke up, and Lady Fillips walked Eloise and her governess to the door. Right before departure, she caught Eloise's hand.

"It was a pleasure to see you again, my dear. Have no fear, once I have my girls settled, I will help your father find you a proper husband. Someone with a strong hand, to contain your boisterous spirit, will do well. I was fond of your mother, but her ideas on raising girls were most peculiar. Miss Samson must have her hands full with you."

The governess curtsied. "Very true, Madam."

Eloise stifled a retort and an urge to roll her eyes. Her stomach tightened when Lady Fillips brought up her mother.

The hostess did not notice and gave her a beaming smile, baring her teeth.

"Please give my warmest regards to your father. It's a

shame he has not joined any recent gatherings. If I can do anything for him, he should not hesitate to ask. We are neighbors, after all!"

Eloise forced her lips into a grin. Rumor had it Lady Fillips' daughters had no dowry, and her late husband's fortune was nearly spent. One could imagine why she wished to be viewed as 'neighborly' by her father, whom she had not seen in months. With a promise to pass on her regards, while having no intention of doing so, Eloise climbed into the carriage with Miss Samson. When the horses neighed and the carriage wheels rolled on the cobbled road, she wondered if this day would only get worse.

After dinner, Eloise took a routine walk around the gardens with Miss Samson. The black dress absorbed the sun's rays, making her back itchy. Fidgeting in her dress, she returned to her room, sweat rolling down her reddened face. Breathless, she fell onto her four-poster bed. At least she managed to collect a lavender-colored flower she had not seen before, and when the governess was not looking, a dead beetle. Later she would check the botany book for the name of the flower and look at the beetle under a microscope, as she used to do when she had lessons.

Father dismissed all her tutors, who had instructed her in music, painting, and foreign languages. Her beloved science instructor, who taught her from biology and chemistry textbooks, and showed her illustrations of human body systems, left first. No need for girls to be too educated; it could give them strange ideas and make them unsuitable for marriage. Yet she longed for those lessons, for the feeling of accomplishment she got when solving difficult problems and the companionship of people who loved to read and learn new things.

After opening Voltaire's *Candide* where she left off, she lost herself in the book for a while. When a maid called her name, Eloise was startled. Susan stood shaking, tears running down her apple cheeks.

"Father?" Eloise guessed.

The young servant nodded with a sob.

"What did he do?"

"I brought him his medicine, and he said that he did not want it. I reminded him what the doctor said, and he…"

Susan broke down and wept.

"Cursed at you? Slapped you? Tell me."

"He grabbed me, tore my skirts, and pushed me down onto the table. I barely managed to get out. Miss, I will not go into his room again. I quit."

Eloise took the girl's hand. She would be the seventh maid to quit in the last three months. Soon enough, they would not be able to find any help for her father. "I understand. I will pass a note to the estate caretaker to pay you for the rest of the week and for your torn dress. I am sorry this happened." She waited for Susan to leave, but the girl kept staring. "Is there something else?"

"Miss, it may be impertinent of me to ask, but would you write me a recommendation letter? I was not sure if you knew about these things."

"Oh, of course I will." The maid was right, Eloise did not know. "What should it say?"

"The usual, I guess. That I am honest, diligent, or whatever you think of my character and my work. You see, these days no one hires servants without such letters."

As Eloise penned, she felt a pang of guilt for not writing such letters for the other servants who left because of her father's outbursts. When she finished, she read the letter aloud to the maid.

Susan gaped. "Miss, I did not clean the entire house from top to bottom in two hours. Nor did I sew a ball gown in one night," she said with hesitation.

"You want to find employment, right? There is no harm in putting your best foot forward with just a tiny embellishment. I know you can clean and sew well."

The girl fidgeted and took the letter with a thank you. When she left, Eloise called for Ivy and asked her to bring another dose of the medicine to her father. The maid was a sturdy and confident woman, able to handle her master. Yet this time, Ivy stared her down with defiance.

"Do not ask me to go into your father's room, Miss. I heard what happened to Susan. I would rather quit as well."

"Fine, bring me what he needs to take, and I will do it." She could not lose another maid tonight.

Ivy marched out with a smug expression. Eloise considered asking Mr. Lewis, but the valet would not coax his master into taking the medicine. Such a job took tact and a woman's touch, so she was best suited for it.

* * *

After accepting the glass from Ivy, Eloise tiptoed to her father's room. She opened the door without a sound and stared at him. His hair, greyed before its time, hung disheveled over his slumped shoulders. His clothes were wrinkled, as if he had slept in them. A week-old, shaggy beard covered his reddened face. The earl sat at his table, which was littered with crumpled papers, crumbs, and spoiled food. In his hand, he clutched an almost empty bottle; he tried to fill a glass, but most of the liquid spilled over.

Despite her heart pumping like mad, Eloise willed herself to sound confident and stand strong as a soldier. She set the glass in front of him and stepped back. "Please take your medicine, Father."

With bloodshot eyes, the earl regarded her like an annoying fly. "Insolent girl. You come here again to taunt me. How many times do I have to call for your mother? Where is she?"

She stifled a cry. "You know where Mother is. You must remember the funeral." Her heart ached saying those words.

"A sham. She ran away to a lover, and you staged that charade to cover for her. Even swooned for the effect. You always regarded yourself quite an actress. You still play the part, wearing black dresses. And you mock me, looking more like your mother every day."

Anger flared inside her. "You think this is a sham? That I want to wear mourning clothes for my mother? That I look like her on purpose? You escape into your drink and your madness, leaving me alone to grieve. Stop with your drinking, see a doctor, and deal with your responsibilities as the master of the house." She grabbed the bottle from the table and smashed it on the floor, breaking it into a shower of glass and blood-colored puddles.

The earl's face grew redder. He jumped to his feet, and the chair crashed with a deafening boom. Eloise backed up to the wall. She froze, limbs rigid, eyes locked on her father's right hand. The one he lifted too often. Red-rimmed eyes regarded her with such fury that she wondered if he meant to kill her.

She shriveled, preparing for a blow. It came at her ear, making her head explode with pain. She stood shell-shocked, when the piercing sound of breaking glass rang next to her head and the side of her neck burst with pain as a shard of glass sliced into her. With a scream, she touched the cut and looked down at her hand, wet with blood.

Her feet found the back stairs on their own. As her father yelled her name, she ignored him and ran, her heart beating faster with each step. He would not follow her to the servants' wing. Blood poured down her neck, darkening the collar of her dress. With a wail, she flew down into the kitchen, straight into Mr. Lewis' arms.

"My God!" the elderly valet exclaimed, holding her, and turning her head towards him. "Ivy, don't just stand there! Do you see your mistress is bleeding? Bring gauze and a basin with water. Jimmy, take a horse and fetch the doctor."

Mr. Lewis pressed his fingers into her neck. Eloise closed her eyes, shaking with her whole body. Something wet washed her neck, dripping down her dress.

"Good," he said. "The blood is not gushing anymore. This cut will need a needle and thread, but you will be fine."

"That's too bad."

"Please don't say things like that, Miss. What did he do to you? Cut you with a knife?"

"With a wine glass. I broke his bottle." A string inside her, drawn to the maximum tightness, broke under the strain. She wondered if that was what people called a heartbreak. Tears came like a stream, rushing down her cheeks.

Mr. Lewis looked around the kitchen to ensure it was empty, then kneeled to her and whispered into her ear. "You should leave, Miss Eloise. Forget that you are an earl's daughter. I've seen milkmaids and serving girls happier than you. Last week, he beat you to bruises. This time he cut you, and it could have been worse. It is easier for him to cause pain to others than to deal with his own. When he rages, he could snap you like a straw. What's worse is that he will break your spirit. Get away, while you have some left." He pulled out a handkerchief from his pocket and wiped her tears.

"Where would I go? If I hide with one of the families we know, he will find me. And I should be taking care of him. What will happen to him without me?"

"You can't help him; you can't even convince him to see a doctor. Don't you have friends somewhere far from here? Take some money, walk to the coach station, and go live with them. After his drinking, he will not be coherent enough to search for you for a while. I will make up some story about you visiting neighbors. We'll manage without you."

"But what will I do after the money runs out? I cannot live on charity forever."

"Your mother prided herself on giving you an excellent education. Find how to use it, or learn something new."

She composed herself and considered. "I do have friends in Cornwall, where I went on a holiday. There are young children in the family who may need a governess," she lied. Better give Mr. Lewis a false lead in case the father or the police interrogate him.

The man smiled. "That's a good plan. You could sail there from Port of Tyne. You will have a roof over your head and be useful to your hosts." He pulled her into an embrace. "Don't come back while he is here. Make your own way in the world."

Could she leave her home behind? Was it still her home now that Mother was gone? It had become a hostile and gloomy place, like a fairy castle cursed by an evil witch. She had no friends or protectors here other than Mr. Lewis, and he was only a kind valet.

The same doctor who had tended to her mother in her last moments examined Eloise's wound after he arrived. When he applied stitches, she prided herself on not fidgeting or crying.

Instead, she stared straight ahead and did not answer when he questioned how the cut came about. When he asked for the third time, she replied through her teeth that she slipped on broken glass. Her explanation satisfied him, and he hastened to make it home before complete darkness fell.

Exhausted, she trudged to her room and rang for Ivy to get her ready for bed. The maid performed the nightly routine in silence, unbuttoning her dress, slipping a nightgown over her head, and closing the heavy curtains.

When her tired head fell on the pillow and she was hidden under the blanket, Ivy spoke. "Miss, I am sorry I let you go to your father." Her voice quivered. "I should have asked Mr. Lewis, or another male servant. Or had the courage to do it myself." When Eloise did not respond, she added, "I brought out your dresses from the storage to see if any needed mending. They are in the yellow guest room. I will accompany you wherever you plan on going tomorrow. Please ring for me when you wake."

Eloise kept silent, and the maid picked up her skirts and sauntered out with dignity. There was no need to patch those dresses, and they both knew it. Ivy checked and mended them before putting them into the storage room at the start of Eloise's mourning. She had obviously eavesdropped on her and Mr. Lewis and was offering her assistance so Eloise could run. Run away from this room, filled with her books, figurines on the mantle, paintings on her walls, most of them selected with care by her mother. Leave this house, where they played, ran through the gardens, played piano at parties. But her mother was no longer here, and constant reminders of her tore at Eloise's heart.

Her father had become increasingly violent, and she doubted she could ever feel safe living under the same roof with him. Her elbows still wore the mustard-yellow bruises from last week's beating. The scar on her neck would heal but never disappear. Her trust that her father, despite his madness, would never injure her, was shattered like the glass he threw at her.

Mr. Lewis was right; a fifteen-year-old girl was not the right person to deal with a sick man. She had to escape, but not to any friends far away, and she wouldn't take Ivy or anyone else. When the maid woke the next morning, Eloise would be gone. The journey would be hers alone. When sleep came, she dreamt of a majestic ship, sailing in the gentle waves.

CHAPTER 2

I t was early morning when the coach stopped at the port. Eloise jumped out, paid the driver, and added a generous tip. She took her bag, filled with clothes, shoes, and some books, and joined a crowd that swept towards the docks. Port of Tyne was the busiest place she had ever been. She did not dare stop moving for fear of being trampled. The masts of massive vessels towered in the distance. Eloise wondered if these were passenger or merchant ships, or maybe even warships. Her eyes darted, searching for the ticket agent. Struggling to find one nearby, she asked a passing couple, who directed her to an inconspicuous grey building. Relieved, she entered and stepped up to the window, but a man behind her yelled and pointed towards a queue. Reddening and muttering apologies, she took her place at the back.

When her turn came, she forced a confident tone. "One passage to London, please."

"Which ship?" the burly agent barked.

"Whichever leaves the soonest."

"*Pamela* leaves in two hours, but all I have left are the first-class cabins. How many people are traveling with you?"

"Only me, and I will take that first-class cabin."

The agent named the fare and widened his eyes when Eloise gave him the named sum without flinching and added a tip. Frugality would come later; she needed to leave with haste. The money she took from her father's bureau while he slumbered in a drunk stupor should last her about two months. Hopefully, she would not have to sell her mother's necklace and earrings, and would secure a job before the money ran out. Meanwhile the agent reassured her that she would find her cabin comfortable and summoned a boy to help with her bag. Onlookers stared as she followed her helper to a ferry boat, their prying eyes scrutinizing her.

I escaped! I am free! Eloise leaned over the railing, watching the glittering, silver-lined waves. Her lungs filled with crisp air, and she could almost taste the sea salt on her tongue. The sun tickled her skin, and the gentle motion of the ship made her feet dance a new rhythm.

She took a seat at one of the benches and reached into her pocket, taking out a letter she had written that morning.

Dear Sir or Madam,
I employed Miss Ella Parker as a governess for over a year,
and her conduct was exemplary. She taught my two daughters
to behave as young ladies, especially proper posture,
curtsying, and table manners. Additionally, they significantly
improved their piano playing and mastered the finer points of
French and Spanish languages. My girls miss her already.
Sincerely,
Lady Fillips

A triumphant smile spread on her lips. With this letter she would find employment in busy London, a city so enormous that her father would have no chance of tracing her. How fortunate that her tutors had taught her to speak like a Londoner. No one would think she came from Newcastle. Yes, she was a bit of a cheat, writing her own recommendation letter, but she could teach little girls to play scales and converse about the weather in perfect French. Fifteen was young for a governess, but she could pass for eighteen if she put her hair up and mimicked Miss Samson's stiff manners. And the position would be temporary, until she figured out what she wanted to do with her life.

Her heart danced a jovial beat in her chest, and her feet tapped in unison. She whispered, "Ella Parker" several times; her new name sounded exotic on her tongue, like her first sip of champagne. From this moment, she would be Ella; a new name for a new life.

High above her, the seamen climbed the rigging. She wondered what the view was like from such height. Even higher, the seagulls circled in a dancelike pattern.

I am free like those gulls!

This moment deserved a celebration. She rose, checked that no one stood close to her, opened her arms wide, and spun, letting her broad skirts swish and spread like an oversized ivory parasol. No more wearing black! No more Miss Samson telling her what she could or could not do! She made several pirouettes, and the world whirled in front of her eyes. Suddenly, the ship rolled on a giant wave, and Ella found herself stretched on her back with her head throbbing. Nausea came up to her throat, burning it. She attempted to sit up, but a hand gently pressed her shoulder down.

"Miss, do not get up. Let me check you are not injured." The voice belonged to a gentleman with overgrown grey hair, who kneeled next to Ella, looking her over with concern. "I am Doctor Joseph Pesce. Does anything hurt?"

Ella shook her head, but the motion made her wince.

"Your head?" The doctor's dexterous fingers pressed on Ella's forehead and temple. "How did you get that cut?" he asked, examining her neck.

"It's from an old accident," she lied.

Dr. Pesce frowned and opened his mouth to ask more, but Ella moaned to distract him from staring at her scar. He continued his exam, pushing on her ribs and feeling her arms. His eyebrows rose. "What are all those bruises?"

"I can be extremely clumsy at times," she answered, rolling down her sleeves.

After giving Ella a hand up, the doctor made her take a few steps. "Nothing is broken, but you had better take some rest. Are your parents in the cabin? I will walk with you and speak to them."

Ella fidgeted. "No, I am traveling alone."

Dr. Pesce widened his brown eyes. "Is someone meeting you at the port?"

She shook her head.

With a tap of his foot, he said, "Let's have you repose, and later we may discuss if I can assist you further. London is a large city, and not safe for a young girl traveling alone."

The ship swayed as Ella staggered towards the cabin. The doctor offered his arm, and she leaned on him to steady herself. They neared the door, when a scream, a moan, and a cry for help came all at once. Startled, they turned in the direction the heart-wrenching sounds came from. The doctor inhaled sharply. "I am afraid my services are needed again. Quite unusual for two emergencies to happen within minutes on a passenger ship."

He asked her name and her cabin location and promised to come back and check on her as soon as he could.

Ella stepped inside and stretched out on the narrow cot. The first-class cabin was not the standard she was used to, but it suited her fine. The porthole gave enough natural light to illuminate the space of fifteen by fifteen feet. The closet had room for a couple of her nice dresses. The cot was a good size for her; she just had to be careful getting up without bumping her head on the shelf above it. The accommodations did not matter, really, the cabin was just for sleeping, after all. Soon enough she'd be in London, starting a new life.

Unable to relax, she tossed and turned, risking a fall from her tiny bunk. Her head no longer ached, and her curiosity prevented the prescribed rest. She rose and clambered back onto the deck, scanning the crowd for the doctor. Not seeing him, she proceeded in the direction the scream came from. A conversation between two seamen perked her ears.

"Poor Johnson. What an awful break. One of the worst I ever seen."

"A shame, but at least Dr. Pesce knows his tools. He is a learned man, not some quack."

Despite her timidness, she approached these men, trying not to gape at their long hair and the ink drawings on their muscular arms.

"Excuse me, could you please tell me where Dr. Pesce is?" she asked.

"He is underdeck in the sick berth, but he is busy," one of the sailors replied with a brusque bass.

"Thank you. He forgot something in my cabin that I need to return to him urgently," she babbled and hurried toward the hatchway.

Moans and wails directed her into a space large enough for a handful of people to stand, and she tiptoed inside. In a gloomy light from flickering lanterns, she observed the injured man fastened to a waist-high table. His left arm bled and lay twisted at an impossible angle while his pallid face contorted with anguish. His shipmate, a bearded man of significant size, put a bottle to the injured seaman's lips that smelled strongly of alcohol. Dr. Pesce, wearing a smock over his clothes, placed a variety of surgical tools on the table, absorbed in his work.

"All right, the tourniquet is on. Put a strap into his mouth, and then hold him hard by the shoulders, Skiles," the surgeon ordered the large man while deciding on which of his instruments to use. With his nimble fingers, the doctor selected a scalpel and turned towards the patient, but stopped, startled. His eyes fixed on Ella, who stood about a foot away from the table, still as a statue.

After a few moments, he spoke in a kind but urgent voice. "Miss Ella, you should not be here. You need to leave."

Ella was still rooted in her spot. With an effort, she made a move to go, but halted when the injured man gave a heartbreaking cry. His pain resonated inside her from head to toe. Somehow it was familiar to her, despite never having broken a bone in her body. It was not that different from the heartache she felt when her father injured her. Scared but determined, she approached the hurt man and took his uninjured hand.

"Miss, please go," the surgeon pleaded. "I have to amputate his arm. This is nothing for you to watch. It may upset your nerves and give you nightmares. There will be a lot of blood. Please go, I need to get started."

Ella looked up at the doctor and willed her voice to sound firm. "Please do what you need to do and pretend I am not here. If I cannot stand it, I will leave." With a squeeze of the seaman's hand Ella focused on his eyes, and whispered, "I was hurt, but I am healing. And you will too."

Put this on to protect your dress," Dr. Pesce said and handed her an apron.

Spellbound, she watched the surgeon cut through the skin in one swift motion. The wounded man struggled and wailed, biting into the strap in his mouth, but Skiles held him with his great strength, and Ella clasped his hand tighter. The doctor cut deeper with a catling knife. She remembered the name of the instrument from her science lesson in which her tutor dissected a frog. The surgeon tied off the blood vessels with cords, which she guessed to be catgut. The metallic smell of blood was sickening her, and she breathed deeply through her mouth to keep the bile from coming up into her throat.

"Could you please hand me the amputation saw?" the surgeon asked her. "It's the thickest one." Ella let go on the sailor's hand and found the saw he needed. With trembling hands, she passed the instrument to the doctor, and resumed her position by the patient.

The surgeon hacked through the bone, and the patient moaned weakly. He seemed to lack the strength to struggle at this point. She made herself watch, wondering if she would see the muscles and bones like in the anatomy book, but it was all one bloody mess. The amputated arm came off and fell to the floor, and she stifled a gasp in her throat. After filing down the bone and pulling the skin over it, the doctor threaded a needle and applied the sutures. Exhaling a long breath, Ella told the seaman that the surgery was over and praised his bravery. His face was bloodless, and his eyes closed, but his chest rose and fell. After checking the patient's pulse, the doctor asked Skiles to stay with his shipmate until he came back. As he gathered his bloodied tools, he motioned for Ella to follow him.

"Well, that's that," the surgeon said, leading her out to the deck. "Are you feeling all right? And how is your head? Many medical students come out from their first surgery as white as these sails, but your color looks healthy. I am sorry about your dress. The blood washes off best with cold water."

She looked down at her clothes, startled to see that they were stained from her collar to her shoes despite the apron. "I feel fine, and my head does not hurt anymore. What about that poor man? Will he recover?"

"Most likely, yes," the surgeon assured as he walked her towards her cabin. "Emergency amputation gave him the best chance to avoid a deadly infection. Once at port, he will be taken to the hospital to finish his recovery."

"Do you live and work on the ship, taking care of the sick and injured?"

"Yes, that's what ship surgeons do, although I am taking a break after this voyage. I served on men-of-war, as well as passenger ships, for years. Caring for the injured is draining work, but such a life has its rewards. I take great pleasure in looking out on the sea. In my travels I have seen hundreds of stars reflected in the still water, dolphin pods chasing the ship, the flying fish jumping in the waves. A ship surgeon's life is dangerous, especially in wartime, but I would not trade it for any other profession."

Ella's heart raced as if she could see the wonders the doctor described, and her brain buzzed with ideas. Why go to London to become a governess when she could travel to other countries? What if she could become a doctor's assistant? She could not think of anything she had accomplished so far in her life as significant as supporting that wounded man through the amputation. *What if she learned how to treat injuries?*

"Could I become your assistant and help with surgeries?"

she asked. "I had a great tutor for biology and chemistry, who thought I had an inclination for those fields. And once I fixed my dog's broken paw." The last was a lie, but she thought it sounded impressive.

The doctor looked at her with confusion. "You want to be a surgeon's assistant? Why?"

"Seeing you work, doctor, was scary but also incredible. Our bodies are such interesting mechanisms, with all those muscles, nerves and organs working together. And it felt good to help the injured."

The doctor gave her a smile. "Miss Ella, you seem like a valiant young woman, and you impressed me with how you handled yourself during the amputation. Surgery as a profession, however, is considered improper for women. Perhaps you could assist midwives or join a convent to learn how to nurse the sick."

Midwives and birthing brought unhappy associations Ella did not want to ponder. Convents did not appeal either, with their discipline and horrible-looking clothes. And she planned to marry someday – very far in the future.

"That is unfair," she argued. "I bet I can be as good as any boy who wishes to be a surgeon's apprentice."

Dr. Pesce heaved a sigh. "I agree with you. My daughter Lindsey was a wonderfully intelligent girl. Her quickness made me think how unjust it is that women are barred from many professions." He looked like he wanted to say more but stopped himself. "I am sorry, but no. Consider midwifery; it's a solid profession. Well, here is your cabin. You need to wash and change, and I better go check on my patient." He hurried away, leaving Ella crestfallen.

CHAPTER 3

At teatime, the ship's dining room for first-class passengers hummed with the conversations of ladies in elegant dresses and gentlemen in stylish coats. Two fashionable ladies joined Ella's table, discussing their plans to visit Drury Lane and the Royal Opera. The doctor sipped tea in the corner, and she considered asking him again about becoming his assistant, but decided that would be impertinent of her. The waiter set a platter of sandwiches, fancy cakes, and pastries on the table.

One of the ladies took a tiny bite into a pastry and closed her eyes. "Oh my, these tarts melt in my mouth! I could eat them all."

"And your waist would not suffer a bit. Not me. Two of these scones, and my corset would burst," her companion said and began nibbling on a cucumber sandwich.

Ella helped herself to a roast beef and horseradish sandwich and a lemon cake. Soon the platter emptied, with the exception of anchovy sandwiches left untouched.

When the waiter refilled her tea, she asked, "Do seamen eat these sandwiches too?"

"No, Miss, these are for passengers only," the waiter replied, his eyebrows rising slightly.

The women stared with curiosity as well, and Ella decided not to ask what would happen to the leftovers. When the waiter walked away, she wrapped two sandwiches into a napkin. This food was likely superior to whatever seamen ate, and the injured man needed some fortification after his ordeal. She would bring him the sandwiches and later casually mention her good deed to the doctor, and maybe he would let her be his assistant after all.

The ladies continued watching her, so she explained, "My mother is terribly seasick, but maybe she will be able to eat this later."

Both women nodded with sympathy and suggested chamomile tea for nausea. Sandwiches in hand, Ella hurried underdeck where the injured sailor was recovering after the amputation. With slight trepidation, she crept into the sick berth.

"Mr. Johnson!" she whispered across the room, recalling the seaman's name. "How are you feeling? Would you like a sandwich?"

Not hearing an answer, she tiptoed to the cot and discerned the pallid face and closed eyes. "Mr. Johnson?" she whispered louder this time, realizing the patient may be sleeping. With her heart skipping a beat, she slipped on the puddle of blood, staining her skirts, and the sandwiches fell out of her hand. Her eyes followed the trail of blood up to the stump and watched more of it seeping through the sheets above the spill.

She bolted towards the stairs but then returned promptly. Remembering how Mr. Lewis applied pressure to her cut, she searched in a frenzy for something she could tie over the stump. After finding gauze and scissors among the supplies in the drawer, she secured a tight bandage above the wound. Dizzy from her heart beating like mad, and her hands trembling, she ran back to the dining room, praying for the doctor to be still there.

Diners froze in silence when she flew into the room, screaming for Dr. Pesce. Her eyes darted over the tables, as her brain failed to remember where the surgeon was sitting. The ladies who dined with her approached with their eyes wide.

"Did your mother swoon?" one asked.

The other gasped and put her hand to her mouth. "She has blood on her dress. Her mother may have hit her head fainting!"

Not wasting time to explain, Ella called for the doctor again.

"He just left," one of the waiters answered. "Check the stern. He likes to watch the sea from there."

Hoping she was running in the right direction, Ella hurried, calling for the doctor every few steps. His tall figure appeared near the place where she fell earlier. When his head whipped around, Ella caught up to him and told him what she had seen in the sick berth, breathing hard with every word. He headed underdeck before she finished talking, and she hastened after him.

* * *

"Good thing you decided to visit him, Miss Ella. I was going to check on him in fifteen minutes, but I might have been too late," the doctor said after applying clean bandages. "The suture I used to ligate an artery came loose. He could have bled to death if you did not intervene."

Ella steadied her breath and peered at the patient, who

was oblivious to the world after the blood loss. "Is there anything else I can do?"

The doctor scanned the berth. "You could mop the blood. The mop is in the corner."

Ella stared back with hesitation.

The doctor jumped up. "I am sorry, Miss. That's not a job for you. I don't know what I was thinking. You are dressed in your finest, and here I am asking you to mop. I will get a ship boy to do it."

"No. I asked to become your assistant, and this is a proper assignment for me." After mopping the floor, she glanced back at the doctor, checking what else she could do.

The doctor's brow knitted. "You must be tired, Miss, and in need of rest. I wanted to discuss your plans in London, but it better wait till tomorrow."

Ella's feet felt dead, but she perceived the doctor may extend her an offer and feared he could change his mind by morning. "I am fine to speak now. As for my plans in London, I wished to find a job as a governess. Here." She took out the recommendation letter.

The doctor fixed his glasses and read. "You secured the position?" he asked.

"No. To tell you the truth, I wrote this letter myself. I can do all the things listed, but I never held a job before."

Dr. Pesce frowned. "It's wicked of you to lie. A governess, caring for the children, must be trustworthy."

"I meant no harm. A servant told me I would not find employment without such a letter, and I had no one to write it for me. And after what happened today, I am not sure I want to be a governess anymore. I want to help with patients."

"You don't have family or friends in London? No anxious parents searching for you?"

"No." Her father would not be anxious; rather, he would rage in fury.

"Unfortunately, I don't have a need for piano or curtsying lessons," the doctor teased with a lopsided grin. "Here is what I can offer you, Miss Ella. I am planning to spend the summer with my sister, Matilda, in London. You can assist her with her clients and housework, and study from my medical books. Also, since your letter says you are fluent in French, I would like you to translate medical notes from my Paris colleague into English. Maybe in time you will be useful with my patients as well."

"Your sister has clients? What kind of clients?"

"She is a midwife and an herbal healer. You will see more of her than me. I don't spend much time at home, to Matilda's vexation. Don't say anything now. Sleep on it. If it's a yes, I would appreciate some help with the patient in the morning."

When Ella stretched out on her cot, her confidence vanished. What made her think she could be a surgeon's assistant? Did she even know what the job involved? The doctor was a curious man, and it felt good to help the patient, but she never heard of women working in a medical profession. And he wanted her to help not him, but his sister, a midwife. After her mother's death, she wanted nothing to do with childbirth. It would be safer to continue with her plan and become a governess.

She would establish herself in some good household with children, teach them piano and good manners. Her mind drew pictures of nice little girls singing with her and painting beautiful scenery. The happy family would enjoy riding horses and boating, celebrate joyous occasions, and invite her on their holidays. There would be a library full of books available for her and the children to read. Her mind drew lovely pictures for a good hour.

Then her gut reminded her of a catch. What if the family was not happy? What if they were secretive, miserable, controlling, or unpleasant? In other words, they could be like her own family, or worse.

She mulled over the doctor's offer again. *He said if I did not intervene, the patient could have died. Did I save a life?* The thought made her heart pump faster and she sat up on her cot, painfully hitting her head on the shelf. If she studied medicine, she could save more lives. This time it was luck, but in the future she would apply knowledge. Somewhere deep inside, the matter was settled.

CHAPTER 4

Despite her exhaustion, Ella slept poorly, with the ship rolling on the waves, the wind chilling her cabin, and the bell tolling every half-hour. When she woke up at dawn, her head swam with the extraordinary events of the day before, from leaving her home, to the amputation, to Dr. Pesce's job offer. Then she remembered that the surgeon might be waiting for her, and hastened to wash and dress.

The doctor snoozed in the chair next to his sleeping patient. She touched Dr. Pesce on the shoulder, waking him. He squinted, as if trying to recall who she was. Then he smiled brightly and said, "I take it you have decided to accept my offer. I will rest for a bit and come back around noon. Soon after that we will be disembarking." He instructed her about feeding the patient, and where to find him if needed.

Mr. Johnson slept most of the time Ella watched over him. When he woke up for a brief time, she fed him broth. Once the doctor came back, she ventured to the dining room for dinner, but soon regretted it. People stared at her as she ate, and several came up to ask about her mother's condition. She gaped in confusion until she remembered yesterday's scene in the dining-room and reassured the patrons that her mother was recovering but could not be disturbed.

Disembarking took longer than Dr. Pesce anticipated. After the ship docked at about three o'clock, they waited for the transport to take the patient to the nearby hospital. When they climbed into a coach, the doctor gave the driver his address, and Ella leaned toward the window, eager to watch London's sites. The first impression disappointed her. Numerous grey buildings crowded the busy streets. Soot covered the roads, sidewalks, and even people. The stench of garbage and manure made her gag. Eventually she dozed off and when she opened her eyes, the horses had come to a stop outside a handsome two-story, brown-stoned house with maples in the front garden.

"Good evening, Matilda. I am home," the doctor called out to his sister when they came through the door.

"Supper is almost ready," came a curt reply.

The doctor led Ella into the small kitchen, where a woman of about fifty, with a brown braid wrapped around her head and sharp, dark eyes, cut vegetables at the table. Upon spying Ella, she put her knife down with a thud and crossed her arms.

"Who is this?" she demanded.

"This is Ella Parker, a… young woman I met on the ship. And… She will help you with your work," the doctor replied.

Ella made a graceful curtsy. "How do you do, Madam?"

Matilda stared at her as if she had fallen from the sky. "What in the world is she doing here?"

The doctor glanced down at his shoes. "Matilda, you complained of having too much work. Now you have help. Ella can translate some French medical texts for me and… sell your herbs."

"Aha, medical texts, books, then help with your patients.

And sell herbs because she is too good to sweep or dust. I see what you are up to, brother. You think this woman can replace Lindsey? Our girl deserves better than some stranger taking her place."

"No one is replacing Lindsey! Miss Ella helped me with a patient and will learn how to assist us further."

"Show me your hands, girl," Matilda ordered.

Ella, shaken by the strange reception, obeyed, and the woman smiled with satisfaction. "These hands have never done difficult work." She felt around her fingertips. "Maybe a little sewing, that's all. Speaking of sewing, let me see your dress."

With her lips pursed, Matilda looked Ella up and down. "Are you a thief? Such fine satin costs a fortune."

"I never…" Ella protested.

"No, you are not. This dress fits you like a glove, I see that now. Do you sew this well yourself?"

"I wish. A well-known modiste made it for me."

"A modiste? Not even a seamstress, but a modiste." Matilda chuckled and mimicked Ella's pronunciation. "Joseph, where did you find this exotic bird?"

"Can we talk privately, sister?" Dr. Pesce said with a stern expression, leading Matilda out of the room.

When they came back, the doctor asked, "Ella, are you being truthful about no one looking for you? Going to prison for kidnapping would be extremely inconvenient for us."

Ella reassured them that no one would come for her. No one knew she had traveled to London, and if someone caught up to her, she would find a way to keep the Pesces out of trouble. Then, staring at his shoes, the doctor asked if she would work for room and board and the learning they could give her. She agreed with eagerness.

Matilda showed her a room on the second floor where she would sleep and brought her a tray of fish and vegetables.

"Do not go exploring on the lowest level," Matilda warned before leaving her for the evening.

That night, Ella slept like a baby. When the light entered her room, she observed her surroundings with curiosity. The bedroom had simple furniture: a table and a chair, a wooden stove, and a wash-basin. Curtains with pink and yellow butterflies, a dollhouse of three floors in the corner, painted scenes of children playing, as well as butterflies and cats possibly drawn by a child.

Ella moved the curtains out of the way, but the view showed nothing more interesting beyond the lush maples than the road and nearby houses. By noticing the morning glow, she judged it was about six. Since she heard no sounds inside, she decided the doctor and his sister still slept, and apparently, they had no servants living with them. She welcomed a chance to explore the house on her own.

After getting dressed, she came out into the hallway. There was only one more door there, and when she tiptoed closer, she heard deep breathing and soft snores, leaving her to guess this was Matilda's bedroom. With nothing more to see on the second floor, she headed downstairs. Besides the kitchen, where she had been yesterday, she found a sitting room with divans, and another room with shelves and cupboards full of jars with various labels, such as: chamomile, lavender, ginger root, cinnamon. It reminded her of a chemist's shop, but smelled sweeter, of flowers and berry teas. Moving on, she went along a different hallway, and discovered an exam room, with a table to lie on, as well as a desk for the doctor, and a shelf full of books. She heard loud snores from the room next to it and guessed it to be the doctor's bedroom.

With the tour of the house finished, she reached for one of the books in the exam room, Hippocrates' *De Materia Medica* and attempted reading it. She found many terms alien and the text difficult, but the illustrations were curious, showing bones, muscles, and organs. Then she remembered Matilda's warning and realized her tour was not finished. You do not forbid people from seeing a certain room and expect them to follow through. It's like giving a child a wrapped gift and presume he or she would not unwrap it and peek.

Just one peek, she thought. *No one will know.*

It took Ella a few minutes to find the door that led to the lowest level. With a lit candle in her hand, she descended the stairs that complained with squeaks. An aroma of wine filled her nose. Did Matilda own a wine cellar? A wall of large, sickly green jars eerily reflected the light of her candle. She approached to examine their contents, bringing her candle closer. Her heart hammered and she gasped when she saw what was inside them. Instead of wines, she recognized the human organs she had seen in the book illustrations: brains, hearts, livers. The largest jar contained a baby with its eyes shut. The labels read: 'Amanda Pikes, brain, age 38', 'Jerald Warren, liver, age 64, tumor', 'healthy heart', 'Lindsey Pesce, lungs, age 17, consumption', and many others she could not stomach examining. Her body shook from head to toe. How could she be so stupid to follow a stranger to his home? Something evil must be happening in this house, for no Christian man would collect organs. And where would he get them, if not by killing his patients to explore what they have inside? She had to get out of there as fast as possible before she became his next victim!

Panting, she ran upstairs and straight into Matilda, who was waiting in the kitchen. The doctor's sister glared with disapproval.

"If you wanted to impress me, you could have made some breakfast. There is no time for idleness in the morning."

Then she perceived Ella's condition and threw her head back laughing. "You snooped downstairs! That's what you get for being nosy."

"I am sorry, this has been a mistake. I will get my things and go," Ella stammered.

"Joseph!" Matilda called out. "The girl saw your treasures downstairs and is keen on leaving."

"Tell her not to hurry," the doctor said from his bedroom.

Ella hesitated, wondering if she should lock herself in one of the rooms and escape through the window. She took a step towards the stairs, but Dr. Pesce came into the kitchen, and his expression, kind and sympathetic, stopped her. Murderers could not look this sweet, she hoped. He beckoned her to sit in his exam room and asked Matilda to make something calming. His sister muttered about wasting valerian root and strode to her herb room. After drinking a spoon of potent liquid, Ella's heart slowed to a normal rhythm.

The doctor gave her a perceptive gaze. "I should have explained about the downstairs, but I thought it could wait. Of course, a girl curious enough to follow me to the sick berth and watch an amputation would take the first chance to explore where she was told not to. You were not prepared to see that room. What did you think it was?"

"Something sinister."

"You had to connect it with my profession, but maybe you were too scared to use your reasoning. Have you ever heard of postmortem?"

Ella shook her head.

"When a patient dies, doctors, and sometimes the family of the deceased, want to know what illness killed him or her. Dissections help doctors progress in our field as well.

Sometimes, I preserve organs for further study. Now do you understand?"

"Yes." She wanted to crawl into a hole. "I've been so stupid."

"No, only unprepared. I noticed you started reading a medical textbook; an excellent one to start with, by the way. Of course, Hippocrates had to dissect corpses to make his illustrations."

He stared at Ella's face. "I think you are restored now. Have breakfast, and Matilda will get you started on your chores. When you get a chance, please begin translating these notes." The doctor handed her a thick folder.

Ella peeked at the writing. "There are medical words here I don't know," she confessed.

The doctor handed her a thick medical dictionary.

After breakfast, Matilda said, "Since you are familiar with the needle, you can do some mending while watching me with my clients." She brought a chair for Ella in the herb room and handed her a pile of ripped clothes.

While Ella struggled with the needle, Matilda answered the door in the back, and brought in women with various complaints and questions.

Several clients named the exact herb or potion they wanted and left within minutes. Others described their problems: a child with a cough; a frequent feeling of exhaustion; a bee sting. Matilda would listen, ask a few questions, and recommend one of her bottles or packages.

The women were dressed in modest clothing. Most were in their twenties and thirties, some in the late months of pregnancy. They spoke to Matilda with deference.

When the last woman left at around five in the evening, Ella asked, "Why don't these women summon a doctor for their complaints?"

Matilda snorted. "Because they are not rich. The wealthy send for a doctor for every cold. The poor go to a charity hospital only for something awful and struggle through everything else. My clients are working women or wives of workmen."

"And only women see you?"

"Yes, women and children. Sometimes wives buy something for their husbands, but often they sneak the remedy into the food. Herbs for coughs work the same on men and women, but men won't hear of it. They will suffer until they cannot take it, and then see a doctor. It's all fine and well with me. Women see a physician when they catch something serious, but otherwise they are happy to buy my remedies for less money. I tell them if I cannot help. I would never sell herbs to a client who needs to go to a hospital."

Matilda busied herself with dinner preparations, and Ella helped her, contemplating all she had learned that day.

* * *

Within a month, Ella settled into a new routine. She learned to perform various household jobs: sweeping, cooking simple dishes, washing clothes, and ironing. Some, like mending clothing, came easy, but her first omelet burned, and she spent the rest of the morning scouring a pan. The first trip to the market proved disastrous as well. She became lost several times among crooked streets and, after hours of wandering, she brought home the goods only to have Matilda rage about the spoiled meat and the outrageously expensive peaches.

The second time was not so bad; she learned to navigate the market and insist on a fair price, and soon enough began to enjoy the trips. Outside of housework, she listened to Matilda helping her clients, made teas per her instructions, and fetched herbs from storage. Once the herb shop closed at five, Ella worked on translations for Dr. Pesce and, if she had energy, she read from the medical books. She rarely saw the doctor, who left after breakfast and returned late in the evening or slept somewhere else.

"Where does he go every day?" Ella asked Matilda.

The woman shrugged. "Men's world. He spends time with fellow doctors, and they discuss various patients or medical news. He also stops by to visit his old patients, but since he spends little time in London, most move on to other doctors and don't want to see him. I don't know why this man cannot be like others and stay home to run his practice. Just watch, by the end of summer, when he has a trickling of patients and a bit of money comes in, he will say that he has had enough and take a ship's surgeon posting."

The translating progressed well, and Ella was eager to show the doctor. Once she got a hang of the French doctor's handwriting and common terms he used, the work became fascinating. Many notes read something like: "A female of forty-seven years presented with a fever, paled skin, grey tongue, and a tender abdomen. After bloodletting at six in the evening, the fever reduced. I prescribed purging by grains of calomel every four hours, and the patient improved. When I left her at ten the next morning, her fever was gone, and her abdomen felt normal." This was one of few good outcomes. Much read similar, but the last sentence often revealed that the patient had succumbed to the illness.

About two weeks after Ella came to live with the Pesces, the doctor warned that he would be going out of town for a couple of nights to visit a friend. When Matilda and Ella finished their stew for supper, a chime came from the backdoor, and Matilda rushed to open it.

A boy of about eight shifted his feet at the door. "Ma said to bring you. Said it is her time."

"And who is your Ma?"

"Mary Tucker."

"Good, I expected her to go into labor a week ago. Are you her oldest, Billy? I delivered you and all your siblings. You will have a new sister tonight, I predict."

Matilda grabbed a bag by the door and shot a glance at Ella. "Do you want to watch a delivery?"

Ella lowered her eyes. "I would rather stay and work on translation, if that's all right."

"Suit yourself." The door slammed behind Matilda and the boy.

Ella arranged her notes and became absorbed in the translation. The case was particularly compelling, about a gendarme stabbed in the chest, his right lung penetrated. With bated breath, she hoped the young man survived the ordeal, and as she read of his full recovery, the backdoor bell chimed again. She rushed to open it, fretting that it could be another woman in labor, and she regretted not asking Matilda where to find her.

The woman at the door was not pregnant or fetching a midwife to attend a birth. Instead, she held a screaming baby in her arms. When Ella ushered her to come into the herb room, she recognized Mrs. Weaver, who came in a week earlier, complaining that her little one cried after eating. The young woman tried to get into the chair but missed it and almost fell. Ella took the distressed infant from her, noticing that the mother was white as a sheet, with grey bags under her eyes.

"I am terribly sorry to have come at such an hour, but I don't know what else to do. Mistress Pesce told me to stop eating dairy, then not to eat any beans, carrots, or cabbage.

I've tried eating nothing but bread, and this one is still screaming, especially at night. She is my third, but I never saw a child with such a sensitive stomach."

Ella scanned the potions and teas, wondering which would restore the mother best. There was nothing she could give a baby this small, as far as she knew. Then it hit her that some hours of uninterrupted sleep would benefit the exhausted woman better than potions.

"Mistress Pesce is away delivering a baby. Why don't you sleep while I handle your little one? You can rest in my room upstairs and will not hear her cries."

Mrs. Weaver gave a doubtful glance, likely torn between the fear of giving her child to a stranger, and the desire to sleep: sleep won. Ella led her to her bedroom and gave her one of her nightgowns.

"Is there anything I can do to make your baby feel better?" she asked while the woman changed.

"If you could lay her down and massage her belly in a circular motion clockwise, that could quiet her for a bit. Then walk around with her but put a rag on your shoulder in case she vomits. And that would be a good thing, because after she empties her stomach she sleeps for a while."

Ella spent a busy night comforting the baby, who screamed bloody murder. Once she got a knack for the massage, the screams quieted down to a whimper. The baby traveled every nook and cranny of the first floor on Ella's shoulder but did not oblige to throw up or go to sleep. When Matilda came home at around five in the morning, sleepyheaded Ella answered the door with the little one still wide awake and squeaking.

"Phew, I thought this would be easy, but the baby grew large, and the mother had a hard time. I almost called for the doctor with his forceps, but we managed in the end. At least I was right that it was a girl. Now, who do we have here?" she exclaimed, staring at the baby. At that moment, the infant threw up all over Ella's shoulder and neck.

"Finally!" Ella cheered, even though she forgot to put the rag in place and her dress was now a mess of reeking wetness. "This is Mrs. Weaver's baby. The mother literally fell off her feet from lack of sleep and food. I let her rest in my room. Is there somewhere we can put this one to sleep?"

"Hold on." Matilda left and then came back shortly, carrying a basket on a stand. "Let me dust it first. It has not been used since Lindsey was a baby."

They put the sleepy child into the basket, swaddling her in a small blanket. When Ella returned after changing her dress, Matilda clicked her tongue. "So, eliminating gassy foods did not work. Time to try goat milk instead of her mother's. Can you run to the market and buy some? Tell the woman who sells it you need the freshest she has."

When Ella returned with the milk, both Mrs. Weaver and her baby were up, and the mother looked much refreshed. They tried to get the baby to drink some goat milk, but she fussed and spit out the strange-tasting liquid. Matilda reassured the mother that the baby would eat when hungry enough.

When Mrs. Weaver left with her baby, Matilda gave Ella an approving nod. "You can be useful after all. I would like to catch up on some sleep after the night I had. You did not sleep either, but at your age, you have more energy. Why don't you manage the customers yourself? As you've seen over the last month, most know what they need. For others, read the labels and notes to figure out what should work. And wake me if someone is in labor, or any other emergency."

Ella found her day in the herb room pleasant. She had a couple of customers in the morning, who asked for ginger root, hickory, and a calming tea. During a lull, she ate breakfast and worked on Dr. Pesce's notes. In the early afternoon, a woman came complaining of insomnia, and Ella sold her chamomile tea. There was a lull again, and Ella thought to surprise Matilda by making something special.

In the pantry, she found apples. Remembering warm apple cakes one of the cooks used to make, Ella searched through Matilda's recipes and found one she could follow. She slid the batter into the oven, congratulating herself on managing all the work without help, when the doorbell chimed again.

The woman at the door was dressed fancier than most customers, but her heart-shaped face wore an expression of great alarm. She held a pretty girl of three by her hand, who resembled her mother, with golden blond hair and blue eyes. She looked around fearfully while holding one hand to her belly. When Ella brought them into the herb room, the mother burst into tears.

"I don't know if you can help us. I brought Violet to the physician first, but his wife said he left to see a patient and may not be back for hours. This is awful."

"What's wrong?" Ella asked, puzzled, since the child was rosy-cheeked and did not show distress.

The woman gave a loud sob. "I brought out various buttons to pick for my new dress. Violet wanted to play with some, and I let her. When I was not watching, she put one in her mouth and… swallowed it."

Ella inhaled sharply. "I will get Mistress Pesce," she told the mother and ran to Matilda's bedroom. Matilda slept, but she shook her awake, explaining the customer's problem.

The midwife gave a mischievous smile. "Tell her, like the words on Solomon's ring, 'that too shall pass.'"

Ella stared in confusion. "But surely something must be done at once for the poor child."

Matilda rolled her eyes. "Who is the mother?"

"I forgot to ask. Blond and blue-eyed, the daughter is named Violet."

Matilda clicked her tongue and got up from her bed. "Not that hen, Mrs. Kelley. Brew her some calming tea before she frets and miscarries. And make enough for yourself, if you get this jumpy over a child swallowing something smooth and round."

While Ella brewed the tea, she listened to Matilda consoling the frightened mother.

"Nothing to fret about. The button will come out in three days or so, without hurting the girl. Teach her to jump rope and look for the darn thing in her poop. If she has trouble going, brew her some senna leaves. You may still be able to use that button," she chuckled.

Mrs. Kelley looked unconvinced. "Maybe I should show her to a physician, just in case?"

"And what will he do? Press on her belly with an intelligent expression on his face, prescribe a purgative that will give her cramps, and charge you twice the fee. In all my experience, I never heard of a child dying from this sort of thing, and believe me, she is not the first one to swallow a button. Be sure to keep your pins and needles away from this magpie until she is six or so and can help you with sewing."

After the mother purchased senna leaves and left with the girl, Matilda shook her head with an amused expression. "First-time mothers. She has a second one in the oven, a boy by my guess, and I can bet when that child swallows something, she will give him a proper scolding and hand him a jump rope without drama. Better yet, she will hide all of her small objects. Speaking of ovens, are you baking something?"

"Oh no! I forgot!" Ella rushed to check on her cake and took it out. "It did not burn." She breathed in the sweet aroma of apples and cinnamon. "I wanted to surprise you."

"Apple cake? I did not have tart apples."

"I found some in the pantry."

"Those are sweet ones, to eat. They are too expensive for baking." Noticing Ella's crestfallen face, she waved her hand. "No matter. It will be extra sweet, and I have not treated myself to a dessert in ages. I'll make some raspberry tea, and we will celebrate your successful day. I looked through your notes on the goods you sold, and you've managed quite well."

As they took out cups and saucers, a girl of ten rang the bell, passing a note from Mrs. Weaver that the baby had goat milk and had not cried afterwards.

The girl held out a bouquet of fresh flowers as a gift of appreciation, and Ella put them into a vase as a centerpiece for the table.

They drank their tea and devoured the cake, while Matilda smiled and talked. "Now you know how to help with colicky babies and children swallowing buttons. I learned those things from other midwives, from the apothecary, from experienced mothers. Sometimes I read pamphlets or medical papers for women, but most of my knowledge comes from talking to others and from experience. I never thought of taking on an assistant, aside from Lindsey, but this job suits you. If you don't want to deliver babies, there is still plenty of work in selling herbs. What do you think?"

"I am happy to help you, but I would like to assist Dr. Pesce as well."

"Why? Women are not supposed to help with surgeries or

cut up bodies to learn what's inside. It's a bad idea, trust me. Those dreadful things are for doctors. You may think my brother has forgotten all about you, but when he reads your translations, he will light up like a lantern. It will be Lindsey's story all over again."

"What happened to her? Was she your niece?"

"I prefer to say daughter, but she was neither. She was a child I delivered. Her mother died of childbed fever, and no one wanted the poor thing. I raised her, taught her to put herbs into the jars, sent her to school to learn reading and writing. At twelve, she attended births with me. She would've made a great midwife. One day, she decided to read the books from Joseph's exam room, and when he appeared here, she asked him questions. He was thrilled by her interest and spent more time at home, growing his practice and teaching her." Beaming at the memories at first, Matilda covered her mouth, her eyes sparkling as she blinked away the tears.

"That's when he started his collection downstairs, and had Lindsey help him with preserving those organs and labeling the jars. I disapproved, telling them the lines are drawn between women's and men's work for a reason. They laughed like I was ignorant, and Joseph declared that Lindsey was as smart as any male apprentice he ever came across, making the girl blush with pride. Then, when she was fifteen, Joseph announced that Lindsey would study in medical school. I don't know what they had planned, because universities do not accept women, but their eyes shone like new coins. It did not come to be."

Matilda looked away and sighed before continuing with the story. "A woman must know her place, or she gets punished. Joseph started taking Lindsey to help with his patients. She went into bad neighborhoods, cared for people sick with various maladies, and soon enough became sick herself. It was a dark day when my brother told me our girl had consumption. Instead of medical school, we spent our savings on her medicines and special hospitals, but she died at seventeen." Matilda grew quiet, staring into her teacup. "Doctor's work isn't only inappropriate for women, but it's also dangerous. Medical men catch diseases in the hospitals, cut themselves with scalpels and die of infections. If they take postings in the military or navy, they perish in the war. Anytime Joseph takes a ship surgeon warrant, I fear he will not come back."

Ella reached for Matilda's hand. "I am sorry about Lindsey, but I still want to learn. If Dr. Pesce has a way of sending me to medical school, I would go."

"I was afraid you would say that. I wanted you to hear my side before Joseph fills your head with his grand ideas. But I see you already know what you want."

When Ella came down for breakfast, Dr. Pesce was at the table with her notes next to his plate of eggs and bacon. "This is great work, Ella. Excellent translation and perfect handwriting. Matilda told me you've been helpful with her clients as well. I hope you are enjoying your time here."

His cheerfulness was infectious, and Ella smiled back. "I like helping her clients. And I am glad you are home because I wanted to ask a few questions about the cases and the medical books I read."

The doctor bobbed his head with enthusiasm. After finishing his breakfast, he invited her into the exam room. They talked until noon about the texts and illustrations; the doctor provided anecdotes about his patients. Then Matilda called Ella to sort through the fresh herbs delivered from the country, while he left to see a patient. Matilda's brows were pulled together, and her speech curt, a change from yesterday's approachable demeanor.

After the doctor returned, the doorbell rang several times, with a couple of clients purchasing herbs, as well as a gentleman, and later a lady to see Dr. Pesce. Soon after the doctor led the female patient to the exam room, he came out seeking Ella. "Miss Little is complaining of sharp pains in her back and side but would not let me examine her alone. Maybe she would be more comfortable with you there."

Ella strode in with the confidence of someone who helped the doctor regularly. "Miss Little, you know that at the doctor's we must put away our modesty for the sake of our health. Please lie down here."

She helped the patient onto the table and lowered the skirts just enough to expose what the doctor needed to see, covering the legs with a blanket. As the doctor fingered the back and abdomen, the woman yelped in pain, and Ella took her hand. When he finished, Ella helped her sit up and straighten her clothes. The doctor stared with a serious expression and explained that it was a kidney stone that caused the pain. He wrote a prescription for a medicine to help it pass and advised Miss Little to drink water with a few spoons of vegetable oil.

When the patient left, the doctor regarded Ella with a spark in his eyes. "Look at you, Ella. You translated much of the notes, made great progress with the books, and helped me with a patient. What do you think now of the room downstairs? Would it scare you?"

"No, I don't think so. I want to see it again."

"In that case, let's conduct a test."

They descended into the room with the wall of jars. The doctor gave her a few minutes to look around, and she examined the contents with curiosity. Brains, livers, hearts, and bones did not spook her anymore, though she avoided looking at the jar with the unborn infant.

The doctor pointed at one of the jars. "Can you identify the organs you see without reading the labels?"

"Small intestine and colon."

"Yes. Can you show me spleen, gallbladder, and pancreas?"

When she pointed at those organs, the doctor nodded with approval. "I find the digestive system intriguing. All those organs working together each time we eat. We are not too good with treating digestive illnesses, short of emetics and clysters, I am afraid. I heard rumors that Dr. Miller is experimenting with stomach surgery, but it's all hush-hush. You should read his articles, by the way. I dare say he is the brightest surgeon of our time."

"I would love to. I know it's not ladylike to admit, but I find medicine fascinating."

"Do you want to learn how the body works? Maybe even watch a dissection?"

"Yes. Very much so."

"You have passed my test. When you asked me to become my assistant, I had to say 'no' because my sister and I are still reeling from Lindsey's death. Yet, I passionately believe a talented woman should not limit herself in her learning, including medicine. You should aim higher, not to be an assistant, but a surgeon. I will tutor you this summer, but you will learn much more than I could ever teach you if you enter medical school. We spent much of the funds I saved for Lindsey's education on her treatment, but there is still some left. Let me use it on your schooling. Lindsey would want this; she was a kind soul. If you become rich someday, you can pay us back. What do you say?"

"This is incredibly generous. I want to go to a medical school. But I don't understand. I thought universities don't accept women."

"Of course. I forgot to explain. You would have to pretend to be a man."

Before she knew what happened, her backside hit the floor, and her chair crashed next to her with a thud.

CHAPTER 5

The scissors snipped right above Ella's ear, and she did her best not to flinch. Her eyes shifted to the window where the maples flaunted their first gold and red among the green. She shamed herself for her desire to cry over her waist-long locks and told herself it was a small sacrifice for her future.

The image in the full-length glass, which the doctor and Matilda brought into her bedroom, became more boy-like with each clip.

"All done," Dr. Pesce declared with a smile.

Matilda, who stood in the corner with arms crossed and a sour expression on her face, came closer to examine his work. "I thought surgeons make straight lines," she barbed. Taking the scissors from him, she trimmed the uneven hair. "That's better."

Ella shook her head, surprised at the lightness of it.

Dr. Pesce nodded with approval. "Now, please put on the clothes on the bed for the full look."

They stepped out while Ella changed out of her dress. When she finished and called them, a green-eyed youth with neat black curls, dressed smartly in a white shirt, black trousers, and a plain brown jacket stared back from the glass. She turned around to let Dr. Pesce and Matilda view her from head to toe.

The doctor fixed his glasses. "Yes, I no longer see a girl. You make a handsome young man. At your age, the transformation is easy."

"That's because you are still flat chested. When your breasts grow, it will be harder to hide your gender," Matilda cut without mercy.

"What will I do?" Ella asked, heat rising to her cheeks.

The doctor frowned. "I suppose you will have to bind your breasts and wear loose clothing."

Matilda clicked her tongue. "Awful thing to do to yourself. You may have trouble breastfeeding later. At least sleep without any binding, or you will deform your bosom."

Ella blushed deeper red. "Maybe I will be fortunate and stay as I am."

"If you can call that fortune," Matilda answered.

The doctor fidgeted and looked away.

Ella clapped her hands. "By the way, doctor, yesterday's medical journal printed an incredible story. This coach driver's leg and foot were terribly swollen. He could barely walk."

"Popliteal aneurysm, no doubt. It's a common malady in his profession. He would need an amputation above the knee and soon. If the aneurysm bursts, he would perish. Unfortunately, even if the poor fellow survives the operation, he would still lose his livelihood."

"Ah, but he was lucky to be seen by Doctor Miller, who had a different solution. The great surgeon made the incision up on the thigh and tied the damaged artery well above the swelling, blocking the flow of blood to the aneurysm. The swelling disappeared in a few days, and six weeks later the patient walked out of the hospital, his leg completely healed. Isn't that astonishing?"

The doctor gave her a wistful smile. "How I envy you, Ella, going to medical school now. It's such an exciting time, so many innovations. All the things you will be learning from esteemed professors. I'm glad you are an avid reader and can absorb information quickly. Don't get cocky, though. My and Matilda's tutoring made you well prepared for the university, but there's no need to show off and volunteer answers too often."

Ella pouted. "I like to offer right answers. My tutors…"

"Forgot to teach you modesty." Matilda cut in, rolling her eyes. "And for heaven's sake, watch how you talk. Your girlish treble rings in my ears when you prattle. Slow down and speak deeper, like a boy would."

Drawing air into her lungs, Ella practices a few simple sentences, deepening her voice.

"You should observe how young men walk and sit and try to mimic their movements," the doctor added.

Ella took a few steps around the room, stretching her arms and legs, sensing the fabric touch her body without restraining it. "These clothes are extremely comfortable. I can run and jump without tripping," she declared.

The doctor cocked his head and spoke in a grave tone. "While men your age do tend to run and partake in various sport activities, I advise you to avoid them. You will lack strength and experience, which may arouse suspicion. Take on the persona of a serious student, interested only in his work. Spend your free time at the library or reading in your room, attend church on Sundays as required, and avoid calling attention to yourself. Do not become that student that everyone is talking about, because popularity will invite scrutiny. Even though you have picked up all I have taught you with great quickness, choose just a couple of subjects in the beginning, such as botany and natural philosophy, as most students do. Add the medical courses later. And, Ella, you may not like this, but hear me anyway: do not trust anyone and do not make friends."

"Do not make friends? Why? I will be lonely."

"Treat it as another sacrifice on the path you have chosen. False friends will discover who you are and tell authorities. Even casual company with other students would do you no good. Most students will be older than you, although university boys as young as ten are not unheard of. Young men tend to drink, smoke, and get themselves into various troubles. Medical pupils, often deemed unworthy of more prestigious professions, have a reputation for being unruly. Ella, heed my advice. You will be keeping a great secret. Do not let people close enough to discover who you are."

The clop of hooves came from the window, and the doctor looked out. "That's your carriage. Mine will come later today."

"You are leaving too?"

Matilda muttered angrily to herself.

"Yes. I've done all I could for you, and now I go where I belong, on a ship. No, Matilda, I cannot be like the doctors who stay in London all year. Prescribing powders and administering clysters day after day drives me batty. My calling is to cut off limbs and sew up wounds. And my reward is watching sunsets at sea. I took a posting to the *Neptune,* a man-of-war. This bloody campaign with France and Spain is not ending anytime soon."

He took out a paper from his pocket and gave it to Ella. "Here is the address of the lodging near the school. Don't expect much, but it's appropriate for a student. Your journey should take about two days, with a stay at an inn. Please write to Matilda often; she will answer and keep me posted. I will receive mail only when at Plymouth. Best of luck, child. We will be waiting for thrilling letters from a medical student named Alan Parker."

* * *

The grounds of the university astonished Ella with their vastness. The buildings reminded her of Roman temples she had seen in book illustrations, the lush gardens boasted trees and flowers from all corners of the world, and the benches beckoned her to sit down and read for hours. Gentlemen of various ages, from adolescents to the grey-haired, hurried along on important business or promenaded in animated conversations. A city within a city, built for learned men.

With a tap of new shoes on the cobblestone path, Ella strode towards the library. A three-story building with stained glass murals appeared to Ella as the fortress of books. She longed to smell the special aroma of old manuscripts, hear the rustle of thousands of pages, and touch the smooth covers of her favorite volumes. With a plan to pick out books for her studies, Ella approached the welcoming entrance. The doors opened, and Ella jumped aside, letting two young men exit. The first one, about her height, raven-haired and hazel-eyed, carried books stacked up to his chin. A tall youngster with red hair and a mean grin tiptoed behind him. The boy that came out first noticed Ella and greeted her, but before she could respond, the other man tripped him, and he fell forward, spilling all his books. The prankster gave a triumphant laugh, yelled a word Ella did not recognize, and ran away.

"Are you all right?" she asked, checking the boy for scrapes as she helped him up.

"I'm fine. Nothing hurt but my pride. You would think there wouldn't be any bullies in this cultured place, but here they are."

"How silly."

"Thank you for your help. I am Oliver Higgins, or you can call me Oli." The young man extended his hand to shake.

"Alan Parker, pleased to meet you," Ella replied, picking up the books. "Human Anatomy. Medical Latin Terms. Are you a medical student?"

"Yes, I am starting the medical course today with Dr. Miller. What about you?"

"I am a medical student as well, but since I just arrived, I haven't signed up for a practical course yet. Do you mean the famous surgeon Richard Miller is teaching your class?"

"Yes, that's him. He's the most popular professor here. I hope I can keep up. He is demanding of his students."

Ella read much of Dr. Miller and the innovative surgeries he performed. A stack of articles written by him sat on the table in her rented room. "Would it be possible to visit the class and meet the esteemed doctor?"

Oli frowned. "Older students told me that Dr. Miller takes his pupils to the dissection room on the first day. Some quit the class after that. You may be better off learning human anatomy from books at first, so you are better prepared for what you will see."

"I think I can handle it."

"In that case, you are braver than me, because sleep eluded me last night." He pulled out a large silver pocket watch. "The class starts in an hour at the medical building."

"That's a beautiful watch."

"Thank you. My parents gave it to me as a going away present before I left for university. I am going to put away these books, and I shall see you in class."

Oli staggered away, balancing his pile with difficulty. Ella tried to ignore the tight feeling in her stomach. Visiting a medical class was contrary to Dr. Pesce's advice. *Surely it could do no harm*, she reasoned.

* * *

The foyer of the medical building was well-lit, spacious, and busy as a beehive, with students darting to classrooms and professors chatting in small groups. Several statues of famous figures in medicine decorated the chamber, and Ella recognized Hippocrates and Ambroise Parè.

To her surprise, there was also a statue of a woman holding a skull; the nameplate said Anna Manzolini. The marble staircase to the second floor drew eyes with its cool whiteness. A bearded, middle-aged man in an elegant jacket descended the stairs with an air of self-assurance. He stopped on a second step from the bottom and made a motion to approach him. About twenty students, scattered around the foyer, formed a semicircle around him. Ella found herself flanked by Oli on one side and the red-headed prankster who tripped him on another.

The man observed the pupils with a stern gaze. "I am Dr. Miller, a surgeon and a professor of medical studies." The doctor's voice was deep and melodic. "Medicine is a profession for lifelong learners, tireless overachievers, and zealous spirits. In this university we continuously push the envelope of treating the most malevolent diseases. As my students, you will conduct research and compose essays, follow me during rounds, and observe my surgeries. As you progress in your learning, you will take shifts at the hospital and assist with patient treatment.

Some of you will find my class too demanding and leave.

I welcome that, because I believe doctors should be held to the highest standards.

The cream of the crop, however, will find limitless opportunities to pursue their passion. Your training in this college will take two years. At the end of your studies, you will submit a thesis and take an oral exam in front of a panel of professors. Those who pass will be ready to pursue one of the noblest professions."

Mesmerized by the doctor's words, Ella nodded fervently.

Dr. Miller swept the students with another unsmiling gaze and continued. "As you likely heard, I start the first class differently than my colleagues. We will proceed to the hospital building, located behind this one, and go down to the dissection room. This lesson may help some of you decide whether you will want to continue or opt for another field of study."

The doctor descended the final step and strode toward the hospital. The students exchanged anxious glances and followed him like ducklings behind their mother.

* * *

The corpse of a man, stark naked, lay on a table in the middle of the room. The skin had greyed, and the face took on an ageless quality. The silence in the morgue was so complete that Ella heard the rapid breath of each petrified pupil. Her nostrils wrinkled at the familiar smell of rotting flesh that she first experienced during postmortems with Dr. Pesce.

Dr. Miller came to stand over the cadaver, facing the crowd. "The people who donated their bodies to science, or whose families allowed us to study them, give us invaluable opportunities to advance the study of medicine. Thanks to them, we can examine organs, discover the causes of death, and practice surgical techniques. We will begin with the cardiovascular system. Would anyone like to volunteer to make an incision and peek at the heart? I must warn you to be careful not to cut yourself. A small nick during dissection could result in a terrible infection. Yet, if you want to become surgeons, practice is vital."

The professor watched the group, offering a scalpel. Ella glanced around, anticipating numerous hands to go up. To her astonishment, the pupils looked at the floor or ceiling, avoiding Dr. Miller's perceptive gaze. *Why are they not jumping at a chance to impress the renowned professor?* she wondered.

"Why don't you try? You know where the heart is, right?" she whispered to Oli but regretted it when she noticed his face turned green. He shook his head and cringed.

Dr. Miller sighed with resignation. "I must say I am disappointed. I expected at least one of you to overcome your squeamishness. This may be the worst group I have to teach. Well, if there's no one—"

"May I?" Ella's voice rang, startling a couple of people.

"Be my guest, Mr.?" He raised his eyebrows, waiting for a name.

"Alan Parker."

"Proceed, Mr. Parker. You want to cut over the sternum."

Ella took the scalpel without hesitation and made a vertical incision over the middle of the chest, cutting through the tissues. Dr. Miller helped her break open the ribcage with a hack saw. This part required stronger arms than Ella's. She made a mental note to practice sawing large bones to build her muscles. Finally, after some brutal chopping, they lifted the ribs towards the head and exposed the lungs and the heart.

"Mr. Parker, you are restoring my faith in this class.

Would you be able to tell me the parts that make up the heart?"

Ella opened her mouth to answer when Oli distracted her by clutching his stomach and dashing out of the room. After composing herself, she started: "The parts of the heart are right and left ventricle, and right and left atrium." Ella pointed out the four parts. "The major blood vessels bringing blood to and from the heart are superior vena cava, aorta, pulmonary artery, and pulmonary vein."

After sharing more facts about the heart, and answering a few questions, Ella inspected the blood vessels. Her eyebrows rose with surprise at her discovery. "This cadaver's aorta is ruptured, a condition called aortic aneurism, usually fatal."

The doctor stared back with marvel. "Excellent observation, Mr. Parker. I do not see your name on the class roster. Why is that?"

"I came to observe."

"Looks like you managed more than just observing. I suggest you register for this class at once. What other classes are you taking?"

"Botany, natural philosophy, and Greek."

"Afraid to overextend ourselves, are we? Add my class, chemistry, and anatomy. That goes for everyone, by the way."

Ella nodded with vigor, and at the next moment jumped at the thud of someone hitting the floor. The man who swooned was Oli's red-headed tormentor.

"Every year someone faints, and it's often the largest man. I wonder what did it, the dissection, or the addition of more classes to his schedule," Dr. Miller jested as he pulled out smelling salts from his pocket and waved them under the student's nose.

When the young man had been revived and sat up, Dr. Miller turned back to Ella.

"You have shown an impressive performance today, Mr. Parker. How old are you?"

"Fifteen."

"Remarkable. I take it you had schooling in anatomy before you came here. If the rest of your studies go as well as your first day, we can expect a bright future for you."

Ella blushed and thanked the professor. After Dr. Miller dismissed the class, many of the students approached Ella to introduce themselves and shake her hand.

Oli came up last, pale, and covered in sweat. "Alan, that was fantastic. I am sorry I distracted you. You will be the talk of the school by noon after receiving a nod from the professor."

"Thanks Oli. I must go to my next class. I hope you feel better."

"I'm fine but will be remembered for my weak stomach." He gave a self-deprecating laugh. "Dr. Miller probably put a minus by my name. I hope William Jeffers, that's the fellow who swooned, received two minuses. Anyway, I was going to ask if you would have tea with me after classes. My treat, of course."

"Sorry, but I will be busy tonight."

"How about tomorrow?"

"Engaged as well."

Oli looked down at his shoes. "Have a good day then."

"You as well."

Ella's heart gave a pinch as she replied to the crestfallen Oli.

* * *

September 10,

Dear Matilda and Dr. Pesce,

In my two weeks here, I've settled fine in my new lodgings. I cannot say I love them; the room is tiny and smells of boiled onions; the landlady is unfriendly, and the tenants are noisy. This morning I was woken up by the most revolting insect running up my arm. The landlady could not understand why I made such a fuss over a cockroach. On the upside, the place is all I need and close to the campus.

My first day did not go as planned, but better. I attended Dr. Miller's class: yes, the famous Dr. Miller I read so much about. When no one volunteered to perform a dissection, I could not help myself and raised my hand. After that incident, I became well-known around the school. Dr. Pesce, I know it is not what you recommended, but I view it as a positive. Other classes are going well, although chemistry is quite hard. The students are friendly, especially Oli Higgins. I think he likes me because we are the shortest people in the room, although he is three years older than me. I am following your advice and not making friends. Instead, I am studying and sawing bones in the dissection room till my arms ache. Good health to both of you and a safe voyage to our dear doctor.

Love, Alan Parker.

* * *

October 2,

Dear Alan,

I am glad that you are finding your studies exciting and challenging. That's why you went to school after all. It was not to live in luxury or to enjoy yourself with new friends. However, I am much concerned for your showing off during

your first class and becoming 'well-known' among students. I am sure my brother will be as well. You may think yourself popular and special, but no one likes a know-it-all. You should not make friends, and you may easily make enemies.
Last night Mrs. Kelley went into labor with her baby boy. She had a straightforward delivery, but if you heard it from her, she went through the nine circles of Hell. It was one of my hardest births, and all from her fretting. I don't know how this woman will survive any real trouble in her life.
I went to bed completely exhausted.
I will send Joseph your love. Please take to heart all he said to you.
Love, Matilda Pesce.

CHAPTER 6

The chemistry instructor, Professor Spears, asked the students to turn in their assignments, but only a few, including Ella, handed in their papers.

Some pupils voiced their displeasure at the difficulty of the task.

"That homework was impossible. How did you do it?" Oli marveled.

"I searched in the library. You should read Joseph Priestley's paper on dephlogisticated air," she answered.

"Dephlo – what?"

A folded paper landed on Oli's desk; he glanced at it and reddened. Hearing Jeffers sniggering from his desk in the back, Ella grabbed the paper from Oli.

"Don't read it, please," he pleaded.

She crumpled it into a ball.

Mr. Spears, a feeble-looking man with a long beard and a monotonous voice, asked the students to quiet down. "The point of the assignment was to set the tone for the class and broaden your thinking. I did not expect anyone to come to the right answer, but I wanted you to try. We had one student who designed the experiment. Mr. Parker, please show the class how to make oxygen."

Ella jumped to her feet and strode over to the cabinet of supplies. After a quick search through the shelves full of flasks of various sizes, jars with liquids and powders of all colors, and sets of mortars and pestles, she grabbed candles, empty jars with stoppers, a flask, two connected L-shaped glass tubes, and a bottle with bright orange powder. With care, she poured a teaspoon of the orange powder into the flask, stoppered the flask, and placed it on the ring stand, over an unlit candle.

"This powder is mercury oxide. I am going to heat it," she explained, forcing her voice to sound low-pitched.

Using the glass tube, she connected the stoppered flask with the powder to one of the jars. She lit two candles, placed them inside the two jars, and stoppered them.

"As you can see," she said, "the flask with the mercury oxide is connected to a jar with a burning candle by a glass tube. The other jar with the candle is a reference. It's stoppered but not connected."

She then lit the candle under the ring stand.

"As I heat the mercury oxide, the temperature rises, and oxygen is released. It flows into the jar with the candle through the tube. We will observe that the candle that's receiving oxygen will burn brighter and longer than the candle inside a corked jar with just air."

As she predicted, the candle without the flow of oxygen went out within thirty seconds while the one receiving oxygen burned with brightness for several minutes, even after she stopped heating the powder.

Mr. Spears clapped his hands and some of the students joined him while a few glared. "Excellent work, Mr. Parker. What a way to start the school year."

Ella took her seat with a shy smile. Mr. Spears lectured on gases found in the air and their properties, and the class fell under the drowse-inducing spell of his voice. Only a few students, Ella and Oli among them, took careful notes. As soon as the teacher dismissed them, Jeffers scrambled for the door.

With precise aim, Ella threw the crumbled paper. It hit him on the back of his head, like she wanted. Startled, he glanced around, searching for the assailant. Oli and Ella bent down, gathering their books, avoiding his gaze. They heard him stomp out of the room muttering that he would deal with whoever had hit him later.

"Good aim," Oli praised.

Ella rolled her eyes. "I cannot believe that we are medical students and still prank each other like children. Did he call you names in that note?"

"Yes, it's all silliness," Oli answered in a low voice, the corners of his lips turned down.

When they stepped into the corridor, Jeffers blocked their path. A head taller than them, he looked down at Oli like at a disgusting insect. Oli's shoulders stiffened, and he drew a sharp breath. Ella flinched and clenched her teeth.

He isn't likely to attack us right at school, but if he does, we'll run, she thought, willing her pulse to slow.

"Higgins, you scat, I want to talk to Parker."

Oli's voice shook. "No, I am not going. Whatever problem you have with me, Parker has nothing to do with it."

Jeffers smiled. "I have no problem with Parker. Just the opposite. I was going to invite him to visit a tavern after school as my treat. What do you say, Parker?"

"What do you want of me?" Ella asked.

"A bit of homework assistance each week. Show me your answers for chemistry and Greek. In exchange, I'll treat you to excellent dinners with plenty of wine and introduce you to my father. He is on the university board, you know. Connection with our family could give you all kinds of advantages."

"Don't trust him, Alan," Oli said.

The bully pushed Oli towards the wall, making him almost drop his sack of books. "You stay out of this and keep quiet. If you tell, both Parker and I will be in trouble, and you don't want that, right?"

Oli stared down at the floor.

Jeffers turned to Ella and offered his hand to shake. "Do we have a deal?"

Ella ignored his stretched out hand and raised her chin. "No. I can pay for my own meals, and I am not helping you cheat. Excuse me, I have another class."

She walked around Jeffers, looking straight ahead. Oli's hurried footsteps sounded behind her.

* * *

Oli, standing in front of the class, spoke with a ring in his voice, waving his hands wildly.

"Thus, according to Maimonides, a diet rich in fruit, vegetables, and legumes promotes good digestion and prevents diseases, such as constipated bowels and piles. It contributes to the patient's overall health and mood."

He halted when seeing that Dr. Miller crossed his arms and bent his head to one side.

"Mr. Higgins, are you quoting Maimonides, a medieval Jewish philosopher who died six centuries ago? Surely you can find a more current source. A number of my recent articles would do, for example."

Oli touched his reddened face. "If Hippocrates' teaching

is still relevant, why shouldn't we study Maimonides? His ideas on preventive medicine, hygiene, and compassion to patients' suffering were ahead of his time."

"His Treatise on Poisons and Their Antidotes is worth reading, but other works are obsolete rubbish. Your time would be better spent by paying more attention to modern physicians. Not all of them, of course," he said with a chuckle. "I hope you all are reading my publications and the sources I recommend and not falling for the nonsense a few of my colleagues publish. You may sit down, Mr. Higgins."

Oli, sweaty and flushed, took his seat next to Ella. "He hates me. He always makes me look like a fool," he whispered to her.

Ella frowned. "He doesn't hate you, and he is right. We have a fantastic opportunity to learn from one of the greatest surgeons of our time. His publications are outstanding. Do you read them?"

"I do, but I read other experts as well. Not everyone agrees with him."

Dr. Miller wrote the homework assignment on the board while Ella's attention drifted to the vibrant plants on the windowsills that perfumed the air. As one could expect, Dr. Miller's room was the most curious of all the classrooms that she attended. A pair of male and female skeletons, affectionately named Adam and Eve, stood in the corner. Large illustrations of nervous, cardiovascular, and other human body systems decorated the walls. Unlike most of the other dusty classrooms, the professor required his assistants to keep his room spotless.

Finished with assigning the homework, Dr. Miller strolled around the classroom, laying graded papers on students' desks. "Mr. Carrow, well done. Mr. Parker, another excellent piece of work. " He handed Ella her essay on blood diseases.

"Mr. Jeffers, great improvement, but I had the strangest feeling that I read a similar essay before, some years ago. Mr. Higgins, quite disappointing, again. Please see me after class."

He slammed the marked up paper in front of Oli who was engrossed in wiping something written on his desk with a hankie. The young man looked up with confusion. After processing the professor's words, he flushed and stared at his paper in shock. In a whisper no one but Ella could hear, he mouthed, "I stayed up for three nights writing it."

"Ouch, I am sorry," Ella said. She thought to offer help with his future papers, but stopped herself. Such a display of friendliness was exactly what Dr. Pesce warned her about.

Dr. Miller cleared his throat. "Today you will accompany me on hospital rounds. This will become a regular part of the class. I have several interesting cases to show you."

Excited students followed the professor on the short walk to the hospital. Keeping pace with the rest of the class, Ella shivered in the biting wind. Oli approached and stammered into her ear, "He will expel me from his class, I know it. I am working so hard, but nothing I do is good enough."

"Maybe it's for the best, Oli? Perhaps another field would suit you better," Ella suggested.

The young man shook his head and tightened his mouth. They started the rounds with children's wards. Ella lost count of the rooms full of young patients: measles, typhoid fever, smallpox, even scurvy and starvation. While the last two were treatable with proper diet, the other diseases did not have a uniform cure. Dr. Miller described treatment plans consisting of various medications, purging, bloodletting, warm baths, and rest. He also emphasized isolation from patients with other maladies and fresh air. Ella made mental notes, hoping she would retain the concepts in her head until she could write them down in her notebook. Sick and weary children pained her heart, but she told herself those patients had the best chances of a successful outcome in the hospital.

They went through the men's and women's wards, and many of the maladies were the same as the children's, with the addition of work and road accidents. Patients suffered from broken bones, and some required amputations due to infections.

Before entering the last ward, Dr. Miller said, "here you will see some curious cases that I have been treating. Let us proceed."

He stopped by the first bed, occupied by a boy of about ten years old. He pointed to the child's neck that had one vertical and two transverse sutured scars. "Can anyone name the surgery this patient underwent? You, Mr. Carrow?"

"A tracheotomy. A delicate and complicated surgery."

Ella's knees went weak at hearing Walter Carrow's velvety voice. He was by far the most handsome young man in her class, with almond eyes and curly black hair, and an excellent student as well. She pinched her hand behind her back to stay focused.

"Can you give more detail on how it's done?"

Ella waited for Carrow to answer, but he looked away, shaking his head. She raised her hand with eagerness. "The procedure consists of an incision at the front of the neck and the insertion of a tube."

Dr. Miller nodded with a smile. "Correct. When this patient was brought to me, he could barely breathe. Diphtheria produced membranes that blocked his airways. I put in a silver tube that allowed the air in." Dr. Miller asked the boy to open his mouth, letting Ella and other students look inside.

"Incredible." Ella whispered to Oli but stopped gushing

upon seeing his dejected expression. "Try to answer some questions. Show you are putting in an effort," she suggested.

Coming over to the next bed, Dr. Miller introduced the case. "This good fellow came back from travels around Africa, where he contracted malaria. Can anyone tell me how this illness is treated? Mr. Higgins, you have your hand up, finally?"

"Malaria's primary symptom is fever, which is commonly treated by bloodletting or leeches," Oli said but halted when Dr. Miller shook his head.

"Many doctors would do just that, Mr. Higgins, and see their patients weaken and worsen. There is a highly effective cure for malaria. I see Mr. Parker knows it."

Ella forced herself not to jump like a pup. "Jesuit's bark."

"Right again, Mr. Parker. An expensive remedy that comes to us from Peru. Besides malaria, it cures yellow jack and even atypical pneumonia. I treated patients with relentless fevers, and nothing worked but the powder of Jesuit's bark."

Ella sidestepped to whisper to Oli. "It was a good attempt."

"Yet wrong again."

Dr. Miller moved on to the last bed, which contained a patient with a wounded arm. The doctor pointed out the signs of infection: ooze and a putrid smell.

"What do you propose as a treatment? Let's hear from someone new. How about Mr. Jeffers?"

"With an infection like this, the arm must be amputated."

"You would make a good army surgeon. Lose a limb but save a life. How about you Mr. Parker, do you concur with Mr. Jeffers?"

"Yes, the arm must be amputated to prevent gangrene," Ella responded, unsure what the professor was hinting at.

With a twinkle in his eye, the doctor explained. "I have been looking for a treatment for infected wounds, and I have found some success with diluted gin. The wound looked worse yesterday, but after soaking it in my solution overnight, I see some improvement. We will continue observing the progress, and maybe this patient will keep his arm."

Ella gave the professor an astonished look which made him chuckle. If Dr. Miller's cure worked consistently, he would be lauded as a hero. The doctor spoke of some of the dangers of infections then dismissed the class.

* * *

At the doors leading out of the hospital, Ella remembered Oli. After waiting for him for ten minutes or so, she returned and saw him a short distance away conversing with Dr. Miller. She moved away, giving them privacy, but they spoke loud enough for her to hear.

"I asked you to stop by and talk to me after class. Where did you go?" Dr. Miller reproached.

"I went back to the children's ward to see if the girl with pox, who was crying during the rounds, calmed down."

"Her physical condition was satisfactory when I examined her. Did she complain of something?"

"She missed her family and wanted to talk about a brother she lost."

Dr. Miller checked his watch. "Mr. Higgins, I am sure you will not be surprised to hear that I am recommending you leave my class. Your essays do not reach the standard set for my students, and your attempts at surgical techniques are atrocious. I suggest you switch to botany; plants will not scream when you mangle them."

The young man stood staring down, flushed, and

breathing hard. "I was meant to be a doctor. There is nothing else I want to do but help the sick."

"I keep only those pupils who show potential. Retaining you as a student will waste your time and mine."

Oli's face contorted with agony, and his whole body shook.

After weighing caution against kindness, Ella approached the two men. "Doctor, I would like to tutor Mr. Higgins and help him reach the level you expect of your students," she proposed.

"Mr. Parker," the professor exclaimed, "you already juggle a busy schedule of classes and practices at the dissection room. And I don't normally allow first-year students to tutor. Are you sure you want to take on this responsibility?"

"I would like to try."

The professor stroked his chin. "Some students do master concepts better when they explain them to someone else. Very well, give it a try. If I do not notice improvements in a month, I will see to Mr. Higgin's dismissal."

The doctor walked away, and Oli gave her a look of gratitude. "Alan, thank you from the bottom of my heart. I am afraid Dr. Miller has made up his mind about me, but I appreciate you giving me more time. May I ask, why you are helping me?"

"I think we could learn from each other. I may have better grades, but you helped a patient. Authoring brilliant essays and performing successful surgeries are skills acquired with practice. When you went back to visit the distressed child, you reminded me of why I want to become a doctor. Let's see your papers first and then review your suturing technique."

* * *

At a table in an empty classroom, Ella leafed through pages covered with neat handwriting and marked with blood red notes and strike-throughs. While the remarks and pointed out mistakes were fair, overall, the essays deserved better marks in Ella's opinion. Puzzled, she kept reading for clues in the professor's comments. Finally, the answer dawned on her.

"In your research, you refer to Dr. Miller's papers and then argue against what he wrote."

"Yes. Oftentimes other doctors make a more compelling argument," Oli explained.

Ella gave him a hard stare. "Don't you see a problem here?"

"Shouldn't I be free to express my thoughts?"

"Yes, of course. How well does that go for you?"

"Could he fail me for disagreeing with him?"

"Not officially, but he can find plenty of other faults and build a case for your dismissal. If you want to stay, stop irking him with every paper, and support his views. In my opinion, it's arrogant of you to argue against the great doctor with volumes of experience. I suggest you read his feedback and expand your research where he indicated. Allow me to read the draft of your next essay, and I will have you read mine. Now, let us proceed to a practical exercise."

With the school year two months in, the dissection room was full of students working at each table. The crowded space was hot from the blazing fire, and the stench of a dozen corpses was stifling. The experienced second-year students sliced their cadavers with great enthusiasm, while the first-year pupils held their instruments in tight fists, their eyes widened, as they made careful incisions or stitches. At the table next to Ella's, a couple of young men hacked into a skull. At the table behind them, their classmate, Walter Carrow, sweated and panted while sawing off leg bones with a capital saw. His shirt stuck to his body, and Ella had to force herself to stop gawking at his muscular chest.

"This one has remains of his last meal in his stomach. I think it was meat stew," someone yelled.

"Great. Now I won't eat stew for a week," his partner answered.

The body in front of Ella and Oli was that of a man, rather young, judging by muscle structure. Ella covered the face and genitals because Oli kept staring at them. It gave the body some dignity as well.

Oli blanched, and his eyes darted around like those of a frightened deer. "Can't I practice on the pig first?" he pleaded.

Ella crossed her arms. "No. We are fortunate to have a body available. Why are you afraid of this cadaver? You cannot hurt him. Here, I'll show you."

She grabbed a scalpel and made a long, vertical incision. Then she threaded a needle and sutured with practiced movements, sewing through layers of tissues.

"How are you so good at this?" Oli asked.

"Embroi- I mean… practice. Now do the same on the other leg."

With his hands shaking, the young man picked up the scalpel and made an incision. His stiff fingers began threading the needle, but he could not get the thread through the hole. He kept trying and trying, becoming more flustered with each attempt. Sweat appeared on his forehead and his breathing became rapid.

Ella sighed with exasperation. "If this were a patient, he would have bled out by now. Not to mention the pain he would have endured. Surgeons conduct operations in a couple of minutes, or the patient can die of shock."

Oli's expression became dejected, and Ella saw that her

outburst hurt him. She threaded the needle for him, and he made hesitant, wide stitches. She had him try again, but he did just as poorly.

"We'll practice together every night until you get it right," Ella said.

They switched to sawing bones, since both lacked the strength required for the job. After an hour of grueling effort, they left the dissection room sweaty and weary.

* * *

After three taxing days, they'd made little progress with suturing. Oli was as scared and stiff as on first practice, and Ella's patience ran out.

At the end of her wits, she yelled, "Oli, you are an army surgeon, and I am brought to you with my leg sliced by a sword. Are you going to stand there for ten minutes threading the needle and let me die of blood loss?"

"Alan, it's bad luck to say such things!" Oli protested.

"Are you a superstitious peasant or a future doctor? Show me how you will save my life. If you don't get this needle threaded in ten seconds, I will cut myself with this scalpel and you will have to suture me for real."

"No! The infection!"

"I am counting: ten, nine…"

Oli glowered and tightened his mouth. He stopped tremoring, and his movements became determined. After a couple of close attempts, the thread jumped into the needle's eye. He made several wide stitches, connecting the layers, then corrected, making tacks smaller and tighter. The last few sutures he sewed quite well and with a good speed. When he finished, he gripped the table and exhaled with relief.

Ella clapped him on a shoulder.

"Would you have cut yourself like you threatened?" Oli asked, breathing hard.

"No, not in the dissection room. I am not mad."

"You were convincing. If you don't become a doctor, you should try acting."

She had Oli cut and suture again, and this time he threaded the needle on the first try and made a better and faster job of stitching. His manner became more relaxed and confident.

After closing another cut, Oli confessed, "I thought I couldn't do it, but it was all in my head."

"Practice two hundred more times and it becomes easy." Ella teased with a wink.

* * *

November 5,

Dear Matilda and Dr. Pesce,

I hope this letter finds you well. I am receiving top marks in all my classes. We started rounds with Dr. Miller, and some of the cases are extremely fascinating. He is a true innovator and attempts procedures others would not do.

Yesterday we watched the professor perform a lithotomy, an operation to remove a bladder stone. I will not go over the details or poor Matilda may hit the floor. The stone was about the size of a walnut, and the twenty-seven-year-old man was in terrible pain before the surgery. The procedure itself was agonizing for the patient as well, but Dr. Miller was lightning fast. It was a privilege to see the master at work. The recovery went well.

I turned out to be a natural at suturing. Who knew that embroidery would pay off so well! Several teachers remarked that my stitches are always even, neat, and nicely placed. I

*even tutored Oli, and he improved his technique and speed. I
help him with his essays and research as well. Don't worry,
we stick to my rules. We meet in the classrooms or the library,
discuss school subjects only, and never go out to taverns or
theaters like other students. We do well as study partners. He
was in danger of expulsion from our class, but his grades
improved enough to stay.*
I hope you are well.
Love, Ella Parker

Ella heated the wax to seal the letter when her mistake
dawned on her. With a sigh, she dipped the pen into the ink
again and rewrote the letter, signing 'Alan Parker' in case her
message fell into the wrong hands. The original she burned
on the flame of her candle.

Can't be too careful, she thought.

* * *

December 3,
Dear Alan,
*I hoped my previous letter would bring you down to earth, but
no, I see your head stayed in the clouds. Now you are
flaunting your knack for suturing. Would it kill you to
struggle with the needle like everyone else? I hope you did
not share your secret to success. I can almost hear you boast,
"I tried a little embroidery as a child!" The way you are
going, you will be discovered before Christmas.*
*Please stop this madness with tutoring Oli. If he fails his
classes, so much worse for him. I see no benefit to you with
having such a study partner, especially one that cannot keep
up with the schoolwork. I suspect that your 'partnership' has
more to do with your tendency to show off by contrast,*

*thinking you shine brighter in comparison to a poor student.
Or maybe you fancy this Oli more than a friend, and if that's
the case, there is even more reason to break all ties with him
at once, before you accidentally reveal your feelings and your
gender.*

*I am busy preparing the cold and influenza remedies ahead of
the season. Soon enough my doorbell will ring non-stop with
women chattering their teeth from fever, or mothers falling
over after sleepless nights with their coughing babies. You
should stock up on mint, ginger, and black pepper in case you
catch a chill.*

Love and take care of yourself,
Matilda Pesce

CHAPTER 7

The yew tree, lit with candles, beckoned Ella inside the shop. The dancing flames mesmerized her, and the smell of the evergreen tickled her nose. She felt warmer just standing near it.

"You like it?" the shop owner asked with a thick accent and a welcoming smile. His round belly and a white beard reminded her of Father Christmas.

"It's beautiful. What is it?"

"A Christmas tree. We have them in my native Prussia. I hope they catch on in England someday. Are you shopping for presents?"

"Yes. I need something for my… aunt and uncle."

The shop owner pointed her towards a display of woolen gloves, hats, and scarves in bright colors. "These are of excellent quality."

Ella fingered the thick knitting. The Pesces could use warm clothing; Matilda traversed London in all weather delivering babies, and Dr. Pesce sailed the north seas which must have been horribly cold. "I will take the red set and the grey one as well."

"Great choice. If you like, my daughter will wrap them in a special box with a bow."

Ella agreed, and a girl of thirteen busied herself with golden ribbons and silver wrapping paper.

"Anything else?"

Ella was about to say 'no' when she remembered Oli. In his last letter, Dr. Pesce stressed caution regarding her acquaintanceship with him. Yet, she could no longer go three days without seeing her study partner. Bouncing off ideas and debating opposite points of view brought out the best in both. A Christmas gift would be a nice reciprocation for the medical papers he translated from German for her.

"I need a gift for a friend."

"A lady friend?" the shopkeeper asked with an amused grin.

"No. A fellow university student."

"Perhaps he could use a pair of warm gloves as well."

Ella shook her head. Gloves seemed personal, something a girl would give.

"Then something you can enjoy together. A bottle of wine or a chess set."

She shifted her feet. "No, I am thinking something useful for his studies."

"How about this writing set? Quill pens from goose feathers, India ink, fine ink well, letter seal and wax."

The set was handsome, especially the white ink well with the gold border, but the price tag made Ella cringe. She had already splurged on gifts for Matilda and the doctor. "It's too expensive for me."

After rubbing his chin, the shop owner offered a ten percent discount in honor of the holiday. Ella bargained to fifteen percent, and the man agreed. With her presents wrapped and her heart singing, Ella exited the shop.

* * *

When she came to call on Oli at his rooms, she heard the clicking of flatware on plates and smelled a mouth-watering aroma of rosemary and sage. Oli dined with other tenants, most of them students at the university.

"Alan, please join us!" he called out to her. "We are feasting on goose. I did the carving, and that's why the poor bird resembles a war casualty. We've been talking about holiday plans and have refrained from political quarrels for a whole hour."

"Now, that's Christmas spirit," one of the diners jested.

She surveyed the group, who drank tea and wine, and stabbed their knives and forks into the bird. It was a similar scene to what she might see in her own building's dining room, which she avoided regularly. Some of the men at the table were medical students and knew her. She longed for conversation and news, but the idea of eating with them made her self-conscious.

Hungry students wolfed down food in big bites. They even held their mugs of tea differently than her: cradling their cups rather than holding by the handle and extending their pinkies, as she had learned from her governess.

"Thank you, but I already ate. I have something for you."

Oli rose and followed her into the hall. "You made a list of assignments for me?"

His tone was serious, like he expected her to do such a thing. And why not? She planned on studying during the break.

"No, I have a gift for you." The silver paper rustled as she handed him the box. "Merry Christmas!"

Oli gaped as he accepted the box, and his cheeks flushed burgundy.

"Thank you so much. Oh Golly, I am so sorry, I did not think of getting you something."

"You don't have to—"

"No, I will fix this and get you something today. You are not leaving yet?"

She considered visiting Matilda, but a trip to London was expensive. "I am not leaving at all. I will be here for the holidays."

Oli shifted his feet and bit his lip. "I leave tomorrow morning to visit my family. I would love to invite you to come along, but my family is large and noisy, and our house is small."

"Oli, I did not expect you to invite me. I will enjoy catching up on reading. There are some French texts I've been meaning to translate."

"You have such a great work ethic. Again, I am terribly sorry."

"Stop apologizing and open my present."

Oli pulled on the golden ribbons and tore the wrapping. His smile widened as he opened the box. "It's a marvelous set, Alan. Thank you, and have a great holiday."

* * *

When Ella stepped into her building, hungry for dinner and anticipating a quiet evening, the landlady called to her in an annoyed tone. "Mr. Parker, these gentlemen have been waiting for you for over two hours."

Surprised, Ella surveyed the three strangers. One was grey-haired, medium in height, and thin; he regarded her with penetrating blue eyes. He had a large jaw that characterized him as decisive, and he had the air of a leader. The other two men were much taller, younger, and large-framed. While their clothing was ordinary, they made her think of policemen. A chill went up her spine, and Matilda's warning ran through her mind. The midwife foretold her downfall; she called attention to herself with her success in school, and someone must have guessed her secret.

"Mr. Parker, why don't we speak in your room," the older one addressed her, keeping his tone pleasant. All three of them rose. One of the tall men walked behind Ella, cutting off any escape to the front door.

They strode up to her room. The older man pulled out Ella's chair, sat down facing the bed, and motioned for her to take a seat on it. The other two remained standing, their backs rigid, arms behind their backs. One stood near the window, the other by the door.

The older man spoke first. "I am detective Charles Stone, and these are my associates, Mr. Bates and Mr. Kinsley." He did not clarify who was who. "Let's save time by acknowledging you are Eloise Parker, daughter of the Earl of Greenwoods."

Ella said nothing, but her heart drummed against her ribs so hard she thought they could hear it. *How did they find me?*

"Your family physician described a scar on your neck. Shall we look for that scar?"

"No," she lowered her eyes, "you don't need to look." She wanted to cry, but she would not give these men the satisfaction. Giving her voice serenity and keeping her expression blank, she asked, "Did the university send you?"

"No. We were hired by Mr. Hastings, your father's lawyer. We will take you back to your father."

Her stomach lurched. "I don't want to go."

"You are a child and have no say in the matter."

"My father could harm me, which is why I left home in the first place."

"I am sure you exaggerate. I've met your father and found him to be a reasonable man. Your maid reported that he beat you, but that's a parent's job to punish impertinent children."

"Do you know how I received the scar you mentioned?"

"Your doctor said you slipped on glass, and your father confirmed the injury was accidental. I believe them more than your maid, who said your father gave you that injury. But it does not matter what I believe. My job is to find you and bring you home before you come to more harm."

"You are confused. I am safe here, but I could come to harm at home."

He raised his brow. "No, Miss, you are the one who is confused, and it's no wonder after all you've been through."

"You mean my mother's death and my father's violence?"

"No, all the terrible things that happened to you after you foolishly left home. Your father made a grave mistake, waiting for you to come back. He finally went to the police after a few months, and those buffoons blundered, never searching beyond your friends and neighbors. A couple of months ago, Mr. Hastings came to me. When I learned you'd been missing since May, I told him the chances of finding you alive were slim. But here you are, safe and sound, physically at least. It's a Christmas miracle." He smiled, but his eyes remained cold and calculating.

"How did you find me?"

"Child's play, miss. It helped that you did not change your surname. We discovered our lead when we searched through passenger lists at the port. We were looking for a ship to Cornwall, from the lead we got with great effort from your valet, Mr. Lewis, but the agent remembered selling you a first-class ticket to London. We interviewed the passengers and the seamen. There was some red herring story of you traveling with your mother, who fainted and cut her head —

not sure what that was all about. Several accounts, however, indicated you spent time in the company of the ship surgeon, Dr. Pesce, and were seen leaving the sick berth covered in blood. We found an explanation to that from one sailor, who recalled you assisted the doctor during a surgery. That was perhaps the beginning of your troubling story."

She kept her silence, and Mr. Stone continued. "In London, we found Dr. Pesce's residence. He was not expected to be home for many months, serving on a warship, but we interviewed his sister, Matilda. At first, she was most unhelpful, but we encouraged her, reminding her of illegal activities we could report to the police."

"She did nothing wrong."

"She is treating patients without education or license. If you are paying attention to the medical news, there have been poisonings, accidental and not, by herb healers like her. If policemen dig thoroughly enough, they would find some questionable cases. But we found even more disturbing things downstairs."

Ella balled her hands into fists. "You had no right to search her house."

"We were looking for you, or your remains. I take it you know what Dr. Pesce keeps downstairs. Even I, with a long career solving crimes, was overwhelmed by what I saw there. I suspected we would find your organs in one of those jars."

She snorted. "Doctors and anatomists preserve organs for further study. There is nothing disturbing in that room."

"Calling a collection of human organs 'nothing disturbing' confirms the degree of your confusion. While we have verified the doctor is not linked to any murders, an investigation will likely reveal grave robberies and unauthorized postmortems. Both Dr. Pesce and his sister have much to fear from the authorities."

"Leave them alone! They have shown nothing but kindness to me."

"I am most concerned by the doctor's actions. No doubt he distressed your delicate mind by showing you those organs, maybe even corpses. The result is what I see in front of me; a young woman who believes herself to be a man and continues to traumatize herself further by viewing surgeries and dissections in medical school. When I learned of your fate, I wrote to Mr. Hastings at once, suggesting we take you straight to a reputable mental asylum."

She jumped to her feet. Her eyes swept the room, searching for an escape route. The large men were blocking the door and the window, and she could not imagine how to get past them.

"Calm down, young lady. Mr. Hastings and your father wanted us to bring you home instead. If you cooperate, we will not bother the doctor, or Mistress Pesce. We will also keep things quiet with the university, the papers, everyone. Unlike the police, we will protect your privacy. Alan Parker will leave for Christmas holiday and not return. But if you start resisting, screaming, or showing violent behavior, we will take you to the asylum for your own good."

Her mind searched for a way out but could not find one. These men were large, muscular, and trained in their work. She could not escape all three of them. And they held excellent leverage: Dr. Pesce's and Matilda's livelihoods, and the threat of a mental hospital. She heard chilling stories of women disappearing into institutions like that, never coming out. Any way she looked at the situation, she lost.

"Fine. I will go."

Once again he gave her a cold smile. "Glad to hear it. My associates will help you pack. Let's make haste and you will be in your father's arms by this evening."

* * *

When Mr. Stone and his associates escorted her downstairs, the landlady stopped her work and gawked at them. Mr. Stone said Mr. Parker was leaving for good and paid the remainder of the rent. Ella was thankful the other tenants were not there.

In the carriage, with Mr. Bates and Mr. Kinsley by her sides and Mr. Stone across from her, Ella felt deflated and gloomy. Her dreams were snatched from her grasp so soon. Her arduous work came to nothing. Dr. Miller, Oli, the other students, and professors might wonder what happened to her, but would forget her soon enough. She stared down at her knees, not letting herself cry. Her stomach twisted in tight coils.

Thoughts of what waited for her at home were even bleaker. Apparently Father was coherent enough when talking to Mr. Stone, but that was not surprising. There were many occasions when he appeared to be his old self after he moderated his drinking for a few days. Once he completed the important task, he would lock himself with a bottle and slip further into his madness. She resolved not to go near her father. Somehow he survived these months without her. The servants managed to care for him, and they could continue doing so. She would put her own safety first. The tightness in her stomach uncoiled somewhat.

A chilling idea drove away the good feeling. *What if those men lied and are taking me to an asylum?* Her whole body convulsed at the thought. For the rest of the tiring and nerve-wracking journey, she tensed till she ached in her back and shoulders. With eyes closed, she wished for the ride to be over. When she opened them what seemed to be many hours later and saw the familiar outline of Newcastle in the distance, she exhaled with relief.

As the carriage approached her lands, she grew sure of herself. She would muster courage and stroll back into her childhood home, not as a scared runaway, but as a confident mistress. Her servants would not run her life anymore, no matter what her father thought.

"I would like to change into a dress," Ella said when the carriage stopped by the front door.

"Certainly, Miss," Mr. Stone answered. He and his associates exited, and Ella put on the woolen dress and a bonnet that concealed her short hair. As she dismounted, Mr. Stone made a move to help her, but the butler beat him to it, offering his gloved hand.

Her maid, Ivy, waited by the door and hurried to take her coat. "I will bring supper to your room, Miss, after you talk to your father. He is waiting for you in his study."

"I will not see him. I will have my supper and a bath and go to bed. Our conversation can wait till morning," Ella said, loudly enough for all of the servants in the room to hear.

A large man in a valet livery responded. "No, you will speak with him now, and he asked me to remind you of your manners and the respect for a parent. Please come with me so I won't have to drag you." His muscles bulged from his ill-fitting jacket, and his eyes were cold and mean. Ella wondered if he had replaced Mr. Lewis, and her heart pained for the sweet old man who indulged and protected her.

"Your father can take it from here," Mr. Stone said with approval. "Good luck, Miss. I hope I won't have to search for you again." He made a curt bow and left with his associates.

The valet's grip tightened on Ella's elbow, and he pulled her towards the stairs.

"Get your hands off me!" she screamed.

He let go, and she straightened her back and raised her chin. From the corner of her eye, she noticed Ivy folding her hands as if in a prayer. As she marched to the study, she willed herself to display strength and self-assurance. Her father would likely be drunk and raging, but she would not be afraid.

The valet opened the door, and she took a breath, bracing herself for the mess of broken and empty bottles, the smell of rotting food, and the fury and madness in her father's eyes. To her surprise, the room was tidy, the floor cleaned to a shine, not a bottle in sight, and her father, clean shaven and immaculately dressed, regarded her with sternness and disapproval, but not insanity. She could barely remember seeing him sober and was unsure how to behave.

"So, you shamed yourself by disguising as a boy to attend medical school. Even cut off your hair." The earl said, breaking the silence first.

"I don't feel ashamed. And I intend to go back at the first opportunity."

"Mr. O'Connor, did you remind my daughter that she is to speak to me with respect?"

The valet confirmed.

"Please give her a better reminder, like the one you would give your own child."

Mr. O'Connor came to her side and twisted her ear till she screamed.

The earl leaned forward, grinning. "How about the other ear for good measure?"

Ella shrunk away from the valet. "I will not be treated this way!"

Her father chuckled. "After everything you put me through, I think Mr. O'Connor is being rather gentle. If his daughter ran away, making him search all over the country, I am sure the girl would not be able to stand on her two feet when he found her."

Ella hugged herself, chilled with fear. She did not believe her father a mean man, only sick and uncontrollable, but now she saw a cold menace in him, like he took pleasure in seeing her hurt and frightened.

"So, you liked this medical school?" he asked with a cold grin.

She kept her silence, refusing to be mocked.

"You are your mother's daughter. She also had bizarre ideas about women becoming involved in medicine. And not like other fine ladies, who donate money to charity hospitals, but tramping to orphanages, asylums, and other god-forsaken places."

This was news to Ella, and she smiled weakly, imagining her mother caring for patients.

Her father noticed her smile and reddened. "Look at you, grinning, when you should be begging me on your knees for forgiveness. Mr. Stone would have taken you to a madhouse, Mr. O'Connor would have beaten you senseless, and yet you don't appreciate my kindness. I will write a letter to your medical school, telling them who you are, so you can abandon any hope of returning there."

Ella gasped, and her father laughed at her reaction.

"Tomorrow morning, you will be going to a new school. And not some finishing school where you could indulge yourself with music and novels, but a serious religious institution where your days will be filled with prayer, hard work, and contemplation of your atrocious behavior. Mr. O'Connor will accompany you, along with the nuns who would come for you first thing in the morning. You will come back a different woman, meek and obedient, ready to be a dutiful daughter and a good wife, whose sons one day will rule this estate. Now, thank me for my mercy."

Fury flew into her head, and she yelled, "Just months ago

you threw Reverend Father out of our house, but now you want me to go to a convent? You do not decide what to do with me. I tried to care for you, to have you see a doctor, to make you stop drinking, and you wounded me physically and mentally when I was at my weakest, grieving for my mother. It is you who should be asking forgiveness for injuring and abandoning me. Let me go back to medical school and do with yourself what you wish."

The earl jumped from his chair. "Hold her!" he yelled to the valet.

Mr. O'Connor seized Ella by the shoulders, and her father slapped her hard across the cheek, making her eyes flood with tears.

"You lie, as usual. There was nothing wrong with me; a man can drink if he wants to, and it's not for a woman to say what he can or cannot do. You will not go back to some medical school to play a boy. Don't presume that you can ruin yourself and still inherit my wealth. Lady Fillips and I plan to get married this summer, and her well-behaved daughters may be more deserving of my inheritance. You can think on that while you spend the night in the cellar. Mr. O'Connor, take her down there, and bring me a bottle of my oldest whiskey. I have not had a proper drink in three months, searching for this imp."

Ella screamed and thrashed, but O'Connor's prizefighter arms secured her in a grip. He dragged her out of the room, and when she kicked his knee, he lifted her onto his shoulder and carried her down the stairs. She writhed like a madwoman, losing a shoe and her bonnet. When he reached the cellar, he shoved her inside and locked the door.

CHAPTER 8

The cellar was icy cold, and Ella's woolen dress did not keep her warm. Her fingers stiffened, and her teeth chattered. Despite her fatigue, she decided not to sleep, afraid to freeze to death. Instead, she warmed herself by holding her hands near the candle that Mr. O'Connor left her and walked around the confined space stocked with shelves. She also helped herself to some jams, but without a spoon she had to eat with her hands, making them and her face sticky.

She punched and kicked the door while yelling with all the strength of her lungs, hoping someone would let her out, but no one came, and she gave up the fruitless pursuit. Weary, she sat down to rest, and broke down crying.

Only a couple of days ago she received her chemistry paper with her best marks yet. This morning she happily shopped for gifts for the Pesces and Oli, oblivious to what was coming. At her university, she was building a life in which she was useful, passionate about her work, and surrounded by intelligent and interesting people. Father snatched it all away because her way of living differed from that of other women and did not suit him. Instead of letting her learn how to treat diseases, he would send her to some awful convent, where the nuns would try to break her into becoming meek and obedient. She wondered what kind of punishments such institutions employed.

And how could she forget, Lady Fillips had found a way to charm her father into an engagement! The inheritance mattered little to Ella, but the woman was repulsive and two-faced, and would be a nightmare of a stepmother. No doubt she was after their money after squandering her previous husband's fortune. Ever playing a matchmaker, she would get rid of Ella, marrying her off at a first opportunity. Ella put her head into her hands, feeling broken and lost.

There was a rustling sound at the door, and Ella jumped to her feet and spun around. The door opened with a screech, and Ivy, holding a candle, tiptoed in with a finger to her lips. Taking Ella by the hand, she led her out of the cellar to the servants' quarters. When they reached the backdoor, Ivy grabbed a basket, and helped Ella put on her coat and shoes, already prepared for her. Then she motioned for Ella to follow her outside. In the darkness, they went through the yard and out of the gates, where the carriage stood waiting for them. The young groom, Jimmy, sat with the reins held in his hands.

Ivy opened the carriage door. "Get in, Miss. Your bags are already inside."

Confused but excited, Ella jumped in, followed by the maid, and the groom commanded the horses to trot. When they reached the end of the estate, she asked, "Ivy, where are we going?"

"To your medical school, of course," the woman replied with a mischievous smile. "You don't want to go to that religious school your father is sending you to, right?"

"Of course not. But I can't go back to medical school

either. Father is writing to the administration that I am a woman, and they will expel me."

"Are you talking about this?" Ivy took out a piece of paper from the pocket of her dress and handed it to her. It was an unfinished letter from her father to the medical school. "Your Father slept like a log, and I took the letter from his desk without his notice." The maid's eyes shone bright, and her cheeks flushed, making her look years younger.

"What's gotten into you, Ivy? You were always such a reasonable and careful creature."

"Why, it's you, Miss. When I heard Mr. Hastings telling your father you were attending medical school, my heart swelled with pride. I have a sick sister, whose legs don't work. I thought, maybe Miss Eloise will treat people like my Nora, and make them better. And when that devil, Mr. O'Connor, dragged you to the cellar, Jimmy and I planned to get you out and take you back to school. We'll go to the coach station in Newcastle, and travel together from there, while Jimmy brings your father's carriage home. I even found a way to distract Mr. O'Connor. The cook, Bessy, makes cow eyes every time she sees him. I encouraged her to take him some meat pies, and then to give him something else to taste." Ivy giggled but then blushed. "I am sorry, Miss, I shouldn't talk like that in front of you."

Ella shook her head and gave Ivy a sad smile. "Ivy, that's terrific of you, but this plan will not work. Father will write another letter and send Mr. Stone or the police to fetch me again. I cannot go back to school, as much as I want to."

Ivy's face fell. "You are right, Miss, and what a silly goose I am. I got excited and did not think this through. Is there another place we can go? Anything is better than leaving you with your father or going to that convent, right?"

Ella considered, then checked inside her trunk, relieved to

find her money where she packed it when leaving the university. "I can't stay with my friend Matilda in London because Mr. Stone would look for me there. But I am a bit familiar with the city, and I could find decent lodging for us. London is enormous, and all kinds of people live there. We could find work, and… maybe someday I could get back to medical school."

Ivy nodded, but with little enthusiasm. She seemed upset at herself for not seeing the flaws in her plan. Ella reassured her that she was thankful for her initiative.

Ella's mind ventured to something her father said. "Do you remember my mother taking care of patients? Father mentioned her visiting orphanages and asylums."

The maid knitted her brow. "Sorry, Miss, I don't. I started ten years ago, when you were five, and I never saw your mother do such things. Maybe it's something she did earlier."

Ella's shoulders sagged. If Ivy didn't know, she could not imagine who could tell her. She turned to the window to watch the sunrise among the bare trees.

"I have bad news. There are two riders behind us going at full gallop. I am guessing it's the master and Mr. O'Connor," Jimmy shouted from the box seat. "I am whipping our horses to run as fast as they can, but they will likely catch up to us."

The carriage shook, tossing the women with a mighty force. Ella covered her mouth with her hands, and Ivy cried out.

"I am sorry, Miss. I thought your father would sleep late, like he usually does when he drinks. Maybe he wasn't so inebriated after all, and Mr. O'Connor discovered your escape and woke him. If they catch us, I will take the blame," the maid said with tears in her eyes.

"It won't matter, Ivy. They will force me to go to the convent school, and it will be all over for my dreams of studying medicine," Ella said with a sigh. She took note that the trees in her windows flew by more slowly than a moment ago. "Jimmy, why are we slowing down? They may catch us, but let's not make it easy for them."

"The road is icy, and there's a bridge coming up."

Ella's heart sank. The horses slowed to a walk, pulling the carriage over a small river bridge with no railings. As they rode away, she could hear the clop of hooves getting closer. She braced herself for the moment the riders would be upon them.

"We got them now!" her father's voice rang with glee.

"Slow down, sir. You are riding too fast." O'Connor's warning sounded.

"It's nothing for my Storm. Giddy up, you jug-headed nag!"

The crack of the whip resonated through Ella's body, and she felt the horse's pain as it grunted. She hated when her father was rough with his faithful animals. In the next moment, there was a scream so disturbing, that both women startled. Ella never heard a horse make such a painful and terrified squeal before. Male voices shouted, but she couldn't make out the words. Their carriage came to a rough stop.

"What happened, Jimmy?" Ella asked.

"Your father's horse slipped, and he fell into the river. I will go help."

"Come on, this is our chance to get away!" Ivy yelled.

"No!" Ella snapped as she climbed out of the carriage. "The water is ice cold, and he may be injured. We can't just leave him."

She rushed to the bank, from where she watched Mr. O'Connor and Jimmy wade into the frozen river to help her father. The ice crunched under their feet as it broke, and the water covered their knees. They helped their master to rise, but he cried out as he tried to take a step. Taking him by the shoulders, the servants led him to the shore and helped him into the carriage.

While Jimmy fastened the earl's horse with the others, Ella covered her father with warm clothes from her trunks. Her father's face was red with rage, and his teeth chattered as he spoke.

"You will pay for this trick, Eloise! Thought you could sneak out and run back to your school. The nuns who came to collect you will be back tomorrow, and you will come with them, even if I must bind you. You escaped the cellar, but I can find more secure places in the house for you to spend the night. And you," he glanced at Ivy, "are fired. As soon as we reach home, you are to pack your things and go. And don't you dare ask me for the pay or a recommendation letter."

Ivy nodded, sobbing into her shawl.

Ella willed herself to keep a calm demeanor in the face of her father's fury. "My medical skills may come handy today. From what I can tell, you sprained your ankle, and you may catch a chill from a dip in the frigid water."

He took a swallow from his flask. "I don't need you or the doctor fussing over me. If I catch a cold, this brandy will cure me better than any potions or leeches. Lad, why are we not moving yet?" he barked at the groom. "Turn those horses around and take us home."

The carriage rocked as they came back over the bridge, with O'Connor following behind them on his horse.

* * *

Ella arranged a tray to take to her father. When she got word that he had taken ill, she sent for an herbal healer from the village, and the woman came in a jiffy with all the ingredients to cure colds and fevers. She winced at the memory of her last night at home before leaving, when she brought her father his medicine and he injured her with a broken glass. *It will be different now*, she told herself. *I will not let him hurt me, and I will do my duty as a daughter by taking care of him.*

The earl, propped up on the pillows of his enormous bed, looked annoyed to see her. "You had better stay away, Eloise, if you know what's good for you. You've ruined many plans this morning. Lady Fillips is throwing a New Year's ball in a few days, where we planned to announce our engagement. How am I supposed to attend with a sprained ankle and a chill? This headache is killing me as well."

"Your ankle will heal on its own by then if you give it rest. As for your cold, headache, and fever, this should help," Ella said, setting the tray in front of him.

"What is this witches' brew?"

"Spearmint and ginger tea with black pepper, and hot milk with honey. If you want to be well by the New Year's, you should drink three or four cups of this a day."

He took a small sip, looking at Eloise with suspicion. "Well, it does not taste too bad. Better than the nasty concoction the doctor prescribes. Tell the cook how to make this, since you are leaving tomorrow morning."

She gave an innocent smile. "I tried to explain, but Bessy is so thick. She can't tell a mint leaf from parsley or ginger root from a yam. I am afraid no one would be able to make the teas without me."

The earl shook his head. "You cunning little devil. Found a way to make yourself indispensable. Fine, these remedies had better work. If you obey me from now on, you can stay till after New Year's Day. Don't even think about running, because Mr. O'Connor will watch your every move. As long as you behave as a dutiful daughter, you may attend the ball, where you will embrace your future stepmother and stepsisters."

Ella curtsied and strode out of the room, turning away to stick out her tongue. The thought of becoming Lady Fillips' stepdaughter made her queasy, but she relished her two victories: her father had postponed her leave and agreed to drink her remedies. With her wits about her, she may yet change his mind about the convent school, or even find a way to get back to the university.

* * *

The doctor's mouth was tight, and his eyes blazed when he stepped out of the earl's bedroom to speak to Ella. "You should know better than to call on some woman healer instead of a proper physician. It was his headache that needed attention, not the cold and ankle injury. He needed bloodletting and purging right away after the fall. It may be too late now."

She hung her head. Her father was a difficult patient, yet she tried so hard to administer her cures. Besides herbs, she made her father soak his feet in hot water with mustard powder and rubbed goose fat on his chest. The earl, irritated by a persistent headache, bullied and mocked her, and often took swigs of brandy instead of milk with honey. He insisted he did not need a physician, and she indulged him. She wanted to prove her worth as a future doctor and hoped he let her go back to medical school.

How naïve and arrogant of me! I should have known a headache could be more than just another cold symptom!

Her father's illness did not appear serious until tonight. When she brought him tea and water a couple hours ago, she was shocked to find him shaking in a seizure and sent for the physician right away. Humiliated by the doctor, she wanted to hide under the blanket in her bed, like a child.

"Miss Eloise, are you listening to me?" the doctor interrupted her thoughts.

"I am sorry, please repeat the last thing you said."

The doctor sighed. "I was saying he should not have any strong spirits. He asked to see you, but I implore you to keep it brief and let him rest. And don't upset him or let him get excited, or I cannot be responsible for the consequences. I will check on him in the morning." The doctor bowed and picked up his bag, heading for the door.

Ella tiptoed into the bedroom, mustering her courage to face her father. He may be weakened by the bloodletting, but he could still shoot arrows straight into her heart. She found him pale and tired-looking, but lucid. Mr. O'Connor propped him up on his pillows.

"I thought you to be disrespectful and deceitful, Eloise, but I never thought you a murderer," the earl said, regarding her with frigid hate in his eyes.

Ella gaped in shock. "How can you say such a thing?" she finally managed to whisper.

"Yes, the good doctor told me about these so-called women healers who sell fake cures, or worse, poisons. So that was your plan? To kill me and inherit my fortune? Now I see why you were so eager to treat me yourself and make me drink those teas prescribed by some village witch."

"That's ridiculous, Father. Spearmint and ginger cause no harm. I should have sent for the doctor earlier, but you were the one who did not want him," Ella protested.

"I will not listen to your lies anymore, and I will prevent your plans. Mr. O'Connor, please take Miss Eloise to her room and stand guard by the door. Have someone bring Mr. Hastings and tell him I am changing my will. This ungrateful and scheming girl will be left penniless, while my fortune, when I die, will go to Lady Fillips and her daughters. Oh, and before you go, hand me my flask, I am quite thirsty."

"You are supposed to be resting and drinking water or tea. Your lawyer could see you in the morning," she tried to reason, but no one was listening. Mr. O'Connor grabbed her by the wrist and pulled her towards the door. "All right, I am going; you don't have to force me," she said to the valet, as she knew it was useless to fight him. At least being imprisoned in her room would be better than the cellar, and she would catch some much needed sleep in her own bed. Before she left, she saw her father smirk and bring a flask to his lips.

CHAPTER 9

Ivy woke her in the morning by stroking her shoulder and hair. Ella's eyes opened wide with surprise. "Ivy! I thought you were gone."

The maid laughed. "The master does not know me from Ann or Mary. I will keep out of his sight for a while. By the time he recovers from his sprained ankle, he will have forgotten he ever fired me. I am not leaving you to his tortures, Miss. I will see that you are safe."

"You clever woman." Ella rose from her bed and embraced the servant. She went to the basin to wash her face, and let Ivy help her change into fresh clothes.

When she caught her reflection in the looking glass, she shook her head upon noticing her pale complexion and the dark circles under her eyes. Her weariness and the anxiety had taken their toll.

"There was much activity last night." Ivy said, helping Ella put on a wig with long curls. She sported her short hair for a few days but became weary of the shocked looks and whispers of the servants. "Mr. Hastings came into your father's bedroom, and soon afterwards called for the doctor.

When the doctor arrived, he wanted you, but you were so tired that I could not wake you. He checked on you and decided to let you sleep, said your nerves were exhausted. Mr. O'Connor shouted something about the poisoned teas you made for your father, and that the police should be called, but the doctor said that was a misunderstanding, and the teas were harmless. Then the doctor left, and Mr. Hastings went to your father's study. He spent the rest of the night there, working on some papers, and asked that you see him as soon as you are able to."

Finished with her morning routine, Ella strode into her father's study, as her stomach tightened with a premonition. Ivy wanted to bring her breakfast first, but Ella insisted on learning what had happened while she slept and what the lawyer had to say.

Mr. Hastings, a man in his fifties with an unremarkable and forgettable appearance, sat in the visitor's chair but stood up and bowed upon seeing her. With a motion of his hand, he invited her to sit in her father's seat.

"Miss Parker, the doctor was concerned for your health. Do you feel all right, or should I send for him?"

"I was extremely tired after the events of the last few days, but I am quite restored now."

Mr. Hastings nodded. "In that case, Miss, I have a sad duty to inform you of the tragic news. Your father passed away last night. Please accept my condolences."

Ella covered her mouth with her hands, halting a gasp in her throat. *I should have called for the doctor earlier. He died blaming me.*

"I found him in a fit and sent for the doctor. The medical man was quite upset that your father did not take his warnings to heart. We found an emptied flask of brandy in his bed, and I understand he was prescribed rest but refused it, wanting to see me and change his will instead. Unfortunately, this overexcitement in his fragile state led to his death. The doctor suspects the cause was apoplexy."

"Did he say anything before dying? Did he blame me?"

"No, he was unable to speak. And, knowing his self-destructive habits, you should not blame yourself."

Ella's shoulders slumped. "He thought me undeserving of his inheritance. His last wish was to change his will in Lady Fillips' favor."

The lawyer twisted a goose feather pen in his hand. "I appreciate your honesty, Miss. Do you mind telling me why you believe your father wanted to disinherit you?"

She described what happened to her after she left home. The lawyer listened with animated interest. When she finished, he remarked, "Your story is extraordinary because it happened to a woman. Young men travel, find their passion, enter a university to pursue it. I hope that happens for my son. He attends law school, but all I receive are requests for money to cover his card debts." He rolled his eyes.

"There's more. After Father became ill, I treated him with herbal teas instead of sending for a doctor. Last night he accused me of poisoning him."

"I heard this accusation from the valet, but the doctor reassured us that while, in his medical opinion, the teas didn't cure, they were harmless. My wife makes me ginger tea with honey when I feel under the weather, and I find it restorative." He drummed his fingers on the desk. "I see nothing in your story that compels me to have your father's will changed. When I saw him, he was not in a state to talk or sign papers, and if he were, I would have prevented him from making a legal decision in his state of serious illness and under the influence of a drink. Lady Fillips was not his wife, and her daughters are not his children. You are his only offspring and a rightful heir. And since you have such fervor for treating the sick and injured, I hope the wealth you are about to receive will benefit more than just you."

He read her the contents of the will, explaining that she inherited her father's full fortune, making her extremely rich. The majority of her money would be locked away in a trust fund until she turned eighteen, with Mr. Hastings as her trustee, but her monthly allowance would be quite generous.

Afterwards, he added, "I hope you are not in a hurry to leave. Mr. Smiley and I managed things as well as we could, but there are many matters that have been neglected. While I will oversee the trust on your behalf, you should take part in the major decisions. We need you to review papers and sign documents. I am sorry to burden you with paperwork, but it would be better if you learn what it takes to manage your wealth now, with us to guide you."

Ella agreed to start after her father's funeral the next morning.

* * *

Her goodbye to her father had been solemn and brief, with only Mr. Hastings, her father's estate caretaker, Mr. Smiley, and the servants in attendance. Lady Fillips replied that she had taken ill with grief and was unable to leave her bed, and Veronica and her parents were on a holiday out of town. Dressed in her mother's mink coat over her black dress, Ella reflected on being at the same spot less than a year ago, burying her mother in the family tomb. At that funeral, she wept on her knees, and fainted for the first time in her life. On this day, she stood with her shoulders slumped, and a heavy rock on her heart, but she did not shed a tear.

Guilt churned her soul, no matter how much she told

herself that her father's death was the result of his own carelessness and destructive habits. Days moved at a glacial pace while she locked herself in her father's study. She slept poorly since the funeral, and often spent the nights seated at the earl's desk. Despite her fatigue, she willed herself to stay alert and keep working. This labor was her penance for letting her father perish, she told herself. Yet she made little progress with the mound of papers in front of her.

Mr. Smiley, a man in his thirties, whose brusque and serious manner did not match his name, explained the urgent issues the day after the funeral. He needed her agreement to repay debts and credits from her father. Then he solicited her direction regarding the purchases and sales of land for farming, investments in the stock market, and repairs to the estate. Her head spun as he described the opportunities she could take advantage of, and the losses she should avoid by swift action. She no longer wondered why her father started drinking soon after he inherited the estate from his own father.

Second in urgency, she read petitions from the villagers, various letters and appeals that awaited her replies. Then there were the matters of numerous estate servants. She inquired of Mr. Lewis and Miss Samson, learning that the governess had found a new position, and that her father fired the valet for suggesting the escape to Cornwall.

Mr. Smiley reinstated him at her request and fired Mr. O'Connor. At the same time, she had to consider what servants were no longer needed, and if any earned raises and promotions. In the back of her mind, she cherished the idea of doing something great with her wealth, such as opening a hospital or a clinic for the poor, but first she needed to come up for air in the sea of documents in front of her.

I planned to spend my holidays reading, and that's exactly what I did, she thought while staring at another letter. This one happened to be from Lady Fillips. The woman accused Ella of being a horrible person who caused her father sorrow and untimely death, and asserted that she and her daughters would never speak to her again. Ella crumpled the letter and threw it in the fireplace. She wished she could do the same with the rest of the stack.

Tomorrow, a new term would start. Oli would wonder where she was, and maybe Dr. Miller would comment on her absence. She longed to walk the university paths, to find out the status of the patients, to check for new books at the library. Maybe she could come back for a day and explain her sudden absence to Oli and Dr. Miller. They would be sympathetic to her loss and new responsibilities. The university administration would grant her a leave of absence. The more she pondered this idea, the more she liked it.

* * *

Her watch indicated she had just missed the rounds, but she hoped for an opportunity to catch Dr. Miller at his office. As she raced towards it, his tall figure appeared from one of the wards.

"Mr. Parker," he called out, "you are late. Holiday travels delayed you, I am sure." His tone was cheerful. "Your last essay was your best so far. I gave it perfect marks."

"Thank you, professor. I…"

"I am operating in an hour. A unique case: I have not seen the like." He strode away before Ella could answer.

Even though she came into the surgery a half-hour early, the room was full of doctors, students, and onlookers. There would be no chance to squeeze between all of them to the operating table. She took her place near Oli, who was in the middle of the crowd.

Oli gave her a smile that illuminated his whole face. "I was so worried about you. The day we last saw each other, I bought you an illustrated medical book. I sent a boy to deliver it, and he came back with a message from your landlady that you moved out. She said you left after three strange men came to collect you."

"No need to worry. I am fine. Unfortunately, my father died, and I had to attend to responsibilities at home."

The young man faced her, and put his hand on her shoulder. "I am deeply sorry. Please accept my condolences."

"I will need to take a leave of absence. I came to file the paperwork and say goodbye."

He bit his lips. "Oh, that's terrible. I know how much this school means to you. Is there anything I can do?"

"Let's talk about it later. What are we about to see?"

"A female patient with an enormous abdominal growth. We saw her during rounds, and her belly was larger than a pregnant woman's. In fact, her physician put her in confinement, but no baby came.

"What ails her?"

"Dr. Miller said it's an extremely large ovarian cyst. The poor woman had it removed twice by a tapping procedure, but each time it came back larger. She traveled from afar and pleaded for an operation."

Ella's heart went out to the patient. Surgeries that involved an incision on the stomach were rare and dangerous, as the rate of postoperative infections was high. Not to mention the pain of the surgery itself, if the laudanum did not make the patient senseless. The poor woman must be at her last straw to beg Dr. Miller to operate.

Meanwhile, the assistants strapped the patient to the

operating table, settling her in a semi erect position. Oli did not exaggerate; the woman's abdomen protruded as though a large baby was inside. Ella could barely see behind the taller men in front of her as she stood on her tippy toes. The man next to her muttered about larger hospitals having surgery theaters where onlookers could watch from their seats.

Dr. Miller marched in and donned a bloody apron over his clothes. He gave a history of the case regarding the previous procedures the patient had and their lack of long-term success. As he spoke, the crowd held their collective breath, and all eyes were on the esteemed surgeon. When he finished, he surveyed the room.

"Mr. Parker," his voice boomed, "you are not a ballet dancer to stand *en pointe* through the surgery. Mr. Jeffers could move and give you a place in the front. He is tall enough to observe even from the back of the room."

This was unprecedented, but Ella did not lose a moment and wedged her way through the crowd. Wide-eyed, Jeffers conceded his spot, and she found herself at the surgeon's side. Exhilarated, she dared to ask, "Could Mr. Higgins come up here? He also cannot see."

Dr. Miller made an impatient shrug, and the stunned Oli made his way next to her.

"All right, time to get started," the surgeon said. "Mr. Parker, would you pass me a scalpel, please?"

Ella handed him his preferred instrument, crusted with the blood from the previous surgeries. She was aware of the honor unexpectedly bestowed on her. With bated breath, she watched the doctor's efficient and confident moves, as he made a three inch incision through the layers of the abdomen, laying bare the surface of the cyst. The patient made involuntary moans; the opium did not take away all the pain. The doctor clicked his tongue upon viewing the cyst.

"I planned to draw out a portion of the cyst, but there are extensive adhesions here. It will be better to open it, evacuate its contents, and insert a plug to continue draining the discharge."

He proceeded with his new plan, and his assistant collected yellowish fluid mixed with blood that poured out from the cyst. "Serosanguinous drainage," the doctor remarked. "How much has come out?"

"Twenty-five pints," the assistant replied.

The doctor nodded. "The plug will remain in place to prevent the closure of the edges of the wound and allow for further drainage. Previous cases from my colleagues tell me the fluid will continue draining for several days, and then pus for next few weeks. If the patient survives, that is."

Ella wondered how good the patient's chances of recovering were. Those who survived the surgeries often succumbed to sepsis or gangrene days later. Dr. Miller began suturing, taking care around the plug. Before finishing, he turned to Ella.

"Would you like to close, Mr. Parker?"

"Certainly." She took the needle he passed her and made layers of stitches, which were almost as even as her teacher's.

"Excellent." Dr. Miller approved. "I heard of the long hours you put in at the dissection room before the holidays. I trust you came back refreshed and ready to continue your efforts."

With that, he stepped away from the table, letting the assistants transfer the patient to the ward. Before Ella collected herself to respond, the surgeon exited the room. The crowd stayed a while longer, discussing the operation. Several surgeons and students shook hands with Ella, some introducing themselves or asking her name.

When she left the hospital with Oli, the dusk covered the

snowy grounds, and ice squeaked under their boots. She lost her balance, but Oli steadied her, gripping her shoulder.

"Could you stay longer?" he asked. "You have momentum now. Leaving would ruin everything you built with your hard work."

Ella inhaled the cold air, which smelled so sweet after the stuffy and odorous operating room. Sometimes being away gives a fresh perspective. "I am not leaving. Things will go on at home without me. I can go back during the summer break."

Oli yelped with joy. "Come with me," he said. "I will give you my present and some fruit cake my sister made for you. It was her first time baking one, so my apologies if it's not good."

They came to Oli's lodging, and while he rushed upstairs to get the presents, Ella asked the landlady for a room. She had none to offer, but recommended Mrs. Bunting's house nearby.

* * *

Ella ended her day in her new room, warming herself by a crackling fire and enjoying a cup of aromatic tea. The place was brighter and larger than her previous one; Mrs. Bunting greeted her with warmth and served a scrumptious supper. The rent was higher than her old lodgings, but she could afford it now.

After devouring a piece of fruit cake made by Oli's sister, Ella borrowed the landlady's writing set, and penned letters to Mr. Hastings and Mr. Smiley, asking them to have Ivy pack her clothes and books and send them to her new address, as well as informing them she did not plan to return until summer. She instructed them to reduce the number of servants, but keep Ivy, Mr. Lewis, and Jimmy. Finally, she requested regular reports addressed to Mr. Alan Parker.

* * *

January 8,
Dear Matilda and Dr. Pesce,
Happy New Year! I hope you received my gifts.
I am extremely sorry for the trouble caused to you by Mr. Stone. That man will not bother you again. I know how he threatened you, and I do not blame you for telling him where I was. I am also begging your forgiveness for not being honest with you about my father. He terrified and injured me, and I was afraid you would send me back to him.
Soon after Mr. Stone delivered me home, my father suffered an accident and caught a chill as a result. I delayed sending for the doctor, showing off my skills by treating him with the herbs and honey you recommended for colds. After a couple of days, he took a turn for the worse and passed. I feel extremely guilty for my actions.
Despite my stupidity, I inherited his fortune. You will find an enclosed check for the money you spent on my tuition.
I will be forever grateful for your generosity. Don't hesitate to call on me if ever you need help.
I've returned in time for the new semester and witnessed an incredible surgery: a removal of an enormous ovarian cyst. Dr. Miller let me stand by him, pass him his favorite knife, and assist with suturing. I pinched myself afterwards to ensure it was not a dream. Unfortunately, the patient died of an infection several days later.
Your suspicion that I fancy Oli more than a friend is ridiculous. We are study partners only. I'd never risk

everything to pursue a good-looking man. Besides, I prefer taller fellows.

Please note my new address. I did not want to return to the previous lodging because the landlady would be suspicious after seeing Mr. Stone and his associates collect me, but this new place seems wonderful so far.

Stay healthy and warm,

Love, Alan Parker.

February 2,

Dear Alan,

I almost tore up your letter, still fuming after the ruckus Mr. Stone and his people made in my house. You should have been honest with us about your situation. We would have taken measures to protect ourselves and you.

Please accept my condolences for the loss of your father. As I told you before, life punishes us more cruelly than any person ever could. You feared your father's vengeance, but now you are learning to live with the guilt of causing his death.

The herbs I told you to administer usually work well, and I would have applied the same cures myself, but I doubt this knowledge relieves your conscience. There are women who purchased my remedies, or whose babies I delivered, who end up dying; those losses weigh heavily on me. I imagine it's no different than for a doctor to lose a patient.

You will need to learn to live with yourself and keep treating people, if you still want to go on with the profession, which it sounds like you do.

Thank you for the check and for your gifts. I understand that you receive no joy from your inheritance, but financial security is a great fortune for anyone.

*I hope you will manage your money wisely and find good
advisors.
Joseph wrote that he's been laid up in his cabin with a fever,
and I've been sniffling and coughing for the past few days.
This winter cannot end soon enough.
Take care,
Matilda Pesce*

CHAPTER 10

The hospital in the evening was an eerily quiet place, disturbed only by stealthy steps of nun-nurses carrying medications or the patients' moans and snores. Lanterns flickered, illuminating the enthralling designs on frosted windows. The heat overwhelmed Ella, but everyone knew drafts caused chills and lung maladies, especially in young children.

A young doctor, with jet black hair and fatigued eyes, greeted her in the hallway. "I am Dr. Shaw. I understand this is your first shift at the hospital?"

"Yes, sir. I am Alan Parker."

The man extended a hand to shake. "I've heard of you. You've made quite a name for yourself around the campus."

"I receive too much credit. It's all Dr. Miller's teaching."

He cocked his head. "Modesty is a refreshing trait around here. Tonight, you will watch over the patients with my supervision in the children's and women's wards. Let's hope for an uneventful night."

Treading softly, the doctor led Ella towards the children's ward.

With windows closed, the room reeked of urine and vomit, making her gag. Sleeping children occupied about a dozen beds, divided by stained curtains. Ella peered at the faces and hands covered with ugly scars and pits.

"Smallpox? So many still catch it?" she asked.

"Unfortunately. Many parents still resist prevention, and this is the result. Were you inoculated?"

"Yes." Her mother told her she was inoculated with cowpox, a milder disease, as a baby.

"Good. You can help by washing away the pus and applying a poultice."

He led her to another ward, with all beds full. "You can guess what these children have by knowing the season."

"Influenza."

"Yes. A couple have high fevers and need to be watched with a close eye. We may need to bleed them."

After examining the young patients, they moved on to a women's post-surgery ward. It was as spartan as the children's, but with only two beds occupied.

Dr. Shaw nodded toward a young woman on the last bed on the right. "This one had her hand caught in the machinery at the mill. Dr. Miller amputated it earlier today. Did you watch the surgery?"

"I did." Not only did she watch, but the doctor allowed her to help with ligations.

"I missed it, resting before my shift. Anyway, she is recovering well, but we need to watch for signs of inflammation."

Ella stared at the patient's blanched face. The woman could not be much older than her.

"This one, however, is not so fortunate." He pointed at the next bed. "She was evicted from her lodgings and forced to spend the night outdoors in this weather. As a result, she lost several toes to frostbite and came down with a fever after the operation. I bled her already, but she did not improve. I doubt she will make it through the night."

Ella approached the bed and felt the woman's burning face. The patient, also around her age, tossed and moaned at her touch.

"Can I put a cloth with vinegar solution on her forehead?" she asked.

He shrugged. "It can't hurt."

After caring for the patient with the fever, Ella hastened to the pox ward to clean the pus. Many of the children slept through the procedure, being used to having it done at least twice a day. She was almost finished when Dr. Shaw called her. "We have a new patient coming, an unconscious woman. The assistants are bringing her."

Ella's ears picked up harsh voices, disturbing the peace of the night. "Does not sound like someone unconscious to me," she quipped.

The doctor did not smile. "Must be her family."

He was right. The young woman carried on the stretcher was accompanied by a man and a woman, who argued among themselves.

"This is your fault for letting her read romance novels and indulging her every whim," the bearded man roared at the woman.

"Me? If only you had bought her that horse and sent her on a holiday, like she asked," the woman hissed back.

"What happened?" Ella yelled to them both.

The mother spoke first. "She's taken sleeping pills I bought from the chemist. At least half a jar."

The woman showed her a small glass container with round balls.

"Do you know what they are?"

"No, but I take two every night and sleep like a baby. My poor girl!"

The mother broke down as the father stared at the floor and bit his lips. Ella learned the patient's name, Amelia Hearts, and her age, sixteen. While she spoke to the parents, Dr. Shaw and the assistants took the patient to another room and lay her on the table. When Ella came in, the helpers removed a silver fur coat from her shoulders, revealing a fancy turquoise dress. Dr. Shaw grabbed the woman's wrist to check the pulse.

"Not as bad as I feared, but not a moment to lose."

"Will you give her an emetic?" Ella asked.

"A stomach pump should work better." When Ella gaped, he added. "It's an invention Dr. Miller brought from America. First time we'll use it in this hospital."

The young doctor's face showed eagerness at utilizing the new instrument. The assistant handed him a rubber tube of about two feet in length and a syringe. Dr. Shaw slid the tube inside the patient's mouth and down her throat. As he pumped the syringe, Ella held a bowl, where the contents of the stomach poured from the other end of the tube. The bowl filled up with the stomach acid, remains of food, and some undigested pills.

"This pump is made to save a patient from poisoning," the doctor explained, continuing the vigorous pumping. "The inventor, a Philadelphian doctor, first used it on three-month old twins who were given a lethal dose of laudanum by their mother. One of the infants survived."

When the patient's stomach was emptied, Ella observed the undulations of Amelia's ribs rising higher and faster. The angular face unnervingly reminded her of her old friend Veronica, who read romance novels and once threatened to poison herself if her parents did not let her attend a ball with her sweetheart, Earnest. At the time, Ella thought her friend bold. Now she perceived the incident with disgust. There was nothing romantic about the stomach pump.

With the procedure done, assistants moved Amelia to a bed in the ward, and Dr. Shaw reassured her parents that she would come around. Despite her placement away from the other patients, and a curtain lowered for privacy, the mother gave a disapproving look towards her daughter's bed.

"Can she have her own room?" she asked Dr. Shaw with her lips pursed. "We donate generously to the hospital and expect the best for our family."

The doctor shifted on his feet, and Ella read the dilemma on his face. There were no private rooms available. He could have the other two patients moved to an infection ward, but that would increase their chances of catching another disease. Yet frustrating an important patron could damage his career. Ella saw him glance towards the assistants and guessed he wanted to ask them to move the poor patients out of the ward. Unable to contain herself, she stepped up towards the group and addressed the mother with a polite smile.

"Mrs. Hearts, the hospital greatly appreciates your generosity, and with your help, gives the best of care to all patients. The two young ladies that share the ward with your daughter are recovering from complex surgeries that were possible because of benefactors like you. They need rest and should not be moved. Your daughter will not be disturbed by them."

The mother's face softened. "Oh, I did not mean to have other patients inconvenienced. If you tell me their names, I will pray for their recovery, along with my daughter's."

Ella was about to answer, but Amelia moaned and opened her eyes, and the parents rushed to her bedside.

"Thanks for appeasing the mother," said Dr. Shaw,

smiling weakly. "Why don't you take the women's ward for the rest of the night while I take care of the children? Make Miss Hearts your priority."

"Surely the woman on the verge of dying from infection needs me more."

"There is little you can do for her, and no one will question her death. The wealthy daughter, on the other hand, will report her experience to her parents. Make sure she is pleased with her care. If not satisfied, they will make all kinds of trouble for the hospital."

She approached Amelia's bed, introduced herself and checked the pulse and breathing. The young woman regained a bit of color on her cheeks. She was wide awake and surveying her surroundings with interest. The parents agreed to go home when Ella explained that Amelia was alright but in dire need of rest. When they left, Ella turned to check on her other patients, but Amelia called her over.

"What did you do to save me?" The girl asked in a breathy voice.

Ella showed her the stomach pump and explained how it worked, expecting the girl to be revolted, but she listened with avidness. "I was the first patient to have this invention used on? This will be the talk of the town for weeks! Even Olivia, with her feeble constitution and never-ending trips to Bath, will not top it. And Baron Cleveland will hear of this and rush to see me."

Ella gave the girl a measured stare. "What you did was reckless. You could have died, if not for your parents bringing you here in time."

"Oh, I told Mum right after I took the pills, so she would send for the doctor. He must have been away, since my parents dragged me to this awful place. And I only took half a bottle. I figured that much would sicken but not kill me."

Blood rushed to Ella's head. "This was a stunt for your parents' attention?"

Amelia sighed dramatically. "I had to do something. Daddy refused to buy me a horse or take me to London on a holiday, and then Baron Cleveland proposed to Katherine instead of me. I never get sick on my own. But after I almost died, they all will be sorry for me."

Ella wished the stomach tube could reach far enough to clean the girl's brain. "If you want to know what sorrow is, look at the two women over there; they are the same age as you. One lost her arm, having it crushed by machinery. The other lost her toes, freezing in the night."

She feared going too far, but the spoiled girl vexed her much because of her resemblance to Veronica. Her old friend could have pulled a number like this to get a suitor's or her parents' attention.

Ella had to admit that she was no better, considering herself the most unfortunate girl in the world when her mother perished, sometimes declaring that she wished to die, and never counting the blessings of her wealthy home and comfortable life. Watching Amelia was like looking into a crooked glass; exaggerated, but recognizable and unflattering.

Amelia glanced with hurt in her eyes. "You think because I am rich I should be happy. I am not!"

"I can believe that," Ella said with pacification. "You should sleep now."

"I am not tired." The girl pouted. "I think I need more treatment. Shouldn't you give me some powder or leeches? I almost perished after all."

Ella's eyebrows rose. Yet she remembered how Lady Fillips used to talk about 'wonderful' therapies she received from various doctors and apothecaries, the more uncomfortable the better, because those were more effective in her view. "Let me ask the doctor what I can give you," she said.

Dr. Shaw bled one of the children in the influenza ward. "Bad night. One died and this one is barely hanging on," he said with a sigh. "How is the princess doing?"

"I am thinking to give her a laxative to properly clean out her system."

The doctor raised his eyes. "That should not be necessary. Some sleep would be better."

"She requested more treatment. It seems swallowing pills to receive a horse from her father or attention from a former suitor did not exhaust her enough."

With a look at the sick children, the doctor tightened his lips. "In that case, I agree. Please administer something potent enough to thoroughly cleanse her. After all, we don't want her to complain of ineffective treatment."

After stopping by the dispensary, Ella handed Amelia a cup with the medication. The girl seemed pleased to receive it but gagged, drinking the oily liquid.

"That tasted nasty. What was it?" she asked after downing the remedy.

"Castor oil. It will nicely supplement your story about having your stomach pumped."

The medicine took effect soon enough. After asking a nurse to help Amelia to the privy, Ella hurried to check on her other two patients. When feeling the forehead of the girl who lost her toes, she determined the fever had lessened. Sometimes strong bodies overcame infections, and Ella hoped this would be the case.

The young woman opened her eyes at her touch, and Ella gave her some water. The other patient was awake as well, tears rolling down her cheeks.

"Are you in pain?" Ella asked.

The woman shook her head. "I won't be able to work by myself without a hand. My little sister will have to leave school and come with me to the mill." After wiping her face on the pillow, she whispered, "I am sorry. There is nothing you can do to help me, and you are busy with another patient."

Ella patted the girl's shoulder. "Don't you worry about her. I can stay with you if you wish to talk." She wanted to comfort the patient more, but the girl turned from her and said she would try to sleep.

After several runs to the privy, Amelia sprawled on her bed, worn out. When Dr. Shaw stopped by in a couple of hours, all three patients slumbered soundly.

"Not bad for your first shift, Dr. Parker," the doctor remarked. "You can go home to get a couple hours of rest before the morning rounds."

He did not have to offer twice. When medical students had time to doze, they took the opportunity.

* * *

"So, Mr. Parker, along with Dr. Shaw, got a chance to use the American invention last night," Dr. Miller said, stopping by Amelia's bed during rounds, his students following behind him. They saw the other two patients first, and the doctor found their condition satisfactory. "Do you mind explaining the case, Mr. Parker?"

As Ella described the mechanism of the pump to her fellow students, Amelia reclined on her pillows and scanned the young men's faces. She seemed to relish being the center of their attention. Her eyes skipped over most of the group without interest, paused on Walter Carrow's tall frame for a second, rested on Oli's face a bit longer, and then stayed on

Ella's figure. Staring at her, she smiled in a predatory way. When Ella finished speaking, Amelia licked her lips and piped up.

"May this stomach pump be used when someone eats too much?" she wondered. Her voice rang melodic like a silver bell. "For instance, my parents host these twelve-course dinners, and one's stomach can feel most uncomfortable when filled with heavy foods, not to mention tighter clothes do not fit the next day."

Dr. Miller regarded Amelia with interest. "Ancient Romans induced vomiting to enjoy more than one feast per night. I do not recommend such use of the pump, or overindulgence with food."

The girl cocked her head and played with her hair.

Oli gave Ella an incredulous look. "Golly, she will make it a fashion. We'll have people flooding the hospital, demanding to have stomachs pumped after large meals."

"Brace yourself for tonight's shift. She will likely be your patient," Ella whispered back.

* * *

"How did your shift go?" Ella asked Oli after the next day's rounds. His eyes were reddish after the sleepless night.

"The patients in the women's ward are recovering well, but the children's ward was busy, and predictably Amelia was a handful. Her friends visited till midnight and made too much noise, with no regard for other patients. They stared at me and other doctors, giggling among themselves. One of the friends, a rather large girl, called me over and complained of various discomforts, asking me to examine her. I told her she would benefit from regular exercise, and she gave me an annoyed look and stomped away. Amelia did not like the plain hospital meals and wanted more elaborate foods. We told her over and over that anything rich would sicken her, but a friend sneaked her a chocolate pastry, which she hid under her pillow. After eating that and having it come back up, she demanded to stay another day in the hospital."

"That's ridiculous."

"Sorry, but you will have her for another shift. And she asked quite a bit about you."

"Me? Why? What did you tell her?"

"Only that you are the brightest student in our class. If I venture to guess, she fancies you," Oli said with a laugh.

"No, she is supposed to be in love with some baron."

"That may be yesterday's news. Be careful, my friend. This girl is a headache."

Ella reddened, and Oli seemed to enjoy her embarrassment.

"On the other hand, she may have enough of a dowry for you to open a practice right after graduation," he added.

"Her fancy would never last that long."

"Seriously speaking, I don't envy you. Who needs such drama from a patient? Please send her home after your shift. We'll all breathe easier."

* * *

Dr. Shaw gave Ella the women's ward again. She perceived that he wanted to avoid Amelia. As soon as Ella walked in, the wealthy girl called her over.

"Mr. Parker, I was so looking forward to seeing you again," she said in a singsong voice and batted her lengthy eyelashes.

Ella had to breathe deep not to burst out laughing.

"I am not feeling so well. Would you please examine me?"

As Ella conducted the exam, the girl smiled, staring into her eyes. She wore a silky nightgown which left her shoulders bare, obviously not hospital issued. The garment accentuated her sizable bosom and slim waist. Most women behaved with modesty or even timidity during exams, but Amelia ogled with no trepidation, showing off her swan-like neck and long arms with graceful fingers.

"Everything is fine. You are ready to go home in the morning."

"But I have an uncomfortable sensation in my stomach, right here." The girl grabbed Ella's hand and put it on her abdomen. "Oh, your hands are small and gentle, almost like women's. But the calluses speak to your hard work," she added when Ella pressed on her belly.

"I found nothing wrong, but we can repeat the castor oil to make sure."

The girl pulled a face. "No, that's quite all right. It must be hunger. I was dreaming of duck with champagne. It's our cook's specialty."

The advice of avoiding rich foods apparently did not stick. Amelia combed through her sandy hair with her fingers and leaned in. "I was wondering, Mr. Parker, if you would like to call on me. I accept visitors every Wednesday at ten."

Ella shifted her feet, thinking fast what to say. "I am afraid a medical student's life is extremely hectic. My studies leave no time for acquaintances."

Her smile was sweet like honey. "What a shame. Maybe an exception could be made once a week."

"I am afraid not. And your parents would disapprove of a connection with a humble student."

"I heard you are a brilliant pupil. If you become a famous doctor, my parents won't object."

"I promise to call on you when that happens."

She sighed, her bosom rising high. "I won't forget you so easily. Baron Cleveland did not visit me, that stonehearted man. I was sure he would rush to my bedside. You, on the other hand, are caring and kind. I will never forget how you saved my life."

"Dr. Shaw deserves the credit. I only assisted."

Amelia squeezed her face like she had bitten into a lemon. "He is married and not so good-looking. You are much more handsome." The frown changed to a salacious smile. "My heart," she touched her right breast instead of the left, "starts beating faster when I see you."

Ella excused herself to check on her other two patients. The young women had improved, both ready to be discharged in the morning.

"Do you have a place to go?" Ella asked the girl who was evicted.

"Yes, my aunt will collect me. She has a job for me in mind, and hopefully I will be well enough to start soon."

The other girl looked at her with concern. "Please write to me when you settle, dear."

Ella opened her mouth with surprise. "Did you two become friends?"

The girl who lost her hand giggled and then whispered, "We bonded over the entertainment from the other patient."

The other girl agreed. "I don't need to go to a show. It cannot be as good as this."

"Do you think if I swallow my mother's expensive medication someone would buy me a horse?"

"More likely you would get a switching so good that you won't sit for a week. Now, I will plan a twenty-course dinner for at least fifty friends, and then arrange for us to have our stomachs emptied so our gowns still fit."

Both girls sniggered.

"That lass has way too much time on her hands."

"She sure does."

Ella agreed. All that energy needed an outlet, or Amelia would continue to be such a pain. A memory of her own aspiration gave her an idea.

Strolling over to Amelia, she said, "I regret that I will not be able to call on you for a while. You resemble a famous actress, but I cannot remember which."

The girl gave her a coquettish wink. "Maria Theresa Kemble? Ann Brunton Merry? I adore them both."

"Yes… Merry, I believe. Have you ever thought of acting yourself?"

She batted her eyelashes again. "Do you think I would be any good?"

"You would be marvelous. You should stage your own play."

The girl gasped. "What a splendid idea! I was moved to tears by *Romeo and Juliet* at the theater. I will play Juliet, of course. My portrayal will be amazingly real after what I've been through. Would you play Romeo? You would suit perfectly."

"I am afraid I have no time or talent for theater."

"That's too bad. Please let me know if you change your mind. Can I go home tomorrow? I am eager to get started on casting my friends and rehearsing."

Ella reassured her she would be discharged in the morning. Dr. Shaw prescribed *Hooper's Female Pills for Purging and Anti-hysteric*, a popular remedy for almost any malady in women. Acting would channel all that energy into something productive as well.

When she met Dr. Shaw later that week, he greeted her with warmth. "Miss Hearts gave you much praise for her care. Her parents were pleased as well and thanked you for suggesting a pursuit for Amelia. They never saw her occupied with such passion before. They pledged a large donation to the hospital, and to the two patients who shared Amelia's ward. Dr. Miller is quite satisfied with you."

"It was only luck," Ella said, reddening. Her heart sang at the thought of the professor happy with her efforts.

"We all could use such luck," Dr. Shaw remarked with a lopsided smile.

* * *

March 1,

Dear Matilda and Dr. Pesce,

I was terribly worried when I read both of you were ill this winter. I hope you are feeling better. The weather has been cold and unpleasant.

Besides classes, I now work shifts at the hospital several nights a week under the supervision of doctors. While I am often tired, I love taking care of patients. When someone gets better, it's incredibly rewarding. I only wish more patients would survive without catching hospital infections, and more diseases could be cured. So many young patients succumb to pneumonia, smallpox, gangrene, and many other illnesses.

On the evenings I don't work, I practice surgical procedures. My arms are now strong enough to saw bones as quickly as most surgeons, but small hands allow for delicate jobs as well, and my professors praise me. I've recently watched one doctor perform a surgery on the tongue to correct a stammer. The surgery was pronounced a success, but when I checked on the patient during my shift, he still stammered when asking for water.

I've read disturbing news in recent medical journals regarding herb healers. The articles warn of the harmful plants sold by ignorant merchants and urge to consult accredited physicians only. One paper even cited examples of fatal poisonings. Of course, they say nothing of physicians' remedies that harm patients. It's easy to see who is benefitting from such press campaigns.

Please take care of yourselves.

Love, Alan Parker

* * *

April 4,

Dear Alan,

In his last letter, my brother wrote that he has recovered from his illness, and I was too busy to get properly sick. Someday, when I retire, I will discover the joy of staying in bed for a few days with some minor illness.

The slandering stories about herb healers occur from time to time. I cannot deny that there are snake oil saleswomen and ignorant fools. Years ago, I knew a woman who accidentally told her client to drink belladonna instead of using it as eye-drops. She ended up in jail after the client died from the poison. Yet the foolhardiness of a few healers does not make the whole profession wicked, as I am sure you know. If you ask me, we do less harm than your surgeons with these so-called scientific innovations. Whoever heard of cutting the tongue to correct a stammer? Lindsey stammered a bit, and I taught her to sing her words when she couldn't speak them. Anyway, a stammer is something one can live with, no need to go under the knife, thank you very much.

I am glad to hear you are progressing in your studies and that caring for patients gives you purpose and joy. Hard work will keep your mind safe from melancholy.
Love and take care,
Matilda Pesce

CHAPTER 11

Every face in Dr. Miller's classroom stared at her, and many whistled and laughed. Even the skeletons, Adam and Eve, grinned. She leaned on the wall for support. Her limbs were paralyzed.

"She is a woman," someone yelled. "How did she ever come here?"

"It's not what you think –" she wanted to explain, but to her horror, her man's clothing turned into a skirt. Her eyes dashed around, searching for someone to help her, but all she could see were jeering and pointing men.

Ella shook herself awake. Her heart hammered and her mouth felt desert-dry. *That dream again*, she thought, hugging herself. Breathing hard, she reasoned: *no one would suspect that the best medical student in the university was a woman.* The idea was too outrageous to imagine, she told herself. And yet that dream disturbed her for the third time that week.

After several deep breaths, she kicked off her blanket and quit her bed. The room felt hot despite the early hour, due to unseasonably sultry weather of mid-May, and Ella's scarlet nightgown dampened with sweat. *Only when I sleep do I get to be a girl*, she thought, removing it. In her undergarments, she approached a glass, scrutinizing her figure. Her body had changed over the course of the year, as Dr. Pesce and Matilda had predicted. Now sixteen, she was no longer flat-chested and wore a tight binder to conceal her growing breasts under loose men's clothing. Her hips grew wider as well, giving her figure a curvy, feminine look, and when she did not suffer nightmares, she dreamed of her classmate, Walter Carrow, kissing her with his soft lips. She gave herself a shake, thinking of the young man. *He does not even know you are a girl. And cannot ever know,* she reminded herself.

After dressing and taking a quick trip to the kitchen, she brought a tray with breakfast up to the room. A cup of aromatic coffee with cream was pure heaven, and she relished every sip. Indulgence was well earned by her hard work. A mad dash from classes to the hospital wards, and from the operating theater to the library, made her feel like a horse on a merry-go-round. Weeks flew by with incredible speed. Exam dates approached, and despite late nights of studying with Oli, she agonized about her readiness. She rejoiced to have a Saturday with no plans but exam preparations.

Busy studying and working, she let numerous envelopes from Mr. Hastings and Mr. Smiley pile up. The stack gave her pangs of guilt. She could get through a few letters today before diving into her exam preparations. With a sigh, she opened and read one, then another. Their formal and ambiguous writing required her to do mental gymnastics to comprehend their messages. She spent a good hour making sense of their questions. Irritated, she pushed the letters away. Instead of a well-earned holiday at the seaside in the summer, she would have to return home to figure out what her estate caretaker and lawyer needed from her.

The room became stuffy to the point that Ella could not bear it. Hoping that walking would clear her head, she hurried to the university gardens. A gentle breeze refreshed her, and the rhythm of her stride and deep breaths calmed her. She paused by a bench and sat down for a spell.

The tap of familiar steps made her look up to find Oli sprinting towards her. He panted, and his face glistened with sweat.

"Have you… heard about… the duel?" he said, catching his breath. His eyes sparkled with excitement.

"Sorry, what?"

He filled his lungs with air. "Two law students argued about Whigs and Tories and decided it was an affair of honor. They fought with pistols and managed to hit each other. They had Jeffers with them, not that he knew what to do, but at least he made sure they were brought to the hospital without delay."

He did not have to ask Ella if she wanted to see the wounded. Their feet strode towards the hospital as soon as he finished relaying the story.

Within minutes they entered the building, and the screams and curses brought them to the right ward. Two of Dr. Miller's assistants held the shouting man, as Jeffers, puffing and groaning, attempted to suture the wound on his leg.

Jeffers gave a sigh of relief when he saw them come in. "Parker, I could use a hand," he yelled.

The patient struggled, causing pain to himself, and frustration to the medical student. Ella shook her head. "People who have this much energy to shout are not in danger of dying. I want to evaluate the other patient first. Jeffers, you need to give your screamer some opium tincture, so he stops wriggling, and you will have less trouble suturing."

Jeffers fetched the laudanum, while Ella approached the

other bed, and Oli followed her. The young man, seemingly forgotten, lay without making a sound. His face was bloodless, eyes half-closed, and he struggled to breathe. She took his hand to check the pulse; it was faint and irregular.

"What is your name?" she asked the wounded man. He looked about eighteen, with fair hair and freckles.

"Daniel Carter," he mumbled.

"Why is he not being attended to? Where are Dr. Miller and the other surgeons?" she called to the assistants.

"Dr. Miller is on his way and should be here shortly. He and many other doctors attended a lecture at another hospital," one of them answered. "There is not much that can be done for him. He's hit in the chest."

Oli inhaled sharply. "Darn, you can't treat a chest wound," he whispered.

True enough, she thought. If a lung or a major artery were hit, the patient would die. If the bullet did not come out through an exit wound, it would remain in the chest, causing a deadly infection. Extracting it without killing the patient would be almost impossible. But the fellow was just out of boyhood, too young to die.

She pressed her ear to his chest, straining to listen for abnormal chest sounds, which would indicate a penetration of the lung. "I think the bullet missed vital organs, and there's no hemorrhage. He could be lucky. I am going to remove his shirt to get a better look," she said to Oli, taking a pair of scissors from a tray.

When Ella moved the fabric away, the bullet entrance hole became visible at the top of his ribs. Ella pressed lightly, and Daniel groaned.

"His rib is broken," she said, turning to Oli.

"Did the bullet come out?"

"Good question," Ella mouthed. She moved the patient

onto his left side and observed his back. "I don't see an exit hole."

Oli gritted his teeth. "That's bad news."

"Wait a minute, what is this?" She pointed to a lump at the shoulder blade. "I don't want to disturb it, but that could be the bullet lodged in the muscles of the back."

"How did it get up there?" Oli asked

"I suppose it changed direction inside after breaking the rib."

Oli gave a short whistle. "Dr. Miller better get here quickly."

As the words left his mouth, Daniel coughed and spit up a mouthful of blood.

"We better keep him on his side," Ella said and called to the assistants, who finished bandaging the other duelist. "This man needs surgery. Prepare the operating room."

One of the assistants looked at her dubiously. "The surgeon will decide what to do."

"Get him on the table, so no time is wasted. Look where the bullet is stuck. Oli, give him some laudanum."

Oli poured a teaspoon and lifted Daniel's head to drink it. Meanwhile, Ella selected the scalpels, forceps, probes, threaded needles, and other instruments needed for surgery and arranged them on the tray the way Dr. Miller preferred, bringing them into the operating room. After ordering the assistants to light more lanterns, she returned to the patient.

"How is he doing?" she asked Oli.

"He spit out more blood while you were gone."

She fingered the vein on the neck, counting the beats, then called to the assistants to take the patient into the surgery. None of them argued with her. They expertly transferred Daniel onto the operating table, keeping him on his left side per her instructions. Ella and Oli threw on the aprons over their jackets. Oli took the pulse again, breathing through his teeth.

"If Dr. Miller does not show up soon, we may lose this man," he whispered. He turned to one of the assistants. "Run and bring any surgeon you can find. Hurry."

"He may rally once the bullet is removed," Ella said while staring at the instruments, her hand itching to pick up a scalpel. "I know how to take out a bullet from under the scapula. I have done it on a cadaver." *I did, but that was on a corpse. I failed to save my father, acting myself instead of calling for a doctor.*

With a deep breath, Ella willed herself to keep waiting through the minutes that seemed to stretch like hours. Daniel stirred and moaned. "Can we give him more laudanum?" she asked Oli.

"I don't know. I gave him quite a bit already."

Ella's hand inched towards the tray with the instruments. *What am I doing? I could be wrong and kill him.*

"Don't even think about it. You, and the hospital, will be in a great deal of trouble for operating without doctor's supervision."

Daniel made another heart-wrenching moan.

Confound it. If the school expels me, I will go play a great lady at my mansion. Ella reached for the scalpel, ignoring Oli's protests.

"Mr. Parker, what are you doing?" She startled as Dr. Miller came into the operating room.

"The patient has a bullet stuck at the inferior angle of the scapula. We believe the bullet first struck him in his rib, and bounced up to the shoulder blade, passing between the bone and the muscle tissue. I found a protrusion where it could be retrieved."

"And were you thinking to remove the bullet yourself?"

"His pulse is weakening, and he is showing distress despite the opium. I have done the procedure on a cadaver. The incision should be made here, avoiding major arteries." Ella traced the spot where she planned to cut.

Dr. Miller nodded. "Proceed then. I will supervise and take over if needed."

Oli gave her a disbelieving look, but Ella, as if waiting for the word, grabbed the scalpel and sliced the skin. The knife struck metal, and she extended her hand for Oli to pass her the forceps. Catching the bullet with the instrument, she pulled it out and inspected it.

Dr. Miller motioned to pass the bullet to him. "Good. You brought it out along with a piece of his shirt." He checked the wound to ensure no more fabric was lodged inside, and instructed Ella to clean it, tie off the blood vessels and apply sutures. When the assistant placed the patient on his back, the doctor showed her how to bind the broken rib. After finishing the procedure, he turned to Ella. "It's too early to tell, but this may be the first life you saved in the operating room, Mr. Parker. The first of many, I predict. How does it feel?"

Ella needed a moment to let the words sink in. "Like nothing else in my life."

"Hopefully, the patient will not disappoint you by succumbing. You were smart to start surgery preparations before I came. We have done all we could. How is his pulse, Mr. Higgins?"

"Stronger and steadier. His breathing is less labored as well."

"Good. We will keep the wound draining and place leeches on it to prevent infection. I am exceptionally pleased with you, Mr. Parker, and I hope Mr. Higgins learned a great deal."

The professor scanned the room, and Ella was surprised

to find it full of people. Absorbed by the surgery, she did not hear them come in. "Since all my pupils are here, I have an announcement. You are close to finishing your first year, and you've come a long way already. At the end of the next school year, after the exams, I will be selecting a single student who has impressed me to be my apprentice. I am happy to say that such apprenticeships have launched many successful careers. Now, please use the day to study for your exams."

The room buzzed with excitement over the announcement, but soon began to empty. Dr. Miller turned to Ella and Oli. "My assistants will monitor the patient and call me if needed. You may visit him when you get a chance to see how he is progressing. I will do my rounds now and see to the other combatant. And, Mr. Parker, I think we both know who the top contender for my apprenticeship is."

Ella did her best not to gape. From the moment Dr. Miller made his announcement, there was nothing she desired more.

* * *

Ella visited Daniel twice during the finals week, but he slept both times. His face took on a healthier color and his slumber seemed restful. The assistants assured her his recovery was going well. When she finished her last final, and her heart sang of freedom and summer break, she stopped by the hospital and tiptoed into Daniel's room again. He was awake and reclining on his pillows as Dr. Miller examined him. A middle-aged couple, Daniel's parents by Ella's guess, stood by his side, watching the doctor anxiously.

"All is going well. I am pleased with your progress, young man. Hopefully, your future battles will be in the courtroom, not on a dueling field," the doctor quipped.

Noticing Ella lurking in the corner, he motioned for her to come closer. "And here is my student, Mr. Parker, whose quick thinking and able hands saved your life."

Daniel beamed and thanked her earnestly. The mother embraced Ella so hard that she felt her body crack then the father shook her hand, making her knuckles hurt. Overwhelmed, Ella wished Daniel a swift recovery and backed out of the ward, blushing, and breathing rapidly.

May 28,
Dear Matilda and Dr. Pesce,
The most amazing event occurred, and no, I don't mean my sixteenth birthday: I performed my first surgery, saving the life of a young man injured in a duel. I've never been this excited in my life. The patient recovered and will leave the hospital in a few days.
Dr. Miller announced that he will select the best student as his intern after the end of next year. Everyone says such an internship would be a chance of a lifetime for any new doctor. The professor hinted at me being the strongest contender, and I intend to win the job. Honestly, I don't have any serious competition, besides Walter Carrow. Personally, I think Oli is excellent as well, but he rarely gets attention in a good way. I received top marks in all my final exams. With the end of term, the campus is emptying, and Oli has already left to visit his family. I decided to go on holiday at the seaside. Matilda, please join me if you like.
I am much disturbed by the latest war news and the battles our ships are engaged in. I hope our dear doctor is safe and sound.
Love, Alan Parker

* * *

May 28,
Dear Mr. Hastings and Mr. Smiley,
I would like to remind you that I am a busy medical student.
Therefore, I am asking the following from you:

- *Please write me your letters and reports in plain English.*
- *Please be clear if you need something from me, or simply want to inform me.*
- *When you do need something from me, please indicate if the request is urgent or not.*
- *You are allowed to make decisions on my behalf. Please act without checking with me whenever you see fit, keeping my interests in mind.*
- *Please send me <u>one</u> new letter summarizing any burning issues I must be aware of.*

If your correspondence does not meet my expectations stated above, I will visit the estate over the summer to have a talk.
Sincerely, Alan Parker

June 25,
Dear Alan,
Happy Birthday, my dear! Your last letter was intriguing, to say the least. Congratulations on saving the young man's life. I did not realize you are allowed to perform surgery already, but that is a great achievement, and you can be proud of yourself. However, I am confused about your plans of becoming Dr. Miller's intern. Surely the doctor would require you to commit to this apprenticeship for a year or longer. How long do you intend to keep up with your way of life?

This may be the opportunity of a lifetime for a young man, but I don't see how you can benefit. If I were you, I would ready an excuse explaining why you cannot accept the doctor's offer and let someone else profit from it.
I received a letter from my brother; he is safe and busy treating the wounded. He writes all about the amputations he has conducted, as if I want to read about those dreadful procedures. He sends you his love, and I will be sure to inform him of your success.
Unfortunately, I cannot play a wealthy lady who has nothing better to do than go on a seaside holiday. Many of the mothers have babies due this summer, and the shop will be busy with clients buying remedies for sunburn, bee stings, and poison ivy. Besides, I never owned a bathing dress and cannot swim.
Be glad of your fortune and enjoy yourself.
Love, Matilda Pesce

CHAPTER 12

August 20,

Dear Matilda and Dr. Pesce,

*I hope all is well with you. I am back at the university,
preparing for the new term. I returned two weeks ago to
conduct research for my thesis — more on that below.*

*My seaside holiday started out lovely. Matilda, you were
much missed. I hired a servant and a companion and became
myself for a while. After a few days in the sun and swims in
the waves, I was as good as new.*

*Several ladies wondered about my hair, but I told them it was
cut short to cool me when I had a fever. Then a tragedy struck
at the beach I frequented: a young woman drowned. While I
was not there when her friends pulled her out, I realized my
ignorance in how to help if I had been there. Frustrated with
myself, I decided to come back to school and research the
topic.*

*It turns out, there is no standard way to revive a drowning
victim. Suggestions I came across included hanging upside-
down, blowing smoke either into the victim's mouth or
rectum, or rolling over a barrel – who has one of those at a*

beach? None of the sources boasted success with their methods. This topic holds potential for my thesis.

I received a letter from Dr. Miller inviting me to take private lessons with a group of other selected students. He will hold them monthly at his house. I accepted his invitation at once. Besides these lessons, I will be adding a couple of classes and working hospital shifts. There is an optional midwifery course, but I don't think I can fit it into my schedule.

Love, Alan Parker.

* * *

September 15,

Dear Alan,

I am glad you had a nice holiday and that you found an interesting topic for your research. However, I am not too happy to hear that you are skipping the one course that could be quite useful to you. Something tells me your choice has more to do with your fears than your schedule. If it's the former, then buck up and get over it. Sorry, I don't have more compassionate advice.

I am also not sure what to make of these private lessons at the doctor's home. The atmosphere may be more casual there than at school; don't drop your guard. Do these classes have anything to do with the internship you are pursuing? I still don't understand the point of it for you, and Dr. Pesce agrees with me. While he understands your ambitions, he thinks that after your medical training you should come back to London to help with his practice or with my clients.

Love and take care,

Matilda Pesce

* * *

A scream came from downstairs, and Ella bolted from her bed. *What is it this time?* Since returning to campus, she had come to the rescue in two household emergencies, saving the landlady's sliced finger and the maid's twisted ankle. Ella managed each case with competence and to her patients' satisfaction.

"Mr. Parker! Are you awake?" The landlady, Mrs. Bunting, called from downstairs.

"I am now."

"I am afraid we need your help. Jane burned her hand."

"Have her soak it in cold water. I will be right down to bring her a salve."

She ran over to her medicine cabinet filled with remedies for cough and fever, emetics, and purgatives, and found a strong-smelling burn ointment. With a jar in one hand, she had her other hand on the doorknob, when she realized she still wore her silky nightgown. After tapping herself on the forehead, she threw it off, then wrapped her growing breasts with a rigid binder, and donned her shirt and trousers.

Downstairs in the kitchen, Ella found Jane, a fourteen-year-old scullery maid, seated on a stool, weeping. Two other young maids dashed back and forth, carrying dishes and utensils to set the table for breakfast, smiling and winking at Ella as they hurried past. Mrs. Bunting turned away from the stove, where she stirred porridge, and greeted her with a smile.

"You are our savior, Mr. Parker."

Ella chuckled and approached Jane, who demonstrated an angry red burn stretching from the back of her palm to midway up her forearm.

"I thought the pot would be cool, but it was burning hot," Jane said, sobbing, as Ella applied the salve.

Rubbing the ointment into the girl's hand, Ella instructed, "The treatment should start working in a few minutes, and the pain will lessen. You need to apply the salve for a week or so, until the burn heals."

"For a week? I have to buy it from the apothecary?"

"No, silly. Keep the jar and bring it back to me when you are done."

The girl gaped and then beamed.

Mrs. Bunting came closer and inspected the injury. "I will make sure you give the medicine back to Mr. Parker." She shook her head and frowned. "You are in no shape to help me today. Go have some rest instead."

When the girl left, the landlady muttered, "I don't know what's wrong with girls nowadays. Sticking her hand into the oven when I told her the roast just finished cooking. And so feeble, always asking for breaks. When I was her age, I was as strong as a mare. Anyway, Mr. Parker, thank you for helping again. How handy to have a capable medical student in my residence," she said with an appreciative smile.

Ella was about to leave the kitchen when Mrs. Bunting called again. "I am so sorry, but with Jane and her hand, I completely forgot to mention: a friend of yours asked me to tell you he will wait for you in the gardens."

Such an invitation could only mean that Oli had returned from his summer holiday. Striding through the rows of blooming flowers, she found him on one of the benches near the pond, basking in the sun. He raised his hand to greet her then stood so they could walk side by side.

"Oh, you are still short. I was afraid you would come back a head taller," he teased. "How was your summer?"

"Fine." Ella considered telling him about her seaside holiday but decided to stick with a safe one-word answer.

"Have you visited patients?"

"Yes. Daniel Carter recovered and sent me a bottle of wine. I saw him walking around the campus yesterday. Lucy with typhus fever went home. Molly, the girl with the broken leg, is recovering steadily." Ella paused before getting to the bad news.

"Who did we lose?" Oli searched her face.

"A number of the children with smallpox, the whole Abbott family with dysentery, and Johnny with scarlet fever," she said.

Oli stood silent for a while, his eyes squeezed closed, and mouth moving as if in a silent prayer. After another moment, he lifted his chin. "Mum sent you apples she picked from our garden."

He handed her the basket full to the brim of yellow and green fruit. They smelled heavenly. Ella asked him to send his family her regards. After describing his mostly uneventful summer, Oli inquired what classes Ella planned on taking.

"I am continuing with the ones from last year and adding medical jurisprudence. I also received a letter from Dr. Miller inviting me to take private lessons with him."

"That's terrific. I did not receive such an invitation. What about midwifery?"

"I am not taking it. I will be busy enough."

Oli gave her a disbelieving glance. "Since when has being busy stopped you from taking a class? You need to enroll in midwifery."

"It's an optional subject, and I have no interest in it."

"It should not be optional. Besides, you have interest in everything medical. Why are you not signing up?"

"I have some objections to how it is taught. For example, why is Dr. Sanders teaching, and not a midwife?"

Oli gave her a crooked smile. "To have a woman teach an all-male class would be too forward thinking for this school.

Also, while many midwives are knowledgeable, there are plenty of charlatans among them."

"And we don't have such among doctors?" Ella replied with a smirk. "Why not organize courses to educate midwives and allow them to share their experience? In Paris, Madame LaChapelle gives lectures to future doctors and midwives."

"That's in Paris, Alan. I understand your reservations, but you must take the class. Someday you may be the only doctor in the vicinity to assist a woman in labor."

"Goodness, Oli. Who is tutoring whom now? Your argument is good, but I would rather skip the class this semester and come back to it some other time. It's too…" Ella halted, unsure if she wanted to use the word on her mind.

"Personal? Did someone you knew die giving birth?"

Ella lowered her eyes. "I don't want to talk about it."

Oli put his arm on her shoulder. "Alan, most of us go into medicine because of something personal. My best friend died of a ruptured appendix. Two of my siblings did not survive their first year and one sister died of consumption. We choose medicine so we can save people. I will be happy to help you work through your fears, like you helped me get over my dread of cadavers. You will thank me later."

She shook her head, grinning. "I trained you too well. You are throwing my own teaching back at me."

"Glad to hear it. And your answer about your summer was unsatisfactory. I am sure you dug up some excellent reading and need to share it." He turns to her. "Why are you chuckling?"

"I missed you, Oli." She wanted to give him a hug but slipped her hand over his shoulder instead.

* * *

Midwifery class commenced at the women's clinic, a short distance away from the hospital. The classroom, sized for fifteen students or so, was gloomier and dirtier than the bright rooms in the medical building. There were a couple of books on the shelf, and a model of the female reproductive system. The single plant in the corner withered from lack of water. The place reeked with smoke from the instructor's cigars.

"Dr. Sanders, will we not only look at, but also touch the female patients?" Jeffers asked, snickering.

Their instructor, Dr. Sanders, a forty-something red-faced man of considerable size, blew a ring with his cigar smoke. "You will look and feel plenty. I suspect many of you signed up for the class for that reason."

"Some of us came to medical school for that reason," another student quipped.

Most of the pupils and Dr. Sanders chuckled, while Ella and Oli reddened and exchanged disgusted looks. She squirmed at the thought of such a man as the doctor examining her, with his rough hands and unprofessional manner, yet women lined up to see him at the clinic.

After the lecture on the female reproductive system, the doctor led them through rounds. Unlike the hospital patients, most of the women who visited the clinic did not stay overnight. The students watched the doctor examine patients with breast tumors and inflammations, ovarian cysts, and postpartum complications.

A young woman stood doubled-over, holding her stomach. Her mother patted her back.

"Bridget has awfully painful monthly flows," the mother complained. "Can you please prescribe something?"

Dr. Sanders shook his head. "Medications during courses, like during pregnancy, disturb the body's humors and cause hysterics. When she is a married woman, I can apply leeches inside. As for now, keep her in bed. Nothing else can be done."

The mother, supporting the girl, shuffled into the corridor, and Ella's heart pained for them. These women likely walked for miles to see the doctor and received nothing helpful from him. With an excuse to use the privy, she sped after them.

"You should buy ginger tea from the apothecary or an herb healer. Also, a warm bath helps," Ella repeated the advice Matilda gave her clients and ran back to the rounds before the mother and daughter could thank her.

She found the classmates by the ward for admitted patients. "Two came in this morning after bungled abortions," Dr. Sanders said in a low voice. "One is sixteen years old and used a knitting needle. The other threw herself down the stairs; a mother of eight children. I gave them laudanum to lessen the pain. Make sure you take the notes you need today, because neither will be alive tomorrow." His tight lips expressed disdain.

Ella stifled a sigh, looking at the two women shivering with fevers. When the reverend in her church talked about abortion as a terrible sin, she thought that the women who committed such acts must be atrocious. Seeing the patients in front of her, she was less sure of her stance.

Instead, she wondered what kind of struggles had made them want to rid themselves of their unborn babies, and whether they knew that they would likely die as the result. She also wished Dr. Sanders would show them more compassion.

Oli's hands trembled as he measured the patients' pulses. When finished, he whispered to Ella, "Why doesn't Dr. Sanders abort the pregnancy, since he could do it safer?"

Ella raised his eyes to him in shock. It was one thing to pity the women, but to imply that the doctor should have assisted them in the illegal and sinful act was a dangerous thought.

"Do you have something to say, Mr. Higgins?" Dr. Sanders rounded on him. Ella put her hand on Oli's elbow, but the young man raised his chin and leaned forward.

"Yes, I do. Why not have a qualified doctor, such as yourself, spare the women from such a fate?"

Someone gasped, and Ella put her hand over her mouth, but Oli straightened and challenged the professor with his stare. Dr. Sanders reddened like a tomato, but after a minute regained his composure. "I am surprised you are unaware, Mr. Higgins. Let me explain to all of you in case anyone else is confused." His tone was full of contempt. "Abortion is prohibited by our laws, and by the Church. Any doctor performing such procedures will lose his license, and likely find himself in jail. We are in this profession to save lives, not kill babies. I hope you all are clear on this, and I will not have to come back to this topic again."

Oli swallowed and looked down at his shoes, and Ella shook her head.

* * *

"I am starting to regret signing up for midwifery," Oli said to Ella as they walked back to their rooms in an October drizzle. "I hope you are not displeased with me for making you take the course."

Ella didn't want to discuss the incident in class any further and thought to share her thoughts on their instructor. "I dislike Dr. Sanders and would not want such a doctor to treat me. If I were a woman, that is." She reddened, mad at herself for the slip. "But I am learning much."

Last week, when they studied human reproduction, she

had silently thanked Oli. While the students were at their worst behavior, yelling vulgarities, her own world turned upside-down. Astonished, she realized Miss Samson had lied when she said babies were conceived by kissing.

As if reading her thoughts, Oli said. "If you mean last week's classes, you can talk to me about those things if you want. I know you are fatherless and brotherless, and it's common for a boy your age to be confused or curious. I will likely be able to answer your questions."

Ella blushed burgundy. She did not like the thought of Oli being sexually experienced; but he was nineteen and good-looking. Her interest was piqued, so she asked, "Do you mean you have been with a woman?"

Oli raised his eyebrows, then said, "I will not boast. I would rather not answer that question. But feel free to ask something else that's not about me."

"Maybe some other time. Do you want to meet at the library after dinner and work on our theses?"

"Why don't you come to my flat instead? We could eat downstairs and have coffee in my room while we work. My place is right on the way."

"No, let's stick to our routine," Ella said with firmness.

"As you wish. I chose my topic, by the way. I read this great paper by Dr. Alexander Gordon where he argues the childbed fever came not from miasmas but from the dirty hands and clothes of midwives. As proof, he foretold which mother would contract the fever by asking which midwife attended the birth. He went on to recommend changing sheets, fumigating clothing, and have the midwives wash themselves between births."

Ella gave him a skeptical look. "How would washing hands prevent infection? They come from miasmas, or putrid air. The correlation between specific midwives and the fever sounds faulty. There could be other factors, like the streets the mothers lived on, the proximity to a sewer or a cemetery, the month of the year."

"I found his logic convincing," Oli said with a shrug. "The same thinking should be applied to prevention of hospital infections, such as sepsis and gangrene."

"Wait, you mean to say that surgeons are making patients sick by operating with unwashed hands, or wearing dirty clothing?"

"Exactly. Did you see Dr. Miller do rounds, check on patients with all kinds of maladies, and then go into the operating room straight after? He puts on his apron, crusted with old blood, and starts surgery like that. I doubt his instruments have ever been washed."

"And why not? All surgeons do this. They are in a hurry. Why stop to wash their hands?"

"After what I read, I know I will be washing my hands more often, especially after dissections."

"I don't know. You should be careful implying that doctors are spreading infections. Our professors will not like such suggestions."

"There are many things they don't like. If they don't hear new ideas, our field will never progress. People think of a hospital as the place where they will likely die. They should not be stepping stones to the grave, but places of healing."

"That would be great but sounds too much like a fantasy. Even so, I will be happy to help you with your thesis even if I don't buy into your ideas."

They parted, agreeing to meet later to discuss more.

* * *

The five students were elbow-deep in the insides of an unfortunate female corpse. Ella mostly worked with her right hand and held a handkerchief to her nose with her left. Despite her wide experience with dissections, the smell of a rotting body, fecal matter, blood, and gastric juices overwhelmed her. Slicing through the bowels took an anatomist with a strong stomach.

Yet Dr. Miller's private students, gathered in the dissection room in his home, jostled each other to distinguish themselves by finding a cause, or more accurately, the instrument of death.

The space reminded her of the dissection room inside Dr. Pesce's house, that once gave her such a silly fright. Here was better light and more space, and myriads more jars of organs on one side and shelves with books on another. The students, wearing aprons over their clothes, crowded around the table. With scalpels out, they were cutting and examining the tissue with careful attention. The first private lesson was nothing like she expected.

Ella aimed to make another incision when she received a painful shove into her arm. William Jeffers bumped her and cut right where she targeted. She hissed like a cat. "Watch it! We all have knives."

Walter Carrow offered her room to work by him, and Ella had to force herself not to grin when his sleeve brushed by hers. Only a year older than Ella, but quite tall and muscular, he was considered second best in her class. Just standing next to him made her heart pump faster.

She did not know the names of the other two students in the room. *Oli should be here, and Jeffers should be out,* she thought with frustration when the tall redhead tried to shove Carrow.

Dr. Miller descended into the room and stood aside,

watching their progress. "How are my chosen men doing?" he asked with an amused smile. No one answered; after an hour of careful searching through the digestive system, there was still nothing to report.

"What exactly are we looking for?" Jeffers asked.

"You can answer the question yourself, Mr. Jeffers, if you tell me how this woman died."

Jeffers pursed his lips. "We don't know."

Dr. Miller knitted his brow. "What? You have not even figured that out? After I told you to check her esophagus?" When Jeffers and the others lowered their eyes, he shook his head. "Mr. Parker, please calm my soul and tell me that at least you have determined the cause of death."

After removing the handkerchief from her nose, Ella explained, "The patient swallowed something sharp that made a tear in the esophagus and later pierced the aorta, killing her."

"As usual, Mr. Parker comes to the rescue of my class," Dr. Miller approved. "I'd been called to this unfortunate woman's house ten days ago. She complained of pain in the epigastric region, made worse by any movement. The pain started soon after dinner, which led me to ask her if there was any chance of her swallowing a foreign body, possibly a pin. She rejected such a possibility and told me that she experienced stomach spasms frequently, although not as painful as these. She reported having pains over the next week and a half, some days unable to leave the bed, and others feeling fine. This morning, after breakfast, she vomited several ounces of blood and died within minutes."

While the other students kept on searching through the bowels, Ella stopped to think. "What did the patient have for dinner the night she first experienced pain?" she asked Dr. Miller.

The doctor checked his notes. "Her cook reported that she served a boiled neck of lamb along with meat soup."

"Then we should be searching for a sharp bone. It pierced the esophagus through but remained stuck as a plug, preventing bleeding for nine days. Today the bone was dislodged, likely when the patient breakfasted, making the tear larger and piercing the aorta, thus killing her."

"That's the conclusion I came to as well. I hope the object we find in her bowels will confirm it."

Carrow raised his hand. "Found it!"

"Well done!" Ella praised with a smile before she could stop herself. *Stop acting like a moonstruck girl!* she chided herself.

Jeffers groaned and threw his scalpel at the table. They all bent over to view what Carrow was holding in his palm. It was a fragment of a bone, long and sharp.

The professor beamed as he inspected the bone in his fingers. "Excellent, Mr. Carrow. Such a tiny thing killed this poor woman. I am satisfied that my initial guess about her swallowing a foreign body has turned out to be correct."

Ella gave the doctor a hopeful gaze. "Would you have been able to save her, if she listened?"

Dr. Miller gave a smile full of affection and replied, "You give me too much credit, Mr. Parker. There was nothing I could have done for her even if she agreed with my theory, unfortunately. The place where the bone lodged itself was beyond the reach of any instrument. Even if I had something long enough to reach that far into the esophagus, the extrication might have introduced immediate bleeding and death. I believe I did the right thing by letting nature take its course."

After finishing with the postmortem, the doctor led the

group upstairs, and encouraged them to have refreshments. Ella drank a glass of water and contemplated an early escape.

The putrid smell penetrated her clothing, and she looked forward to removing the garments and bathing. She reddened when Carrow approached her, horrified how she may look and smell to him.

What does it matter how you look or smell! Stop being stupid when he's merely being polite with some small talk!

She nodded to him with civility. "Congratulations on finding the bone."

"It's you who should be congratulated. You reasoned the cause of death, a rather unusual one. I take it we are the final five for Dr. Miller's internship. I hope to give you worthy competition, but you are always ahead of me."

Ella wondered if he was flattering her, but his tone was sincere. She whispered, "Why is Jeffers here? And Higgins not?"

Carrow raised an eyebrow. "Jeffers is a son of a prominent member of the university and hospital board. His father will try to use his influence for Dr. Miller to choose his untalented son as an intern. I don't believe the professor would agree though. It would be an outrage to choose Jeffers over us. As for your second question, I will not speculate." He took a sip of red wine from his glass.

Ella was about to add more about Oli's absence, when she saw a long red scratch on Carrow's hand. "Did you get this cut while dissecting?"

He turned his hand over to inspect. "Maybe. I don't think I had it this morning."

Wounds received when working with cadavers were bad news. "Did Jeffers nick you? He was terribly careless."

"It might have been the bone itself. Something grazed my hand before I saw it." That bone was covered in dried blood and body fluids. Ella shuddered like something icy had touched her.

"Put some gin or brandy on it and show Dr. Miller."

He took a bottle from the table with refreshments, poured the brown liquid on a handkerchief, and pressed it to the cut with a wince.

"No need to tell the doctor. It will either be fine, or there will be nothing he can do." He said a hurried goodbye to everyone and left.

Ella stood, chewing her lip. Her chest was heavy with worry, but she knew Carrow was right. If he cut himself with a dirty knife or bone, there was nothing to do but hope that infection didn't occur.

* * *

November 1,

Dear Matilda and Dr. Pesce,

I signed up for midwifery after all, at Oli's urging. So far I am quite disappointed in the instructor, Dr. Sanders, especially with his manners and unprofessional demeanor in class and sometimes with patients. I am convinced the ladies he treats would be more candid and comfortable if a woman doctor were taking care of them.

The year started with a tragedy. One of my classmates, Walter Carrow, cut himself during a dissection and his wound became infected. A sharp bone fragment one unfortunate woman swallowed claimed two lives: hers, and the medical student's too. Dr. Miller amputated Carrow's hand, but even that did not save the young man. He died of gangrene a few days later.

When I heard the news, I was devastated. All medical students attended the funeral, and I broke down crying.

*Oli comforted me and was tearful as well, but he seemed
surprised at me displaying such strong emotions.*
I hope you are well,
Love, Alan Parker

* * *

November 30,
Dear Alan,
*I am glad you saw sense and signed up for midwifery, even if
it took Oli to set you straight instead of me. Silly of me, I
imagined it would be an experienced midwife teaching the
class, but of course, male doctors know better. Never mind
Dr. Sanders' manner, just learn what you can from him.*
*I am sorry about Walter Carrow. I take it he was someone you
liked, and I hope you did not reveal your feelings to be more
than grief for a fellow student. I've heard such infections are
not uncommon, and I always fretted when my brother
performed postmortems downstairs. Hopefully, you will
remember to be extra careful.*
Love, Matilda Pesce

The woman at the harpsichord played hymns with wonderful musicality, and the worshippers' voices rose to the painted ceiling. Ella always loved the Christmas Eve service because of its uplifting and jovial feeling. She went to church each Sunday morning as well, as was required of all university students, and found that her mood often improved from singing or hearing a spirited service. Oli usually arrived late, stayed in the back, and was among the first to leave. If attendance were optional, he would never go, Ella suspected.

Tonight, instead of praying, her friend volunteered for another shift at the hospital. They both decided to stay at the university to keep up their studies and care for patients during holidays.

The service ended, and the churchgoers shook hands and wished each other Merry Christmas. After greeting acquaintances and strangers, Ella put on her heavy coat and made her way towards the exit.

On the steps, she heard a small voice interrupted by frequent coughs. "Please, kind sir, would you spare any change?"

Another voice, which sounded young but not as childlike as the first, begged, "Please help the poor and hungry." After the plea, the speaker rasped and hacked.

A woman in a lavish fur coat, and a girl of around twelve walked past Ella. "Mum, can I give some coins to the beggars?" the girl asked.

The mother took her daughter's hand and pulled her away. "These people should be at a workhouse. Don't go near them! Do you hear how they cough? They are filthy and will give you their diseases."

The girl gave a sad glance towards the beggars. "But what about charity on Christmas?"

"We put plenty in the basket tonight. Let the church take care of them," the mother answered, leading the girl to the waiting carriage.

With a few coins in her hands, Ella approached the paupers who continued to beg from a dwindling crowd of worshippers. Most of the patrons sped by without stopping to spare their change. Ella put a few silvers first into the hand of a small girl, no older than six, then a woman about her own age. The child blessed her kindness but doubled over in a coughing fit. Ella observed that she had nothing but a knitted shawl to protect her from frigid wind. The woman was huddled in a coat that must have known better days. Something was familiar about her angular face.

It took Ella a moment to make the wild guess, but she thought herself wrong until she recalled the coat in its former glory.

"Amelia Hearts?" she asked, shocked to see her former patient.

The woman looked up, and for a second, there was an expression of a former capricious princess in her features, as if she were only acting the part of a beggar and stepped out of character. Then despair and shame revealed themselves in her eyes.

"Mr. Parker, what a meeting," she said with bitterness. "I take it you will not be calling on me during my visit hours." She cracked a smile, revealing a couple of large gaps between teeth.

"What in the world happened to you?"

"It's a long story. If you add more silver, I'll tell you."

Ella gave her some more coins but stopped her from beginning her tale. "You need to come inside. You don't look well, and the child will catch a chill of death in this weather with no coat. Who is she?"

Amelia shrugged. "No one. Her name is Abigail. I found her today and thought we would get more change begging together."

"They don't let us inside," the girl complained. "The big man did not want us there. 'Don't bother the good people who came to celebrate the holy day,' he said."

The big man was likely the caretaker.

"Where are your parents, Abigail?" Ella asked.

The girl broke into a coughing fit again. When she got her breath back, she replied, "We only had Mum, and she died last week from a fever. Our neighbor took the babies, but she did not want me. Said I am too big to love her like a mother and too small to help her with chores. This nice lady," she nodded at Amelia, "shared some bread with me and taught me how to beg."

Ella stared down at Amelia.

"What? She was hungry and did not know to ask for change or food. There are worse things than begging, you know," Amelia said with her chin raised.

"All right, I am getting cold standing here, and I have a coat on. Do you have a place to sleep?"

"Sure. Anywhere we can find that's warm and dry, like a barn or a stable."

"Then you both will come with me to the hospital."

Amelia shook her head. "They will not take me. I spent the entire day last week in the waiting room, then the doctor sent me away. Consumption is incurable, he said. Take Abigail; she coughs but without blood."

Ella chewed her lip. What a turn of fortune for a once wealthy girl who talked of horses and trips to London! Their hospital did not treat consumption, but she could get a bed for Amelia for a night or two.

"I will get both of you in. Let's go."

They walked at a slow pace, both Amelia and Abigail stopping often and coughing into their hands. Halfway to the hospital the child became too tired to go on, and Ella wrapped her into her own coat and carried her the rest of the way.

The children's wards were full of coughing, sneezing, and shivering young patients. Other than the plum pudding that some of the children were eating with supper, nothing reminded her of the holiday.

Ella remembered a Christmas tree she saw at a shop last year and wished there was one to cheer up the sick little ones, but when she took in their feverish faces, she doubted that even a lit wonder could lift their spirits. Influenza and pneumonia were relentless this winter.

Oli went around to each bed, administering medications. When he noticed Ella, he came over. "Who did you bring, Alan?" he asked, looking at her bundle.

"A little beggar who sat on the church steps with no winter clothes. She's coughing her lungs out."

"Poor thing. A bed emptied an hour ago. Over here," he took Abigail from Ella's hands and placed her on the bed. "Is that her mother?" he said glancing towards Amelia.

"I remember you, Mr. Higgins. But I see you don't recognize me," Amelia said with a bitter laugh.

"Amelia Hearts?" Oli asked with disbelief.

"Did I change that much?"

"She has consumption," Ella said. "Is there a bed in the women's ward for her to spend a night or two?"

Oli shook his head. "All other wards are full. Only this ward has room, with several patients perishing. She can take the bed in the corner."

As Oli examined Abigail, Ella had Amelia remove her coat and lie down. Under her coat, the young woman had a shimmery canary dress, resembling a stage costume. She was much thinner than Ella remembered her.

"Sorry, it's the children's ward, but at least you can sleep in a warm bed," Ella said.

Amelia laughed with a hysterical note. "My mother was displeased that I did not get a room to myself. Now I am lucky I am getting a bed at all. If I knew what was coming, I'd have that full bottle of pills and get it over with."

"Don't talk like that. Where are your parents?"

"At home, resting after a holiday meal, I suppose."

"Why are you not with them?"

"Right, I owe you a story. You paid for it. But I would rather eat and sleep now."

"Fine with me. I'll listen to your lungs and then make sure you get some supper."

"You are an angel," Amelia answered in a breathy voice and batted her lashes, giving Ella a glimpse of a former coquette. Then she burst out laughing.

Ella shook her head with a smile, as at a naughty child. "Hush."

Amelia quieted, letting Ella examine her. When she finished and asked a nurse to bring hot food, the young woman stared at Ella with her head tilted to the side.

"What's your verdict, Mr. Parker? Don't be afraid to say I am dying. I already know it."

"It's too early to say so. Last time I saw you in February, you were healthy, other than that stunt with pills that you emerged from unscathed. When did you start coughing up blood?"

"A month ago, maybe less."

"You could still recover if you are cared for."

"No one will care for me. Not my parents, not my former friends. I will die somewhere like a sick dog."

"I am sure things are not as dreadful as you say."

The nurse, a young nun from a nearby convent, brought a tray with supper.

"Eat and get some sleep. Maybe your spirits will be better in the morning," Ella said, and Amelia pounced on the hot porridge, risking burns to her mouth. She coughed violently as she ate.

Oli administered a cough medicine to Abigail when Ella came to check on her. "You found her just in time," he said to Ella. "Pneumonia has not set in yet. I had the nurse put hot bottles in her bed to warm her and applied goose fat to her chest. She should recover with diligent care. I wish I could say the same for most of the other patients here."

"Are you working by yourself? Where is the doctor?"

"Dr. Mead lay down for a nap. He was not sober after a party he attended." Oli twisted his mouth with disapproval.

"I can stay and help." If she went to bed, she would wonder all night what had happened to Amelia.

"It's kind of you to offer, but you have better things to do tonight than watch over perishing children. This is going to be a miserable Christmas."

"Even more reason not to leave you alone. Tell me what needs to be done."

They spent the next few hours bloodletting, applying cloths with vinegar solution to burning foreheads, and giving out medicines. Oli grimaced, preventing tears after closing the eyes of an eleven-year-old boy who stopped breathing.

"His parents walked five miles with him to another hospital, where he was not allowed in because the admission hours were over. They had to trudge all the way back and more to get here. By the time I saw him, his lungs sounded something awful."

Ella let out a sharp exhale. Such stories were common. Most large hospitals accepted patients within certain hours or on a particular day of the week. People received a number and waited for hours to see a doctor, who would decide to admit them or not. To get a bed, they had to be sick enough to warrant admission, but not considered incurable, as consumption patients were.

The night became a blur of listening to little hearts and lungs, and coaxing children to drink water and take potions. Many children could not sleep, as congested noses and body aches kept them awake.

Ella checked on Abigail; the girl, warmed and fed, dozed. She had a touch of fever and coughed but fared better than many other patients, as Oli predicted. Amelia was asleep as well; her pillowcase stained with crimson spots.

When they had a lull in their work, Oli sat at the desk and jotted down notes about the patients. His hands shook with weariness. Ella collapsed in a chair by him, aching everywhere, especially her tightly bound chest, which she was dying to massage.

"What a terrible Christmas night," Oli said with a sigh, as he completed his notes. Death harvested the lives of three children with pneumonia. Last year, they would have sobbed after a night like this. Now they accepted death with a degree of indifference, like a tiresome visitor they could not dismiss. They ignored it and focused on the living.

"How is Amelia?" Oli asked. "I saw she gobbled up the hospital food like manna from heaven. No more caprices."

"Don't joke about her, please. I am flabbergasted as to what could have happened to her. She said her parents are fine."

"I presume she ran away on a whim, got herself in some trouble and wanted to come home, but her parents had had enough. Not to sound callous, but foolishness has consequences."

"You don't know! Maybe there was a good reason for running away." Ella felt heat rising to her cheeks.

Oli gave a lopsided smile. "What is a good reason for a wealthy young woman to run away from home?"

"All kinds of things could have gone on in her seemingly perfect estate. She was miserable when she swallowed those pills. It was a cry for help."

"You read too much into her predictable story."

"She was unlucky meeting trouble after running away. It could have worked out differently."

"Have you ever heard of a runaway story that ended up well?"

"Yes, in fact… I knew a wealthy girl who ran away from home and… and she became a governess."

Oli gave her a disbelieving look. "Well, that woman was fortunate. I still say Amelia was thoughtless. I have much more sympathy for Abigail. That child did nothing to deserve her fate."

"That little girl will need to go somewhere after she gets better. She cannot stay on the streets."

"We'll think of something," Oli promised.

Before leaving at dawn, Ella checked on Amelia. The young woman was awake and sitting up, and her face was fresher and more animated than the previous evening.

"I am going now. You behave yourself if you want to stay another night," Ella said.

Amelia smirked, then looked down on her blanket. "Mr. Parker, you've been kind to me," she said in a soft voice, with no hint of flirting. "I want to ask you for another favor. Could you bring my mum here?"

"You think she will let you come home?"

"I don't know. I heard what Mr. Higgins said, and he guessed right. I ran away to join a theater troupe. Soon I learned that my employers expected me to entertain not only on stage. I wanted to come home; many of my expensive things were stolen, and I was out of money. I wrote to my parents, but my father sent an angry letter back, saying I will not get a penny from him. If he only sent me money then, I would not have done a quarter of the disgusting things I did later. I ended up earning money with my body for the trip home, and I even sold two teeth. It hurt so bad when that horrible man pulled them out, but I finally had the money."

She pointed to the gaps in her mouth. "I came home and begged my parents to let me in several times, and I thought Mum wanted to, but Father would shout at me, and I would shout back. The last time, he yelled that they have no daughter and slammed the door in my face. Ever since I started coughing, no one wants me. I was evicted from a workhouse, where I tried to take refuge. Last time I went to beg my parents to let me in, I drank a half a bottle of wine for bravery. I guess it showed, because when they saw me, they had a look of revulsion on their faces and said they would not come out to me anymore, and the servants were to chase me away. Maybe if Mum saw me here at the hospital, she would soften."

"It's worth a try," Ella agreed, and Amelia gave her an address.

Ella knocked on the door of a beautiful three-story home on one of the most sought after streets in town. A couple of workmen swept the pathways free of the shimmering snow. A white-gloved butler answered the door, looked her over with suspicion, and said that the mistress was not in. After Ella handed him some money, he told her that Mrs. Hearts had gone to a Christmas soiree given by her friend. Her husband stayed home with a headache that he often got before visiting his wife's acquaintances. In exchange for some silver, the butler gave directions to the soiree, and Ella hurried there.

The merry music echoed for the whole neighborhood to hear. When she approached and could see through the enormous windows of a large estate, she spied a ballroom full of dancing couples. The party was in full swing with people enjoying the holiday. She wondered how the mother could take pleasure in a party when she knew her daughter had no roof over her head. *The woman must have a heart of stone,* she thought.

Once again, Ella gave a few coins to the servant who wanted to dismiss her for not having an invitation. She explained that she must see Mrs. Hearts for urgent business, and the man disappeared inside to find her.

Amelia's mother took a while to come out. When Ella gave up on waiting and turned to leave, the door opened, and the familiar woman came out in her fur coat and muff. Her face had aged with wrinkles, and her hair, curled in the latest fashion, was greyer since last time she saw her.

"I am sorry to take you away from the celebration," Ella said.

The woman made a tiny shrug, and her face puckered as though she had bitten into a lemon; Amelia's face took on the same expression at times. "I was glad for an excuse to leave. My friends are kind to support me by inviting me to their gatherings, but it breaks my heart to watch their well-to-do families. Last year I gave such a party myself, and Amelia was the jewel of the ball. I take it you are one of her friends and spotted her begging on the street, or perhaps in a house of ill repute. I heard all kinds of reports of her atrocious behavior. If she sent you, please tell her there is no coming home for her."

"Please madam, have mercy. I did see your daughter begging, and I brought her to the hospital. You might remember me; I am a medical student, Alan Parker. Amelia has consumption. She needs you."

Mrs. Hearts stood for a few moments in silence, but her shoulders slumped, and her face tensed.

Ella pushed on. "Her disease manifested recently. There are treatments that may save her. If not, at least you will get to spend time with her before the end. You were a loving mother to her when she came to the hospital last February. She needs you even more now."

"I remember you, Mr. Parker," the mother spoke after a long pause. "You were the one who piqued Amelia's interest in theater. What a disaster that proved to be! Not that I blame you in any way. Are you sure this is not one of her tricks?

That she is not pretending to be ill? Last time we saw her, she claimed to be on the verge of dying, but her breath reeked of wine, and we did not believe her."

"I am certain, madam. The hospital will not keep her beyond tomorrow morning. You may save her life. She will not live long if she is not cared for."

The woman stared down at her boots and chewed her lip. She seemed to have a silent dialog with herself, sighing and shaking her head at times. "This will not be easy," she said finally. "My husband wants nothing to do with her. Friends will turn away from us, the few we still have."

"Be steadier than your husband and forget your fair-weather friends, who don't know how fortune flees. Show everyone what a mother's love is."

She gave a sad smile. "You are right, Mr. Parker. A mother's love is stronger than anything. I will go to the hospital to see my child, and I will take her home."

Mrs. Hearts told a servant to bring her carriage, and within minutes she and Ella reclined on the velvety cushions, and the horses carried them to the university hospital. During the ride, Mrs. Hearts asked a myriad of questions about Amelia's condition and how to care for her. The idea of taking her somewhere warm especially appealed to the woman. When they entered the hospital, she flew through the halls with such haste that Ella had to trot behind her and yell directions.

Both out of breath, they ran over to Amelia's bed. "My darling!" the mother shouted, but the gasp stayed on her lips. Instead of Amelia, there was a little girl moaning in her sleep.

"Did you make a mistake? Is she in another ward?" she rounded on Ella.

Ella reassured her that they were in the correct ward. Dr. Shaw appeared with a lancet, and she hastened to ask him.

"I discharged Miss Hearts, as her consumption cannot be treated. Another patient needed the bed," the doctor explained. Ella knew he was right, seeing the child delirious with fever.

"But where did Amelia go?" Mrs. Hearts cried.

The doctor shrugged his shoulders and apologized for not having more information.

"She might have gone to your house," Ella suggested.

The woman put her hand to her heart, as if trying to still it. "Oh, that's not good. My husband is home, and he might rage and throw her out. And our servants are instructed not to let her in."

"I know where she is," a little voice said.

Mrs. Hearts and Ella turned towards Abigail, who was in one of the beds behind them.

"She said she will go to the church and pray that her mother will forgive her and take her home. If they won't let her into the church, she would pray on the steps." The little girl stared at Mrs. Hearts with her pink mouth gaping. "Did God answer her prayer already?"

"I forgive her a million times!" Mrs. Hearts exclaimed. "Let's go."

They found Amelia right where Ella spotted her the previous evening. "Mum," she cried. "I am so sorry."

Mrs. Hearts kneeled by her daughter and took her stiff hands into hers. "Hush. I am the one who should be sorry. I should have let you come home the first time you asked. Take my muff to warm your hands and don't cry in this chill. You are coming home with me."

Mrs. Hearts helped Amelia into the carriage. Ella declined a ride with them and wished them her best. Her spirits were high, and the walk on such a bright winter day was pleasant.

As she traversed to her lodging, her thoughts switched to the other desolate girl, Abigail. The child would need a home.

* * *

"Oli, did you see how I decorated the children's wards?" Ella asked a few days after Christmas.

When she hung branches of holly and yew, many children smiled despite their sickness. She gave each a small present as well.

"It looks wonderful, Alan. So good of you to do it. And thank you for the gift."

Ella presented Oli with a microscope for Christmas. It was a popular gentlemen's toy, revealing slightly more than was naturally visible to the human eye, though with some distortion.

Oli would enjoy looking at leaves or tiny insects through the lenses. He, in turn, gave her a beautiful set of studs for her jacket.

"Where have you been?" she inquired.

"I went to see my family. And I brought Abigail with me."

"What? I don't understand."

"You said that she needs somewhere to go after she recovers."

"Right. I thought to bring her to an orphanage and make a donation on her behalf."

"I am sure you meant well, but who knows how she would be treated, even with a donation. My parents can take care of her."

"They agreed to take her in?"

"Yes. Mother was not even surprised. Said after all the puppies and kittens I brought in, naturally, a foundling would follow. We are a large family, and my parents always act like the more the merrier. My married sisters live nearby and help with little ones as well."

"And how is Abigail doing?"

"Great. She took to everyone like a fish to water, especially to my mother's cooking."

Ella wanted to throw her arms around Oli. The school break turned out to be a merry Christmas after all.

* * *

December 30,

Dear Matilda and Dr. Pesce,

I hope you had a Merry Christmas and received my presents. Thank you for sending me the tea and spices, they smell wonderful.

Dr. Miller showed great enthusiasm for my thesis topic. He provided me with a source by Dr. Hunter, which I found extremely useful. The paper advocates for reviving a drowned victim by blowing air into his nose and mouth. That makes so much more sense than tobacco enemas! Tell me, is it true that a society patrols the River Thames, ready to revive poor souls who have fallen in, by tearing off their clothes, sticking a tube into their bottoms, and working the bellows? Imagine waking up on your stomach, with a strange man exposing your posterior for everyone to see while he is blowing hot tobacco smoke into it! I know women who would rather die than be saved like this.

You wondered why I am so interested in the apprenticeship with Dr. Miller, if I do not intend to continue keeping my secret beyond medical school. I must admit that the masquerade is becoming quite burdensome. However, I believe that if I do my best in my studies, Dr. Miller may accept me as I am. Such genius would not be shortsighted like other medical men.

I intend on winning Dr. Miller's internship, and then revealing my secret to him.

You may think me mad, but lately I have noticed him looking at me more than usual, and I perceive he knows already and approves.

This winter keeps bringing scores of patients with lung maladies to the hospital, and the youngest and weakest often do not make it.

Please take good care of yourselves. I hope Dr. Pesce is sailing somewhere balmy right now. Some days I would risk a storm or battle to warm myself in the southern sunshine.

Love, Alan Parker

* * *

January 23,

Dear Alan,

Thank you for the presents, the shawl is quite lovely. I am not accustomed to wearing such fine things, and there is no need for you to spend that much.

Your idea of telling Dr. Miller who you are is TERRIBLE. I will never believe that your famous professor would agree to have the real you as an apprentice. Please come to your senses and pray your professor has guessed nothing.

As far as drowning, yes, there is a society of volunteers patrolling the river. I quite agree that I would rather die with dignity than have my rear end exposed and heated with a tobacco enema. If you ask me, these gentlemen are hoping to get a peek of what's under the ladies' skirts.

Never heard of anyone coming back to life after such a save. I might come back, just to smack some sense into these

'rescuers'. I can tell you as a midwife, that when a newborn is not breathing, we blow air into his or her mouth, and sometimes the baby revives. Sounds like your doctors are approaching the problem from the wrong end.
Not sure where my brother is right now, but he wrote that he's safe and sound, and that's all I need to hear. It's been an awful influenza season here as well, and I can barely keep up with the demand for the cough and fever remedies.
Love, Matilda Pesce

CHAPTER 14

Dr. Sanders stood with his arms folded, his prominent jaw clenched. "Push, woman, push! You can scream all you want, but you have to give a strong push with each contraction!"

The medical students returned to studies after winter break, and with no time to acclimate, followed Dr. Sanders into a delivery room where a woman with an enormous belly reclined on the pillows and held her legs apart under a blanket. Sweat rolled from her forehead down to her neck, and her matted hair gave her a wild look. Her face was a mask of focus and pain. The midwife, Mrs. Brooks, a bespectacled woman with silver hair peeking out from her bonnet, patted the patient's back. Ella felt sorry for the patient, having her suffering observed by a group of curious students.

With each push, the woman's grunts became louder. "Please, no more," she yelled after another contraction.

"It's not long, dear." The midwife pacified her, rubbing the mother's back and shoulders. "A few more pushes."

The mother sobbed. "I can't do it. I am going to die."

"No, dear, you will be fine. Keep pushing!" the midwife encouraged. "The baby's head is showing; you are almost done."

Dr. Sanders gave the mother a cross stare. "Look at me. You will have this baby in a few minutes if you listen. Take a large breath, count to ten, and push with all your might."

The woman filled her lungs with air, paused, and then gave a piercing cry of a warrior as she pushed. Dr. Sanders put his hands under the blanket and yelled to the mother to push one more time. As she struggled and shrieked, the doctor pulled the baby out. The midwife accepted the baby from his hands, while he grabbed a scalpel and cut the umbilical cord. Ella strained her neck to look at the newborn. The head with strawberry-blond hair was comically large, compared to the rest of the tiny, pink body.

The mother fell back on the pillows, covering her face. Then, seized by sudden panic, she bolted upright. "Why is the baby not crying?" she shouted.

Ella sucked in air sharply.

"Don't worry, dear. The child is alive and breathing," Mrs. Brooks soothed. The midwife patted the baby's back and sprayed a bit of water on the face. After another agonizing moment, the baby gave first a squeal and then a demanding cry. Ella exhaled with relief and saw Oli put a hand over his heart.

After helping the mother deliver the afterbirth, Dr. Sanders cracked a smile and spoke to the mother. "Congratulations, another son. Your third, if my memory serves me right."

The woman beamed and thanked him. Mrs. Brooks washed and swaddled the infant and passed him into his mother's waiting arms.

When the students assembled in the classroom, the doctor

commented, "This was as easy as births go. A perfectly healthy woman having her third baby, without complications, and in under six hours. Not all deliveries go this smoothly. By the end of the semester, you will feel lucky you were born men."

A couple of students chuckled.

"If this one was easy, I may have that feeling already," Oli mouthed to Ella.

Chilled, she put her arms around herself. *I am not having babies.*

* * *

Dr. Miller greeted his private students as they settled into his sitting room. Without Carrow, they were down to four, and Ella looked at the empty spot next to her with sadness.

"Glad to have you back. Tonight, Mr. Parker will show us a demonstration," the doctor announced.

Ella stood up from her chair and came over to the table in the middle. From her bag, she took out jars with stoppers, a bent glass tube, a vial with orange powder, and a cage with two grey mice The pests squeaked in panic, as if anticipating their fate. When scientists get hold of rodents, the results benefit humankind but prove disastrous for the mice and rats.

Jane, the young maid, set the mousetraps last night, per her request. Ella noticed that the girl's scrawny figure became curvy, likely blossoming into womanhood. When Jane bent over to give Ella the cage this morning, she gasped and put a hand on her belly. Worried, Ella offered to examine her, but the girl pushed the cage into her hands and ran away to her room.

After clearing her throat, Ella spoke up: "Last year, in chemistry class, I presented an experiment with mercury oxide and two candles. I will conduct the same experiment with two mice. By my theory, the mouse breathing air inside the stoppered jar will suffocate quickly, while the mouse breathing oxygen in a similar jar will survive much longer and be more energetic."

She placed the mice into the separate jars and sealed the containers. The animals ran in circles, squeaking. Meanwhile, Ella used the tube to connect a vial with mercury oxide to one of the jars. She lit a candle to heat the orange powder, holding the vial with tongs over the flame. After a few minutes, she disconnected the tube, stopping the flow of oxygen. By this time, the mouse in the stoppered jar with air lay without moving. Ella put it back in a cage, hoping the mouse would wake up. The mouse who breathed oxygen, as she predicted, ran around with more vigor and excitement than before.

Dr. Miller came to her side, inspecting the mice. "Could you please tell us how this experiment helps your thesis?" he asked Ella.

"I am writing about resuscitating drowned victims," Ella explained. "As you saw, the mouse that breathed air inside the closed jar fainted or died within a few minutes. The one that's breathing oxygen is alive and active. While it would suffocate eventually, it outlasted the other animal. I conclude in my paper that oxygen is preferable to air when reviving someone."

She reunited the active mouse with her mate in the cage and presented them with cheese for their role in the experiment. The one that breathed oxygen ate with gusto, while the other showed signs of life but no appetite.

The students and the doctor spent the rest of the evening discussing thesis topics. The conversation flowed with difficulty as Jeffers rarely had anything intelligent to add, and the other two students were painfully shy and spoke only when Dr. Miller addressed them. Ella made most of the suggestions and comments.

Once again, at the end of the lesson, the professor offered refreshments and time to socialize. Ella contemplated trying wine but chose her usual water instead. Dr. Miller, who stood in the corner, motioned for her to approach.

"I am greatly impressed with your experiment, Mr. Parker," he praised. "After the exams, I would like to help you publish your thesis in leading medical journals. Having your name in print will open doors for you."

Ella's breath caught. "It would be a great honor, doctor."

"You deserve nothing less, my boy. I hope you don't mind me calling you that. I don't exaggerate when I say you are one of the best I have ever taught."

Her heart drummed with such intensity, she imagined others could hear it. The professor strolled over to talk to the other students, and she composed herself, sipping her water. Jeffers approached her with an unsteady gait, holding an almost empty glass of wine. *Not his first one*, Ella guessed from his reddened face. She made a step towards the door.

"Do you miss your little friend?" Jeffers asked with a chuckle. "He's not invited here."

Ella spun on her heel. "Jeffers, you are months away from becoming a doctor, yet you behave like a childish bully. I know you still send him nasty notes. Leave Higgins alone!"

The redhead gave her a mischievous grin. "I bet you know nothing about him. Nothing. He is full of lies. You should choose your friends better, Parker. Help me with my thesis, and I will introduce you to my father and other members of the hospital board. But only if you cut ties with that little piece of dirt."

Anger rushed to her head. "He is a better human being

than you could ever be. I choose my friends based on their character, not their connections. Don't ever talk to me again."

"Sure, you are bold because you are Dr. Miller's pet. What are you without his protection?"

Dr. Miller stepped in between them with his fists clenched. "Mr. Jeffers, you drank too much wine. Please clear your head with some fresh air. You are no longer welcome at these lessons."

Jeffers's eyes bulged. "I beg your pardon, professor?" he mumbled.

"Please leave us."

Jeffers shuffled out of the room. When the door closed behind him, Dr. Miller shook his head.

"I am sorry this occurred, Mr. Parker. Inexcusable behavior."

Ella was lost for words from embarrassment. Her cheeks flushed scarlet.

The doctor continued speaking in a pleasant tone. "Our small group is falling apart. I can barely get a word out of the other two." He glanced towards the remaining students, who stood by the wall. "What do you say to one-on-one lessons, instead? We could hold them here quite comfortably and maybe more often than monthly."

A chance to collaborate closer with the beloved professor appealed to Ella. Yet there was something uncomfortable in being singled out, and a bit too much sparkle in Dr. Miller's eyes. Her gut twisted with a painful sensation, and she surprised herself by her own answer.

"My preference would be to keep the lessons to a small group. And invite more students to join." She hoped the doctor guessed her hint at Oli.

The doctor's lips tightened, and eyes dulled. "I will think on it," he said without enthusiasm.

* * *

January 28,
Dear Matilda and Dr. Pesce,
The school and hospital shifts keep me so busy I barely have
time to repose. We continue to see numerous patients with
lung maladies.
In midwifery, we watched several deliveries, all successful.
The first birth scared me to death, but the next ones less so.
One involved forceps – Dr. Sanders demonstrated how to use
the tool. The law allows only surgeons to utilize it, but in my
opinion, an experienced midwife like you could master the
forceps if given the opportunity.
Dr. Miller hinted at a groundbreaking surgery he performed
at a patient's home. He did not give many details but
apparently he operated in the stomach. Despite his
colleagues calling him a 'belly ripper' after the ovarian cyst
surgery, he continues to break new grounds.
I hope to see the surgery he pioneered. As his apprentice, I
would help him with treatments never done before. I cannot
think of a more exciting future for myself.
Unfortunately, our private lessons may stop as there are only
three students left. I can't explain why I did not agree to
individual lessons at the professor's home – something did
not feel right.
Maybe I was silly to miss such a chance.
I hope you are staying healthy,
Love, Alan Parker

* * *

February 21,
Dear Alan,
It gladdens my heart to read that you are getting over your fears and seeing for yourself what a great profession midwifery is. I truly hope you will come back here and work with me side by side until I retire and leave my clients in your capable hands. Golly, I have not done this much daydreaming since I was a little girl. Silly me! You still cherish hopes of working with your professor and cutting into the patients' stomachs or whatever it is that he does. I don't see how anyone could survive such an operation. I feel queasy just thinking about it.
I am glad you listened to your instincts about these individual lessons your Dr. Miller proposed. You should not be alone with him in his home. Do not allow it.
This winter cannot end fast enough. I cannot remember such an awful start to the year. Too many of my clients have lost children to pneumonia and influenza. My trusted remedies do not seem to work on what's been going around. We'll just have to wait for warmer weather.
Love, Matilda Pesce

CHAPTER 15

The woman fixed her braid, and when she reclined on the cot, it reached the floor, reminding Ella of Goldilocks with chestnut hair. She was one of those ladies whose face glowed during pregnancy, making them a picture of health and feminine beauty.

After the exam, Dr. Sanders intoned with seriousness, "Mrs. Bennett, your baby is positioned across the uterus, instead of head down. We call it the transverse lie. If the fetus does not turn on its own, I will need to turn it to deliver it."

The woman showed little reaction to the news. He asked if the students could feel her abdomen, and she allowed with a shrug. When it was her turn, Ella touched the belly, scared that she would somehow hurt the baby, or cause the patient any pain. She found the head and envisioned the fetus lying horizontally in the womb. The doctor urged the mother to stay at the clinic, but she declined, saying she had other children at home. With a promise to come back soon, Mrs. Bennett jumped down from the cot with the lightness of a young girl. Her jovial disposition revealed no concern about the complicated delivery.

After the students took their seats in their classroom, Dr. Sanders lit a cigar and scanned the pupils' faces, searching for a victim. "Mr. Higgins, what can you tell me about the transverse lie?" he asked.

"Transverse lie? It's not a favorable scenario," Oli stammered, suppressing a yawn. His eyelids stuck together after late nights drafting his thesis with Ella.

"Indeed. Can you elaborate on the danger of such a position?"

"The baby will not fit through the birth canal," he said without confidence.

"Obviously not. How should the fetus be turned?"

No one volunteered an answer.

"What I am planning to do is a podalic version. This is how it's done."

Before he could explain further, Mrs. Brooks shuffled into the classroom, breathing heavily, and wriggling her hands. "Doctor, I am sorry to interrupt your class, but there is a woman in labor, and she is not doing well. Could you please come now? She said her name is Mrs. Walters and you may remember her."

The doctor's eyes bulged and his face reddened more than usual. "Anna Walters? Are you sure? She was not supposed to be pregnant! I told her!" He cursed under his breath, then scanned the room, pondering. After a sigh, he snuffed out his cigar with force. "Come on. You may learn much from this case."

The young woman lay on the cot as if she had fainted there. Her chest rose slightly and infrequently, and occasional quiet moans left her colorless lips. Her swollen belly was the largest one Ella had ever seen before. With her thin arms and legs, she seemed crushed under the weight of it. Dr. Sanders listened to her breathing and checked her pulse, then felt her abdomen. "There are two babies in there. As if one was not enough," he muttered and turned to Mrs. Brooks. "Call her husband."

"Her mother brought her. The husband is working."

Dr. Sanders muttered a curse. "Bring her then."

Ella's knees shook and her chest constricted to the point that she could barely breathe. Her scalp burned, as if on fire, and her heart hit against her ribs, as if trying to escape. The image of her own mother in her last moments appeared in front of her eyes.

Oli touched her hand. "Are you all right? Do you need to step out?"

Ella wished to run outside, inhale the icy air, and throw herself onto the fresh snow to cool. But if she left, she would not learn.

"I need to watch," she whispered.

He blinked with understanding, then fished in his shoulder sack and passed her a flask. "Water. I wish I had something stronger."

Ella drained the flask in two gulps.

An older woman, in a simple grey dress and white bonnet, bustled into the room, followed by Mrs. Brooks. "Anna! My dear!" the mother cried, coming over to her daughter's side and taking her hands.

Dr. Sanders motioned for Mrs. Brooks to approach him and asked her in a whisper to prepare the operating room and take a student or two to help. The midwife winced, then motioned for two students who stood in the back to follow her. The rest of the class remained in dead stillness.

Clearing his throat, Dr. Sander addressed the patient's mother. "Madam, I need to talk to you. Let us step out."

The woman looked apprehensively from her daughter to the doctor and back.

"We have little time. Please come with me. I need a prompt decision from you."

She squeezed her daughter's hand and whispered reassuring words, then turned and followed him into the hallway.

While wiping sweat from her forehead, Ella willed her pulse to slow with each long breath. Oli's fingers tugged on her sleeve. "Dr. Sanders can save her if he hurries. He must be asking the mother for permission to operate. Otherwise, why would he prepare the surgery, right?"

Ella wanted to explain, but her tongue refused to work. Oli frowned, staring at the patient, whose chest undulations became rare and moans no longer audible. With hesitation, he approached Anna and took her wrist.

After a few seconds, he let go and touched her neck. Then he looked at Ella, with alarm all over his face. "I can barely feel any pulse. Alan, could you check? I think Dr. Sanders may be too late."

As if he heard, the doctor stepped inside. "What's happening, Mr. Higgins?"

Oli turned to him wide-eyed. "I think she is dying," he said with difficulty.

The doctor's mouth twisted. "I concur with your conclusion."

"But why the operation then?"

"You will see." He took the patient's pulse and prodded her abdomen, then requested a few students to get the stretcher and bring the patient to the surgery.

Ella came last into the operating room, dragging her feet. It was her first time in the room, but it looked the same as the one in the hospital, only smaller. Lanterns flickered, reflected in the metal instruments Mrs. Brooks laid out on the trays. White linens, stained with blood, covered the table. The sawdust on the floor absorbed the sounds of steps. The air felt cool, but Ella still sweated as if in a fever.

The patient made no move or sound when the students dropped her from the stretcher to the table. Dr. Sanders touched her neck. "She just perished," he announced.

Ella had already guessed that by the woman's unmoving gaze, but the teacher's words still gave her a painful pinch in the heart. Oli covered his mouth with his hands.

"Watch me now and save your questions for later," the doctor said.

Mrs. Brooks lifted the woman's gown to reveal her belly and covered her legs, then passed a scalpel to the doctor. Dr. Sanders made a long vertical slice in the lower abdomen, through the skin and fat, and asked a student to hold the clamps. After cutting through the abdominal muscle, he moved the intestines and the bladder aside, exposing the womb, and made an incision to open it. He reached in with his hands and grabbed a bluish infant. After cutting the umbilical cord, he passed the baby to the midwife. Ella prayed silently as the woman patted the baby on the back. After a few agonizing seconds, the infant gave a feeble cry. A sigh of relief came from many lips at once.

Meanwhile, Dr. Sanders reached in again and lifted another baby. He looked at his students and pointed at Ella with his chin. "Take this one and do what Mrs. Brooks is doing."

Ella's hands shook when she accepted the precious bundle. Supporting the head and neck with one hand, and the buttocks with the other, she came over to the basins where the midwife washed the first baby. The infant Mrs. Brooks held, a small boy, trembled at the touch of the water, and whimpered. Ella stared at the newborn she had in her arms, a purplish girl; light, like a cat.

"Check for the mucus in her mouth and nose and pat her back," the midwife instructed.

Before Ella had a chance to pat, the baby girl gave a displeased cry, much louder than her brother. If the circumstances were different, someone might have joked about the girl already showing her character and outdoing her twin, but this was the quietest birth Ella had witnessed. Mrs. Brooks helped Ella to wash the baby and swaddle her in a warm blanket. Other students busied themselves examining the organs inside the deceased woman before Dr. Sanders closed the wound. After suturing all the layers and covering up the body, the doctor sent a pupil to bring back the patient's mother and asked the rest of the class to go back to their classroom. Ella still held the baby, who squeaked and whimpered. Her eyes opened wider and stared at Ella; they were cornflower blue. *Her mother will never meet her,* she thought with her throat constricting.

As if hearing her thoughts, Mrs. Brooks came to Ella's side and said softly, "Let's put the babies next to her. Maybe she will see them from wherever she is now."

The infants snuggled next to their mother's still warm body, and the midwife whispered a prayer and crossed herself. Then she glanced at Ella, rooted in her spot, and said louder. "The family will come now. Time for you to get back to your class."

Ella stood still for a moment more, and then ran out of the operating room. Instead of the classroom, she sprinted towards the lavatory. In the hallway, she saw the dead woman's mother, slumped near the wall, wailing like a wounded animal. She ran past her and locked herself in the privy, where she retched all she had eaten that day. Then she wept, holding her mouth with a palm to silence her sobs. Her hands and knees trembled, and her teeth chattered.

When numbness took over, she washed her face and returned to her seat in the classroom, taking care not to interrupt Dr. Sanders, who was in the middle of his lecture.

"No, this procedure cannot be done on a living mother, or she would die of shock," he responded to someone's question. "There are some accounts from Uganda that native people have performed the operation, and both the mother and the infant survived, but such stories have not been verified. The name for the operation is caesarean section, and later we will go over the steps in detail."

Oli raised his hand. "What did she die of?"

Dr. Sanders looked down, then answered. "Heart disease. She came in a year ago after a miscarriage and complained of chest pains and difficulty breathing. I sent her to see other doctors, and they concluded she could not do strenuous work or deliver a baby without a peril to her life. It's a miracle she managed to carry her twins full-term. I will talk to the family to ask if they will allow a postmortem as this case is rare."

There was a silence for a moment as students digested the information. Ella's chest pained, thinking about this patient who knew she would die from the moment she realized she was pregnant.

What courage did this woman have to carry her babies for nine months and let them be born while she died! And yet, was it even a choice?

Oli stood up. "If it was known that a pregnancy would kill her, why wasn't an abortion performed to save her life?"

Dr. Sanders rubbed his forehead with his fist, and a few students groaned or glared at Oli. "Again, Mr. Higgins? I thought I explained already. Abortion is forbidden, and doctors would not perform this vile procedure. I made the patient aware she must not get pregnant at peril to her life."

Ella wondered if the patient received any practical advice

on how to comply with such a doctor's order, and what her husband thought of it.

"Which meant, since the moment she learned she was with child, she had no option but to wait for death," Oli said through gritted teeth.

Dr. Sanders crossed his arms. "Not every patient can be saved. She was doomed, but her twins survived, as you saw."

"But in this case, when an abortion could save the mother, why not perform it early in the pregnancy instead of condemning her to death?" Oli insisted.

"Mr. Higgins, we are all clear by now about the abortion laws and the Church's teaching. I will not discuss it in my class anymore. I suggest you talk to the chaplain."

Oli flushed and sat down, lowering his head. Ella gave him a sympathetic look, even though she disapproved of his insistence.

* * *

After class, Ella and Oli stepped through the fluffy January snow, on their way to their lodgings. Snowflakes danced in the air, settling on their clothes and reddened cheeks. Oli broke the silence first.

"I am sorry I made you take midwifery. I had no idea what it would be like. If I knew, I would not have signed up either."

"No, you were right to push me. It's heartbreaking, but we need to prepare for anything as doctors."

"I wish I knew what was coming. Poor woman. Dr. Sanders told her she cannot get pregnant. How helpful is that?"

"What if she knew the risks but wanted to have a baby anyway? Some women go to extreme lengths to get pregnant against their doctors advice. Doctors don't know everything, after all."

"I doubt I could understand such a thing. To condemn yourself to death and have a child that you would never hold? Do you agree with Dr. Sanders then?"

Ella shrugged. "There is nothing to agree or disagree about. The Church teaching declares abortion sinful and forbidden. There is no need for women to choose, since the choice was made for them, to let the baby live instead of the mother."

He glanced around and asked in a soft voice, "Do you think this choice is the same for everyone? What if the patient does not believe in the Church's teachings?"

Ella did not understand. "Do you mean if you practice medicine among non-Christian people? Why do you ask such a question?"

Oli shook his head. "I am having trouble accepting what I saw today. And I could see it was awful for you as well." He paused, then snapped his fingers. "I know we never do such things, but would you like to go to a tavern for a drink? We earned a break. Good brandy will warm us and help us sleep better tonight. And in conversation we can stick to lighter subjects."

She wanted to delay going to an empty room. A lively atmosphere, her first taste of brandy, and Oli's company tempted her. Yet such an outing would be incautious, as spirits could loosen her tongue.

"Thank you, but I would rather be alone with my thoughts," she lied.

Oli nodded with understanding and walked away towards his lodging.

She needed all her willpower not to call after him.

* * *

February 26,
Dear Matilda and Dr. Pesce,
Midwifery confirmed every fear I had regarding the
profession. Days ago, I witnessed a tragic case that affected
me greatly. After the mother died, Dr. Sanders performed a
cesarean section, and the twin babies were saved. I tended to
the newborn girl, but my heart was breaking for the loss of
her mother. Then today we heard terrible news about another
pregnant patient. A woman with a fetus in a transverse lie
hemorrhaged and died at home. Oli and I will attend the
postmortem for both these patients tomorrow.
The private lessons with Dr. Miller resumed with the two
remaining students and me. He is of an opinion that the
mother may survive if the cesarean section is done with great
skill and quickness. Of course, such an operation must be
performed only in the most extreme cases. He also debated
the benefits of bloodletting, and generally the causes of
disease from imbalance of humors. The other students were
shocked, and I was confused. If not for disbalance, what else
would cause maladies? Dr. Miller hopes to find an answer. If
he does, it would turn the medical world upside-down.
Take care.
Love, Alan Parker

* * *

March 21,
Dear Alan,
Unfortunately, midwifery has two sides: a great joy and a
great sorrow. I understand how difficult it was for you to
witness these deaths, but those things happen. It's a miracle

the doctor was able to save those twins, so take comfort in that. And I don't even want to think about having a woman's stomach cut to remove the baby while she is alive and can feel pain.

As for bloodletting, I agree with your professor. Some doctors are a bit too eager to bleed the patient when she may just need rest and some restorative tea. I just visited a young woman whose doctor bled her to treat a migraine. Trust me, such cure did no good to her. He was going to try cauterization next; I am glad she sent him away and called for me. I would not be surprised if that 'balance of humors' is also nonsense.

Love, Matilda Pesce

The crowd filled the dissection room, shoulder to shoulder. The postmortems of Mrs. Walters and Mrs. Bennett drew a record number of eager medical students, doctors, and onlookers, as the event presented a rare opportunity to study the organs of pregnant and recently pregnant females. The place hummed with excited discussions. Ella and Oli, sickened by the occasion and the atmosphere, forced themselves to watch.

The corpses of the two young women with swollen bellies occupied the two front tables. The anatomist chose to start by slicing Mrs. Bennett's abdomen. After cutting through the tissues, he revealed the uterus and pointed out the rupture that killed her. After opening the womb, he showed the fully formed fetus of a boy curled inside, all blue, still in the horizontal position.

Oli cringed. "My stomach hurts," he confessed to Ella. "I ate nothing today to make sure I don't throw up."

Ella did not fare much better. Her chest felt like there were stones strapped to it, and she could not take a full breath. "What was the poor woman's name?" she asked Oli.

"Ella."

"What? How?" Her eyes grew wide.

"That was her name. Ella Bennett. I saw it in her notes."

She barely suppressed a groan, as her chest compressed with excruciating pain when she thought of the unfortunate coincidence.

She locked her eyes on to the tool in the anatomist's hands, trying to match her breathing to the pace of his sawing. He opened Mrs. Walter's belly and uterus, sawing through the bones of her chest. The conversations continued with vigor, doctors discussing the heart disease that killed the woman. The defective organ was extracted from Mrs. Walters' chest and several men came forward to hold it and look at it in detail. One of the doctors suggested preserving it in wine spirits for further examination.

Ella's head ached, and she rubbed her temples. "Nothing to be done for these poor women but learn from their corpses," she whispered.

Oli did not answer, but Ella noticed that he bit his lower lip until it bled.

They made it to the end stoically. Exiting into the cool night was like coming up for air after near drowning.

* * *

"I am starting to fear the rounds," Oli said as they trudged through slush to the hospital. "Every day brings more little ones with lungs full of fluid. I hate feeling so helpless, knowing most of them will die. The night shifts are the worst."

"This season cannot end soon enough," Ella agreed. She worked a shift yesterday and was in tears at the end of it after closing the eyes of several dead patients.

"On a happier note, Abigail sends her love. She added a couple of words to the letter from my parents. They said she is healthy and doing well in school."

They stepped through the hospital doorway. "Good to hear. At least one child is doing well. Please send my regards to your parents. They are true Christians, taking in an orphan."

Oli chuckled and looked as though he wanted to say something, but a shout behind them interrupted him.

"Does anyone know where Dr. Miller is?"

They spun around to see a man slouching, as he was carrying a girl of about six in his arms. The child squirmed, holding her small hand to her belly and clutched a stuffed bunny in her other fist. She was squeezing her eyes and weeping, tears running down her pale cheeks. Ella pointed towards the wards, when Dr. Miller appeared at the end of the hallway.

"Richard!" the man cried. "My daughter Maggie is sick! Her stomach is hurting so bad, she is screaming. I took her to your house first, but your servant said it would be better to bring her here."

Dr. Miller halted, then motioned for the man with the child, as well as Ella and Oli to follow him into a ward.

"Put her here, Frank, and let me examine her. Pull her dress up."

The father laid Maggie onto the bed and started raising her skirts. The girl opened her frightened eyes wide, clutching her toy to her chest.

"No, Daddy, I am scared," she whimpered.

"I have no time for caprices. You are here for treatment and need to do as I say," Dr. Miller chided.

The father hurried to move the fabric layers out of the way and reveal the girl's belly. The doctor palpated around the navel, then pressed with firmness on the right side. The girl twisted and yelped in pain, then vomited onto the floor. Dr. Miller inquired about administered treatment, and the father described a grueling night of purges, emetics, and enemas, prescribed by their physician, that brought no relief. The doctor took the father aside to talk.

Oli rubs his hand over his face and whispered into Ella's ear. "This is awful. She has an inflamed appendix, and there is nothing any surgeon can do."

She was about to answer, but the doctor's discussion with the father grew louder, and she listened to them instead. The doctor implored to perform a surgery, convinced that it was their only hope. The father asked for other cures, but the doctor shook his head and urged him not to waste precious time. The father took his face into his hands and gave his agreement.

Dr. Miller ordered his assistants to prepare the patient and the operating room. Addressing Ella and Oli, he said, "If you see your classmates, tell them to come and watch this surgery. This one may make a sensation in the medical world."

Ella and Oli stepped into the hall and directed other students. Oli wriggled his hands. "Can he really remove the appendix? I am scared to think what would happen if he punctured her bowels. And would the laudanum make her oblivious enough to the pain when he cuts inside her?"

"I have faith in Dr. Miller. Remember I told you he had success with a private patient? He must be sure of his abilities. The surgery would give her a chance."

"Mr. Parker and Mr. Higgins?" an assistant called from the ward. "Could you help us, please? The patient is fighting us tooth and nail and won't take the opium tincture. You both are good with pacifying the little ones."

They rushed over to the room.

"I don't want to do this! I don't want that doctor to cut my belly!" The girl screamed and tried to get down from the bed, but assistants held her firmly by her arms and legs.

Oli exchanged looks with Ella. "Dr. Miller could have been gentler with her," he mumbled.

Ella approached Maggie and took her hand. "Maggie, I know you are frightened, but I can tell you are very brave. My name is Alan, and this is Oliver. He will give you a medicine to drink, and you will go to sleep."

"I don't want to go to sleep!" The child's lips trembled. "I am scared!"

Oli patted Maggie's shoulder. "It can be frightening to think about an operation, but you understand that there is something wrong inside and it is giving you pain. Dr. Miller will fix it. Take a deep breath for me and open your mouth for the medicine."

Ella held the girl into a gentle hug. The child complied and swallowed a spoonful of laudanum Oli put to her lips.

"Can you bring me my bunny? I always sleep with it." Maggie asked drowsily.

"I am afraid bunnies are not allowed in the operating room. When you wake up, your friend will be waiting for you," Ella replied, still holding her.

* * *

Sleeping Maggie lay on the operating table, with her legs and chest covered by sheets and her belly exposed. Dr. Miller scanned the faces of his students, with Ella and Oli at the front.

"Gentlemen, the patient's symptoms - an acute pain in her abdomen on the right, accompanied by fever and vomiting - give me strong suspicion that her appendix is inflamed. I will remove it, saving the patient from the abdominal infection." After a grave silence, the doctor asked for the scalpel and began.

Ella watched the surgeon's confident movements with awe as he made the incision and spread the muscle fibers. As he opened the peritoneum, Ella heard Oli's sharp breath. While the assistant spread the opening with retractors, the doctor pulled out the pouch-like cecum and located the fingerlike structure. Even to her inexperienced eye, it looked enlarged and inflamed. Next he made a cut at its base, removed the appendix, and applied ligatures.

"Mr. Parker, would you like to apply the sutures?" he asked Ella.

Ella reached for the needle when an unexpected thought came to her. "Mr. Higgins would like to do it."

Dr. Miller frowned but did not object.

Oli gasped and his eyes grew wide. "Not on a little girl," he whispered.

"You can do it," Ella encouraged.

Oli accepted the needle and thread Ella passed him and, after a long exhale, started applying layers of sutures with practiced movements. If he were nervous, he did not show it. Ella admitted to herself she could not have done better.

Dr. Miller inspected the removed appendix. "It has not ruptured, and that's good news. I will dissect it later to see if its contents give any clues to the cause of the disease. The first successful surgery of this kind was performed in France quite a few years ago. In that case, the appendix protruded through the inguinal hernia, making the surgery possible without opening the peritoneum. When the surgeon cut inside the appendix, he found a pin that the young patient had swallowed. An interesting find like that would make my publication quite colorful," he said with a chuckle.

He examined the stitching and nodded to Oli. "I have to compliment your suturing technique, Mr. Higgins. You have improved greatly under Mr. Parker's tutoring. I hope you thank him for all the help he has given you."

Oli gave a side glance to Ella, who winked at him. After scanning the room, Dr. Miller spoke again. "The surgery you have observed can save thousands of lives, from children younger than this one to people of substantial age. If no infection occurs, this child has a good chance of making a full recovery in several weeks."

Several students clapped and Ella found herself beaming at her beloved instructor.

* * *

"Could you have told me what you were planning?" Oli confronted her, as they attended to Maggie after the surgery.

"If I had warned you, you would have been nervous. I had complete faith that, after hundreds of practices, you would do fine. Your fingers would remember what to do. Most importantly, everyone saw how good you were and even Dr. Miller complimented you."

"Didn't you want to do it? This was a groundbreaking surgery."

Ella shrugged. "I get plenty of attention from the professor. It was high time for him to notice your work. But golly, wasn't Dr. Miller incredible?"

"Well, sure, he is great, but lucky too. I was holding my breath, afraid the child would wake up. Laudanum does not always work this well. And he has clout to do a risky surgery like this; other surgeons will fear criticism from colleagues and mistrust of patients."

"That's why he is the best, and we are fortunate to be his students."

"I can see why you want that internship so badly. I am hoping you get it."

Meanwhile a half-hour passed, but the child had not stirred from her sleep. Oli paced near her bed.

"The little lady is taking her time waking up," he said, knitting his brow.

Ella took the girl's pulse for the third time in fifteen minutes and put her ear to her chest. "She is only sleeping. It might have been a large dose of opium for her, but her heartbeat is fine."

Oli nodded and sat down, studying the child's pale face. "Alan, do you think she will get better?" he asked in a quiet voice.

"The surgery went brilliantly, as you saw. There is a chance of infection, of course, but barring that, she should be fine. Why?"

"I think I told you I had a close friend who died of a burst appendix. It was so sudden. One day he complained of stomach pain as we walked home from school, then he did not come out to play for a couple of days, and then he was gone. His family learned after the postmortem what he had, but the surgeon said there was nothing he could have done."

"I am sorry," Ella said, putting a hand on his shoulder. "Now we have hope to treat this condition."

He was quiet for a few minutes, pondering something. "It scares me that she is still not awake. This may sound strange, but I talked to a young patient when she was at the worst with pneumonia, and sometimes I felt that she heard me and liked it. What if I talk to Maggie and tell her to wake up?"

"I see no harm in that. Why don't you show me?"

Oli took the child's tiny hand into his. "Maggie, you are

doing very well so far. You are a good patient and will be all better soon. It would be great if you opened your eyes and told us how you are feeling." He patted her hand and exhaled.

"I think that was helpful," Ella responded.

He looked at the floor. "You are teasing."

"I am not. You connected with the patient. Maybe you will conduct an experiment with two groups, a group you talk to and hold their hand, and a group you do not, and compare their progress. I doubt Dr. Miller or other doctors here will perceive this as a serious study, but someday it may be your discovery. I will adopt this practice with my future patients and call it Dr. Higgins' method."

"It makes me feel less anxious for sure."

"That's important as well."

After ten minutes or so, Maggie stirred and squinted her eyes, throwing off her drug-induced sleep.

"Bunny!" she demanded. Ella passed her the furry friend and fluffed the girl's pillow.

"How are you feeling, Maggie?" she asked.

"Belly hurts," she complained, looking at Ella with a pout.

"Not as bad as it did this morning, right?"

Maggie shook her head.

"It will get a little better every day and soon enough it won't ache at all. I am going to change your dressing and make sure everything is well." She opened the bandages and checked the sutures. "Your work looks good," she said to Oli with a grin.

* * *

Maggie improved a bit each day but struggled with pain. Each shift Ella or Oli worked, they spent much time nursing and distracting her, as the doctor forbade more opium. She had no fever or other signs of infection, and Dr. Miller rejoiced at her progress.

One morning Ella stopped by to visit and found a young woman with red hair like Maggie's sitting by the bed. Maggie, who held three ragged dolls in dresses of various colors, turned to Ella, then towards the woman. "Mum, that's Mr. Parker," she introduced.

The young woman beamed at Ella. "Maggie told me much about you and Mr. Higgins. Thank you for comforting her all those nights."

Ella patted Maggie's head with affection. "She is a wonderful little girl. How is she today?"

"She's been playing with the dolls. I am taking it as a good sign."

"It is. Sick children do not want to play."

They observed Maggie converse with her toys. One doll suffered from a bellyache, and the other two, a doctor and a medical student, came to examine her. Maggie's mum told Ella that Dr. Miller stopped by and relayed that he found undigested cherry pits inside the appendix. He was much surprised by the discovery as cherries were not in season yet and must have been lodged inside for nearly a year. Overall, he was pleased with the child's progress and plans to send her home in a week or two.

The doctor and the medical student dolls finished the patient's examination and prescribed a treatment of a lump of sugar and a spoonful of jam every hour. The patient seemed pleased with such a cure.

"Mum, all my dolls are in skirts. Can the doctor and the medical student be ladies?" Maggie asked.

"I don't believe so. I can make you some dolls in trousers and suits if you like."

"I think you should play as you were and have your dolls be the first women doctors," Ella suggested. "They seem to be doing a fine job."

Maggie nodded with a serious expression and told her doctor dolls to check on the pink bunny who hurt his paw.

Ella promised to come back later and left in good spirits.

* * *

A few weeks later, Oli and Ella were on the way to watch a surgery when they heard a gleeful cry across the hall. Maggie handed the bunny to her father and made a beeline into Ella's arms.

"Are you going home, Maggie?" Ella asked.

"Yes. Daddy said Mum made me some new dolls and they are waiting for a tea party with me."

"That's wonderful. We are so happy you are all better."

"I still have a scar on my belly." The girl's smile changed to a pout.

"No one will see it," Oli appeased, but Maggie crossed her arms, pouting more.

"Scars make us special. See, I have mine." Ella lowered her collar to let Maggie inspect the long mark on her neck. "Scars remind us of our stories. Do you have a story to tell?"

"Yes. I have a story about how I ate many cherry pits, and they grew in my stomach. I had to stay in the hospital, and you two visited and were nice to me," Maggie answered.

She hurried back to her father, leaving both Ella and Oli grinning.

* * *

March 24,
Dear Matilda and Dr. Pesce,
I had an honor to witness a groundbreaking surgery
performed by Dr. Miller. He saved the life of a little girl with
an inflamed appendix. How amazing would it be to work with
that great man! Someone that brilliant would be open to
working side by side with a deserving person regardless of
gender; I am sure of it.
This girl's recovery was a ray of sunshine after this horrible
winter that took the lives of so many children. Spring has
arrived, but the weather is still cold, and the flood of
influenza and pneumonia patients has not slowed down. Oli
and I are exhausted, physically and emotionally.
Meanwhile, we have slightly more than two months left before
exams. I shudder at the thought. The classes keep us
incredibly busy, and I don't know when I will have time to
prepare.
Matilda, it would mean everything to me if you came to visit
at the end of the term. We could walk around the campus and
celebrate my diploma – if I survive the exams, that is. Of
course, I would love to see our dear Dr. Pesce as well, but I
know he is somewhere in the Mediterranean, according to the
naval papers.
Love, Alan Parker

* * *

April 22
Dear Alan,
I can't believe how time has flown. You are nearing the end of
your medical school journey. Now is the time to be extra
careful and to trust no one: neither Oli nor Dr. Miller.
Your job is to complete your studies, receive your diploma,

and disappear from the school before anyone suspects anything.

I just came back from a breech delivery. The young doctor had no idea what to do and looked ready to faint from his nerves, but I am an old hand and caught the baby's feet first just fine. Afterwards, I had some tea with that young doctor and gave him a lesson in midwifery he apparently missed in medical school. I hope you would be better prepared for your first delivery.

I wish I could visit you, but I've been incredibly busy with my clients. With the way things are, I cannot imagine leaving, even for a few days.

Love, Matilda Pesce

CHAPTER 17

The flood of patients with respiratory maladies slowed down to a trickle but had not halted. During rounds, Dr. Miller examined three-month-old twins. With a grave face, he told their grandmother the babies had severe pneumonia and would not survive. The unfortunate woman was Anna Walters' mother.

Ella took a long breath, willing away the tears that rose to her eyes. When the doctor permitted, she put her ear to the infants' chests and listened to the bubbling noises of fluids inside their lungs. She had learned enough of the illness's progression to agree with her instructor. The memory of Anna Walters, who sacrificed herself to bring these babies into this world, made Ella's chest ache. The babies would join their mother soon.

In the evening, after classes and homework with Oli at the library, Ella made her exhausted legs climb one step at a time to her room. Every inch of her body ached. She was almost at the top, when she heard a voice from downstairs.

The speaker paused after each couple of words, like it hurt her to talk.

"Mr. Parker, can you... help me? There is something... wrong with me."

Ella turned around to see Jane, the young maid, clutching her stomach with one hand, and holding on to the wall with another. The girl moaned and doubled over. Despite her fatigue, Ella ran down.

"What's going on? How long have you had this bellyache?"

"Since this morning... It was slight at first, but then it became worse and worse, hurting something awful one minute, and releasing the next... Now it's hurting so bad, I can barely walk."

Jane managed to finish her sentence, then grasped her stomach again. After a minute she straightened out and whispered, "I think I am dying. My belly has grown large and heavy in the last few months, and I did not eat any more than usual. There must be a tumor swelling inside."

"You are not dying, Jane. This is not a tumor," Ella responded.

"Do you have medicine for this pain? I would be so grateful, even if I must pay for it out of my wages. It is too much to bear."

Ella shook her head from side to side. "Sounds like this will be a great surprise to you, but you are having a baby."

Jane gasped and her eyes bulged, but then she cried out as another contraction came on and her face squeezed like after biting something sour.

Ella rubbed the girl's back and called out, "Mrs. Bunting! Jane is in labor!"

"What?" The landlady rushed in from the kitchen, holding a spatula in her hands. After staring at Jane, she flung the spatula at the table. "What did you do, girl?" she demanded.

"We need to bring a midwife or take her to Dr. Sanders' clinic," Ella urged.

Mrs. Bunting pursed her lips. "If the baby is in the right position, better summon a midwife and have the baby here. I would not drag her to the clinic if I don't have to." As Jane bent over and screamed, she added, "It may be too late to go there anyway."

She called another maid and asked her to run to the clinic and see if Mrs. Brook was there, and if not, to try her home. Then she put Jane's arm on her shoulder to lead her into a tiny room in the back, which served as the maid's bedroom. After helping her onto the bed, Mrs. Bunting turned to Ella. "Have you learned how to deliver a baby?"

Ella shifted her feet. "I took a midwifery class, but we mostly watched."

"Can you tell if the baby is in the right position and if it's coming soon?"

"I think so."

She took a deep breath and approached Jane. Guessing that the maid had little experience with doctors, she said, "Jane, you will need to let me touch your stomach and between your legs. Don't be afraid. I will be gentle."

Jane gave Ella and Mrs. Bunting a terrified look. "No! I don't want a man to touch me there."

Mrs. Bunting snorted. "Don't be silly. Obviously, you let some man do more than touch you. Mr. Parker will be a doctor soon and will do nothing improper. Lift your skirts up and submit to his exam."

After helping Jane with her skirts, Ella pressed on the hard stomach. It took her a little while to get the hang of what she was doing, but after some searching she found the baby's head near the bottom of the girl's abdomen.

"The baby is in the right position," she confirmed.

"Thank God for that," Mrs. Bunting answered.

"What is that?" Jane asked, pressing higher on her stomach.

Ella put her hand where the girl pointed. "That's the baby kicking. You must have felt it before." She held her hand there a bit more. There was something wonderful about those kicks.

Jane stared at her stomach with marvel. "I really am having a baby," she mumbled, as if she did not believe it until now. Then she screamed again.

"Have you flooded yet?" Ella asked after Jane's face relaxed. The maid did not understand, and she tried to explain. "Did you have fluid rush out of you? Could be a small stream, or all come out at once and make a big puddle."

"Yes. It happened before supper. I thought it was…" the girl looked down in embarrassment.

"Supper was more than two hours ago," Mrs. Bunting piped. "How soon do you think this baby will come?" she asked Ella.

"Why don't you hold her hand, and I will check her cervix," Ella responded.

She asked Jane to relax and spread her knees. Comparing in her mind what she observed with the textbook drawings, Ella inserted her fingers and concluded the cervix to be almost fully open. That meant Jane would be ready to push soon. A chill seized her chest. *What if the midwife does not come in time?*

The landlady read Ella's mind. "We may have to do this ourselves, Mr. Parker. I have attended two births, and the job didn't seem that hard to me."

Ella summoned her courage. "Right. We should prepare water, washcloth, and towels. Oh, and a sharp knife or scissors."

Jane screamed, hearing the last part, and looked at Ella wide-eyed.

"It's just to cut the cord, Jane. It won't hurt."

"I will boil water and get those supplies. You stay with Jane." Mrs. Bunting clicked her tongue and hurried out of the room. Ella's heart raced, but she tried to appear calm. A woman in labor needed reassurance, she told herself. She sat down next to Jane and told her she was doing fine. After another heart-wrenching scream, the girl grabbed her hand.

"Are you sure that all is well?" she asked with urgency. "You don't think I will die?"

Ella's mind flooded with the faces of Ella Bennett, Anna Walters, as well as her own mother. She willed the images to leave. "I know you are scared and completely unprepared for having this baby, but all that occurred so far is normal. Birth hurts something awful and there will be bleeding, but a healthy young woman like you should make it through fine." She reassured the girl and bit her lip wondering if the girl was healthy and if there was something else to check other than the baby's position. Unable to think of anything else to do, she concluded that much was left to chance.

"I wish my mother were here. She died soon after giving birth to me," Jane moaned.

The last image of Ella's own mother, succumbing while birthing her brother, made Ella's mouth dry.

She pressed the girl's hand, wincing at a lump in her throat. "Your mother will help you," Ella said, imagining a woman's face resembling Jane's looking down from above at her daughter about to birth her grandchild. Despite the anatomy books, the educational lectures, the dissections, there was something mysterious and indescribable about birth. Ella sensed the ancient rite of passage, women gathering in caves, huts, humble homes, and palaces, in every country and century, to help one of their sisters bring a new life into this world.

Heaving, Mrs. Bunting stepped in, holding towels, sheets, and a bucket of water. A pair of scissors stuck out from the pocket of her apron. "I forgot all about the pot roast in the oven. It was almost burned," she chuckled.

"The baby is coming!" Jane yelped.

Ella rushed over and looked between her legs. "Jane is ready to push," she said.

"Well, we are ready, right? Come on, lass, birth that baby!" Mrs. Bunting cheered, propping Jane up on her pillow. Ella positioned herself by the legs, while the landlady patted Jane's back and wiped her face.

Jane took on the challenge with bravery, pushing hard, and pausing for rest between contractions.

An exhausting hour passed, and all three dripped with sweat. Ella's scalp blazed with heat, as she agonized over whether all was well. Jane's face went from scarlet to greyish, as she fatigued from excruciating pushing. Ella desperately wanted the midwife to appear, but more than an hour into the pushing, there was still no sign of her.

Another half-hour passed, and the long awaited head showed itself.

After encouraging Jane to give several more pushes, the girl gave an ear-splitting scream, and Ella caught first the head, and then the shoulders and back of the wet, slippery newborn. The rest of the body slid out, and the baby gave a piercing shriek in her arms.

The three women held their breath, hearing that first cry. It could not be more beautiful than a song of angels.

"Mr. Parker, you delivered the baby yourself?"

Ella spun around, startled by the voice of Mrs. Brooks, who shuffled in, followed by the maid who brought her.

"Jane did all the hard work; I only caught the baby. And Mrs. Bunting was an excellent assistant."

The midwife retrieved a knife from her bag and cut the umbilical cord. Then Ella and Mrs. Bunting washed the baby with warm water, while she examined Jane and helped her deliver the afterbirth. After confirming that the mother was fine, she inspected the child with a critical eye.

"Healthy pink color, all fingers and toes in place, and a nice loud cry. You have a healthy baby boy," she grinned at Jane and placed the dry and swaddled infant on the mother's chest. "I am sorry I took so long. I was delivering a baby in another town. On the full moon, babies come one after another. I better get back to see if anyone else has gone into labor."

The midwife rushed away, promising to come back in the morning to help with breastfeeding. Ella peered through the window, noticing the circle of the moon illuminating the silvery dew on the swishing grass. Beautiful clear night for a new life to come into this world.

Mrs. Bunting rocked the baby in her arms, then placed him into a large basket, covering him with a thick blanket. "April showers brought more than flowers," the landlady quipped, then shifted her gaze toward Jane, who snuggled on her side, holding her hands under a cheek like a child. "Lass, before you sleep, tell me how this happened. Why didn't you say you were in a family way?"

"She didn't know even when she went into labor. She thought she was dying from a tumor," Ella explained.

"What? Jane, wake up! Who is the father? Will he marry you?" the landlady demanded, shaking the girl.

"I don't know who the father is. I don't have a sweetheart," the girl protested in a tired voice.

"You are not stupid. Tell me who it was. Think back to early fall."

Jane opened her eyes and mouth wide. "I still don't know. It could be Mr. Collins or Mr. Finn." Both were tenants in the house.

Mrs. Bunting crossed her arms. "I had a better opinion of you. Carrying on with two men at once. You are no longer involved with either?"

Jane reddened. "It was not like that. I was sweeping the hall when Mr. Collins called me to his room asking me to clean there. Mr. Finn was there as well. They were drinking whiskey and poured me some too. They took turns kissing me and said I was beautiful, then poured me another glass and..."

"We have heard enough, Jane," Mrs. Bunting interrupted. "You got drunk with two men and either one could have impregnated you. Unbelievable. Didn't your mother teach you anything?"

"I don't have a mother," the girl wept.

The baby stirred and cried. Ella picked him up and swayed him in her arms.

"Could she go to the police?" she asked the landlady.

With a snort, Mrs. Bunting pointed out that the girl went into the room and drank willingly. No laws protected women even that young from foolish behavior. Ella remembered her own ignorance before taking midwifery. The class delivered many painful but necessary lessons.

"I will not let such a foul deed go unpunished though. Both so-called gentlemen will leave this house in the morning. If they do not pack fast enough, their belongings will fly down the stairs," Mrs. Bunting vowed. "Listen, Jane," she touched the sleepy girl on the shoulder, "You cannot keep the baby here long. I will give you time to recover and the baby to grow a bit, but then he will have to go. Do you have family who will take him in?"

Shaking her head, the girl turned over in her slumber.

With curses that would impress a seasoned sailor, the landlady pulled Jane's leg. "I have a childless sister who lives with her husband in the country. They may want the baby. I will write to them."

Jane turned again then bolted upright. "I am not giving my baby away. He is mine."

"Don't be stupid. You cannot support yourself and a baby with your wages, and I don't run a charity. A good family to adopt your son is the best for which you can hope. My sister and brother-in-law are kind people and have a good income. If they agree, don't miss such a chance. Do you want me to take you to the slums and show you dead babies, whose mothers could not feed them?"

With a sob, the girl asked if the sister may have use for her. Mrs. Bunting pursed her lips but promised to ask.

The landlady took the baby to her room, letting Jane rest. "After such a night, I won't sleep anyway. I hope you can doze before your morning classes, Mr. Parker. Thank you once again for helping us."

Ella took the hint and dragged herself upstairs. As soon as her shoes flew off her feet, she was asleep on top of her covers.

"You delivered a baby practically by yourself!" Oli gaped at Ella as if she committed a heroic deed. They were walking to their first class, showered by a drizzle. Ella covered another yawn with her elbow. The baby cried several times through the night, and then in the morning; when she finally fell asleep, loud protests on the stairs awakened her. Mrs. Bunting was true to her word, evicting the men who took advantage of the young maid.

"Yes, but it's not a happy story." Ella relayed the circumstances how the baby was conceived and how Jane would have to give the baby away.

Oli's smile did not fade. "Many lives start out in poverty, but circumstances can change for the better. If a kind soul is willing to take in the child and possibly the mother, all could turn out well. How are they doing?"

"They rested well. Jane said she will name the baby after me."

"That's splendid. I am so proud of you."

"You look like you had little sleep as well," Ella remarked, noticing grey bags under Oli's eyes.

"I took the night shift and spent most of it with the Walters' twins. The boy died around midnight, but the girl improved. She is named Anna, after her mother. Her fever broke towards morning, and chest became less congested. I desperately want her to pull through. That family has endured enough sorrow."

Ella agreed wholeheartedly. If little Anna survived, she would be another girl growing up motherless and wondering what her brother would have been like. Even when life started out in such an unfair and miserable way, the future may be kind to the child eventually.

* * *

April 29,
Dear Matilda and Dr. Pesce,
Matilda, you will love my news. I delivered a baby! The mother and the baby boy are doing well. He is named Alan

after me. The landlady assisted me at birth, but the midwife arrived when I already held the infant in my arms. She was a great help with showing the new mum how to care for the baby.

If you remember the case of the twins born by cesarean section, they came to the hospital with severe pneumonia and were not expected to live. The baby boy died, but his sister survived and was released home. Her improvement and Alan's birth gave me much joy.

The exams will be upon us soon, and I plan to study daily. I showed Oli a schedule I drew up, and he thought me mad. We will have to keep our noses in the books late into the night. It will be a grueling effort but all worth it in the end. I must excel at the exams to intern with Dr. Miller, and you know how much that means to me.

I am sorry to hear you cannot visit me for my graduation. Since Dr. Pesce advised against friends, I will likely have no one to celebrate with.

Love, Alan Parker

* * *

May 20,

Dear Alan,

I am extremely happy reading the beginning of your letter, and I am very proud of you. Maybe this is the sign that you will embrace midwifery after all.

I will save my ink regarding Oli, Dr. Miller, and this pointless pursuit of his internship. I've said enough in every other letter.

I will see if I can arrange for another midwife to take care of my clients for a few days so I can visit. I make no promises. Remember Violet, the girl who swallowed a button? Her

*mother, Mrs. Kelley, is pregnant again and comes over every
other day or so with various complaints and worries. That
hen has convinced herself that she will have a terrible
delivery. Lord give me patience to deal with that hen.
At least she has money and always buys some remedy for
herself or her children.
There have been some slandering articles about female
healers in the latest papers, and I lost a few customers.
Love, Matilda Pesce*

CHAPTER 18

The library table creaked under the stacks of books and papers Oli and Ella piled on it. The librarian glared at them for taking too many materials. Ella did not see why he minded: at this hour of the evening, they were the only ones still there.

After the library closed, they would continue studying in one of the hospital classrooms and return to their rooms well past midnight. They pored over their notes and asked each other possible test questions in preparation for their exams. The intimidating thought of standing before the committee of professors, and the desire to obtain their degrees on the first try, served as powerful motivators.

Oli asked a question about the lymphatic system, and Ella broke into a cough before answering. He stared at her with alarm.

"You've been hacking all day."

Ella took a sip of water from her cup. "It's just a cold," she replied, shivering.

"Why don't we call it a night? You don't look well."

"We have much left to review!"

"It will do no good if you make yourself sick. Let's go get some sleep."

Oli returned the library books and packed their belongings. Ella wanted to argue but gave in to her tiredness and followed him into the cool evening. He spoke about something, but she had trouble focusing on the conversation. Several times she interrupted him with long coughing fits. Her throat was dry and sore, and the short walk she usually enjoyed left her breathless. Each step took some effort, but she pushed her feet to keep going. Her back and arms ached from the weight of her books.

When they reached the fork where Oli and she normally went separate ways, he stopped.

"I don't like the sound of your cough. Why don't I walk you home and examine you?"

She panicked at the thought of Oli touching her chest. "No. Thank you for your concern, but I am fine," she responded with coolness in her tone.

He looked taken aback. "I just want to help."

"I am not allowed visitors at this hour, and my room is a mess," she reasoned.

"Oh, don't worry about that. You should see my room, it's a pigsty. And your landlady will understand it's not a social visit."

"You don't need to come, Oli. I will go to sleep."

His insistence frustrated her. She wanted to get to her lodging and the comfort of her bed.

"But your cough needs to be checked. It could be more than a cold. I should walk you home and make sure you are well. That's what a friend is supposed to do."

He put his hand over her shoulder, but she shook it off. She was too exhausted to be polite. "We are not exactly friends. We are study partners. I tutored you so you don't fail your classes. Anything beyond that was never part of the deal."

Oli stared with hurt all over his face, then whispered, "It's because of who I am, isn't it? I bet Jeffers told you during those private classes. You would rather hack in your room alone than accept my help. You are right; we are not friends. And since my grades are good now, I don't need a study partner anymore."

He stormed off into the direction of his lodging. Ella stared, not fully comprehending what just occurred. *At least he won't ask to examine me anymore*, she thought as she trudged home, rasping. She crossed the threshold and dragged herself towards her room, carrying her heavy books. Mrs. Bunting offered supper, but Ella shook her head. Each step came harder, and the flight of stairs seemed never-ending. Her lungs ached by the time she made it to the top.

Relieved to make it to her room, she undressed and put on her warmest nightgown, pink with white roses. Then she climbed into her bed, hoping to recover after a good night of sleep. As soon as her head hit the pillow, her throat convulsed in a coughing fit, and she shivered violently. A cup of tea would comfort her, but the effort to get it from the kitchen seemed enormous. Mrs. Bunting or a maid could bring her some, but she was in her nightgown and could not be seen this way. She rose to change, but her head was foggy, and she feared falling. She had to admit she was sick. And she was all alone.

Back in bed, she told herself to calm down and stop being a coward. It was only a cold, and she would be much better by morning. An hour went by, but she still tossed and turned. Melting heat replaced cold shivers.

A voice downstairs startled her. "Did Alan come home?" Oli asked.

"Yes, he went straight to his room," Mrs. Bunting answered.

"I should check on him. He did not look well tonight."

"Yes, I heard him cough as he passed. It's good of you to come."

Rapid steps sounded closer to her room, and then there was a knock on the door. "Alan, it's me, Oli. I know you don't want to see me, but can I come in anyway?"

Ella did not answer. Oli's voice gladdened her, but she could not bring herself to invite him in. Changing into men's clothing seemed a herculean effort. She decided to say nothing, so he would think her sleeping and leave.

"Alan, you are unwell, and I am here because I am concerned. I am sorry for the things I said. Whether you want to be friends or not, I am grateful for your tutoring. Please let me see you, if just for a minute."

Oli's pleads continued from behind the door. Ella guessed he was conflicted between lack of permission and putting politeness aside to check on her. The young man still hesitated and implored when Ella curled into a ball in a violent coughing fit.

The door squeaked and Oli came in. When he walked towards the bed and lit a candle, her eyes squeezed shut. She felt him move the blanket from her shoulders. There was a silence for an infinity. Then she heard Oli's chuckle.

"So, the rumors were true," he said. "And I thought other students gossiped out of envy, saying you look like a girl. Not what I expected. Look how our secrets almost tore us apart. Never mind. Respiratory illnesses are treated in females similar to males. Relax and breathe as deeply as you can."

He put his ear to her chest, listening intently. "Not good. I don't hear pneumonia, but the lungs are congested." He put a hand on her forehead. "And you have a fever."

"Not before exams," Ella moaned.

"We still have ten days. Should be enough time to get you back on your feet. I will go down to the kitchen and make you a drink of tea, rum, and honey to sweat off the illness."

Ella heard him descend and say something to the landlady. Part of her tired brain reeled from Oli's lack of reaction to her secret. He came back and made her drink his concoction. Hot beverage burned her throat but warmed her from the inside.

"Does the landlady know?" he asked.

"No one can know."

"I told her you are contagious, and she better not come up. She seemed concerned for your sake. Do you have anyone who could take care of you?"

She shook her head.

"Fine. Finish your drink and go to sleep. I will stay here for a while to make sure the fever diminishes."

The room darkened when he snuffed a couple of candles. Her eyes closed on their own. She felt Oli straightening her blanket.

Faces appeared and vanished in her troubled dream. Mother, laughing and extending her welcoming arms; Father, his face red, throwing the wine glass. Ghostlike faces of sick children, Walter Carrow, Anna Walters, and Ella Bennett came and went.

A wet cloth smelling of vinegar cooled her forehead. "You need to take something for that fever," Oli urged.

She looked around dazedly in the dark room. "Oli, it must be quite late. You need to go."

He gave her a tense smile. "I would be a terrible friend and a terrible doctor to leave you now. Your fever is worse each time I check. We need to break it. I raided through your impressive medicine cabinet and found these potions. Take them now with some water."

After taking the remedies, she stretched out on the bed, hoping for a better dream.

* * *

Shades of grey, silver, and lavender changed before her eyes. Her head felt leaden, and her throat parched. Two men's voices were audible to her. Someone squeezed her wrist too tight, then put his head to her chest.

"Is it pneumonia?" Oli sounded spooked.

"Could be. Some nasty lung malady," a deep voice with a Scottish burr answered. A rough hand felt her forehead and neck. "She is burning up. I will need to draw quite a bit of blood."

"Wouldn't that weaken her? Her pulse is faint as is."

"Young man, I don't know what they teach in medical schools these days, but bloodletting is the best thing for a fever. Trust my experience. After she revives, give her a couple grains of calomel to purge her. That will clean out the disease from her system."

Her sleeve rolled up, and something sharp jabbed into her arm. She moaned at the pain.

Warm wetness flowed down her skin, while a small, gentle hand patted her head. Then the world turned black.

* * *

She found herself bound to an operating table. Restraints cut into her skin as she struggled.

Dr. Miller, Dr. Sanders, and other familiar faces of the professors and students, watched her with contempt. They wore powdered wigs and black robes. Dr. Miller stepped forward

"This woman is a pretender. She stole knowledge that belongs to men. She earned her punishment." A scream left her throat as she watched them take out scalpels from their pockets with bloodthirsty smiles.

A long coughing fit interrupted her nightmare. Her whole body ached like someone had beaten her with a rod. She was so hot she could melt. The same two voices argued nearby, but she had no energy to respond.

Oli spoke with assertiveness. "Please tell me what you mean to do."

"She needs to be bled again."

"No. I barely restored her pulse last time by pouring brandy into her mouth. More blood loss will kill her."

"Her fever lessened after the treatment."

"Yes, for an hour or so. It rose again after you left, and she was weaker after bleeding. Do you know anything else?"

"I still believe bleeding is the right course. There must be more diseased blood that I need to remove. You said yourself that the potions did not help."

"I will not allow more bloodletting."

"Then I cannot help. Please do not send for me again."

Ella heard hurried steps and a brusque goodbye to the landlady, who inquired about her condition. Then the door slammed closed. For a while, she heard nothing else. Her sleep was dreamless. Then she was not in the room anymore. Her body became weightless and could float. She was inside a fog, thick as milk. Her mind was serene like never before. She knew if she surrendered to this welcoming fog, she could stay in it forever.

* * *

"Please, wake up." Oli's voice seemed miles away. "I don't even know what to call you. I know you are not Alan, obviously. I will still call you my friend. You were afraid to call me that, but you are one of the best friends I ever had. I wish you trusted me. Come on, you must fight this fever. Do you think I can go on to be a doctor if I lose my patient and my best friend?"

There was a sob in his voice. "Not that I should be thinking about myself. What about you? You are so close to graduating, to achieving your dreams. You would help so many people. It would not be fair if you die now. Two years of medical school with the best professors, and I am losing you to some atypical pneumonia and fever. Please, you know more things than me, you know yourself, is there is something I should do? Find your strength and tell me."

She focused on Oli's voice, on his hand that held hers and forced herself to say the words. "Dr. Miller."

"Did you say Dr. Miller? Please, not him. He will see you are a woman, and we can kiss our degrees goodbye." He was quiet for a while. "No, I was wrong to say that. If he can make you better, I will bring him. Your life is more important than a fancy piece of paper. Hold on, I will get him, no matter what he is doing."

He squeezed her hand and then his steps thundered on the stairs.

CHAPTER 19

A drizzle tapped on the window, playing its lively rhythm. The cotton nightgown felt damp with sweat and the blanket too hot and heavy. The sharp smell of vinegar and potent medicines disturbed her nose. Her back ached, and she turned onto her side, groaning. The divan creaked and footsteps hurried towards her. She pried her eyes open and saw Oli watching her with worry. His hair was disheveled, and his cheeks sported the beginning stubble of a sparse beard.

A taste of something bitter was in her mouth. "Water," Ella whispered. He beamed at her, filled a cup, and helped her sit up to drink. Still thirsty, she asked for more.

After draining two more cups, she reclined on her pillows.

"How long was I sick?" she asked.

"Three days. I was afraid," he paused. "I was afraid you would miss the exams."

"That's not what you wanted to say."

"It's all right. You are on the mend now. The fever broke two hours ago. Let's see how you are doing." He performed the routine exam of checking her pulse, listening to her lungs, feeling her forehead, and peering at her tongue and throat. "Everything is much better. This medicine is working wonders for you. Which reminds me that it may be time for the next dose. Do you have a watch?"

"Check the pocket of my trousers. What medicine?"

"I will show you the bottle later."

He found her watch and got busy grinding something at the table. After mixing the powder with water, he gave her the treatment to drink.

Ella took a careful sip. "Yuk. It's so bitter," she complained, sticking out her tongue.

"Bottoms up!"

After making sure she drank to the last drop, he put the glass away and sat at the edge of her bed, still beaming. "What's your name?"

"Ella Parker."

"It drove me insane that I did not know. I will call you Alan in public, don't worry."

"You seem to have little reaction to my secret."

He shrugged. "There were rumors which I dismissed as envy. I considered telling you about them, but I could see nothing to be gained by it."

"You are not angry at all?"

"Angry? I admire you even more. Too bad this will have to stay a secret, and our wise professors and university board will not know that the best student in our class is a woman. I wish you could throw their hypocrisy into their faces like a modern day Agnodice." His cheeks reddened as he talked. "They know women work fourteen-hour days at the mills but proclaim them too delicate to study at the university. They expect mothers, shaking with fever, to get up from their sickbeds and take care of ill husbands and children, but bar them from learning the science of medicine. On what grounds are they stopping women like you from education? That you cannot stand to watch surgery? If only they saw you on that first lesson at the dissection room."

"I am sorry I lied to you."

"I know why you had to do it. You are not the only one who kept a secret. My real name is David Fridman. I am Jewish. Jews are also barred from the university on religious grounds."

Ella stared in confusion. "Sorry, I am ignorant about those things. Jeffers said something once about me not knowing who you really were and picking better friends. Is that what he meant?"

"Yes. He must have suspected but had no proof, otherwise I'm sure he would've reported me to the Board. Besides tripping me the first time we met, he wrote insults on my desk and passed me notes saying nasty things. He stopped when you became Dr. Miller's protégé, and I was protected by association."

"I think he stopped because he sensed your confidence growing. Bullies go for the prey they can handle. Did Dr. Miller know as well?"

"I suspect so, even if he did not say anything. As you saw, he judged my work harshly and wanted to expel me. Unfortunately, that's how it is. You can change your name, wear the same clothes as everyone else, come to work on Sabbath, share a meal of pork chops with a gentile friend - not that I went that far - but people behind your back still say, 'he is a Jew, and look how cunningly he is hiding it.'" Oli sighed. "It does not change anything for our friendship, I hope. We have religious differences, but our values are the same. We strive to learn, to help others, to show kindness. Am I right?"

"Of course. You think I would care about some religious

distinctions, when you have no trouble accepting me as a female? You are the best friend one could hope for, Oli."

She drank some more water as the unpleasant taste of the medicine still lingered in her mouth. "Who was the doctor who came here?"

"Your landlady gave me his name. He was not connected to the university. I let him bleed you, and you got much worse. Dr. Miller was right when he cautioned about bloodletting. Speaking of Dr. Miller, when you seemed awfully bad, I went to get him. I thought you wanted me to bring him because you said his name. When I almost reached the hospital, I realized that you could have meant something he said. And I remembered what treats fevers that nothing else breaks."

"Jesuit's bark. That costs a fortune! Please tell me you found keys to my drawer and took the money from there."

"I would never do that without permission. It does not matter, the point is I did not have to tell Dr. Miller about you, and your secret is safe. You may be well enough to take exams in a week."

"But how did you pay for the medicine?' She looked at him expectantly then gasped. "Oh Oli, the watch that your parents gave you as a gift! Is that why you asked where mine was because yours is gone? Please tell me you pawned it, and I can get it back for you."

He cringed. "I went to the pawnshop, but they offered a fraction of what it was worth. Instead, I went to a jeweler, and he gave me a fair price."

She embraced him by the shoulders as her eyes moistened.

"Oli, that is the sweetest thing anyone ever did for me. Not to mention how you took care of me. How can I ever thank you?! As soon as I can, I will go to that jeweler and buy back that watch, or if that one is gone, I will purchase the best one they have. Don't you worry, I can afford it."

He patted her back. "It was worth it. My parents will love the story once they hear it." He chuckled. "Mmm, I can smell Mrs. Bunting's chicken and roasted potatoes. You should eat to get your strength up, and I am starving as well. Your landlady is the second best cook to my mother. I will go down and tell her the good news about you and bring back some food."

He stood up and opened the door when a deep, melodious male voice came from downstairs. "The least I can do is check on my favorite student while he is ill. Thank you, madam, for the offer, but I have other plans for dinner. I will see to Mr. Parker's condition and be on my way."

They gasped and looked at each other.

Oli whispered, "What if you change quickly?"

Ella shook her head. "He will insist on examining me and know right away. It's all right, I planned to tell him if he chose me as his intern. Let it be now instead." Not hiding, she sat up in bed, exposing the top of her pink nightgown.

Brisk, confident steps sounded on the stairs, and Dr. Miller strode into the room through the door Oli left open. Dressed with his usual neatness, and holding a case, he turned towards Ella's sickbed with a polite smile. As he saw her, his eyes bulged, and his smile changed to a grimace.

"What in the world is this?" he shouted, making her wince.

She put effort into remaining calm. "Dr. Miller, I can explain."

He stared at her with disgust, as though she were a tumor he needed to remove. "There is nothing to explain, young lady. You do not belong at the university."

"But you know me. You have allowed me to assist you at

surgeries and operate under your supervision, you praised my research, and even said I was one of the best students you ever taught."

"All I know about you is that you are an impostor, and your presence here is an embarrassment to the school. There is no question of you sitting for exams. Your name will be removed from the university's register and your records destroyed. There was never an Alan Parker at this school because he did not exist. Pack your bags and get out of here."

Her cheeks burned, and she felt feverish again. Dr. Miller's gaze penetrated her, as if ensuring the words had enough effect. Tears sprang from her eyes, and she covered her face with her hands. The doctor opened his mouth to add more, but Oli, who huddled in a corner, stepped in front of Ella, as into a line of fire. He crossed his arms and stared back with rebellion at his teacher.

"My patient has been dangerously ill and is not ready to travel. I will observe her progress and decide when she is ready to go."

David versus Goliath, thought Ella, holding her breath.

Dr. Miller's mouth twisted, and he looked down. "Very well, but she will not show her face on campus. And I will see *you*, Mr. Higgins, at the exams."

The doctor turned on his heel and stomped out of the room. The slam of the front door made Ella jump. Oli's arms caressed her back, and she put her head on his shoulder.

He whispered, "This is horribly unfair. You were the best of our class and so close to graduating."

A lump in her throat made her sob. Did her efforts and her dreams slip away with Dr. Miller's thunderous steps? Her mind reeled. She thought her beloved professor would accept her. The disappointment in him and in her misjudgment stung like a slap.

"Why did you not tell me to keep him away? I would have said you were out." Mrs. Bunting burst into the room, holding a ladle like a weapon.

Ella pulled back from Oli's embrace, and they both stared at the landlady in her stained apron and her hair sticking out from under her cap.

"I apologize, but the door was open, and I could hear everything. Miss Parker, can I call you that?"

Ella nodded.

"No professor from your school has a right to command you under my roof. You are welcome to stay as long as you need. So good to see you recovering. I wanted to nurse you, but Mr. Higgins said your malady was contagious, and I feared for Jane and the baby. I will ask one of the girls to stay with you at night. Mr. Higgins, you are welcome to sleep in one of the empty rooms."

Ella wiped her tears. "Did you know, Mrs. Bunting?" she asked.

The landlady cocked her head. "I had an inkling. When you took care of Jane, you dropped your guard, and I could sense womanliness from you. I am sorry your teacher found you out, because you would make a fine doctor. I recall a couple of similar incidents, but those young ladies were caught, and their stories hushed up. I will cheer for a woman who will outwit those stuffy scholars, get her degree, and go on to build a terrific career, even if she will have to hide her gender all her life."

She straightened her apron. "I need to feed my patrons. Mr. Higgins, I know you will appreciate my culinary talents. What can I bring for your patient, a broth or a hearty soup?"

Ella did not have much of an appetite, but Oli insisted she ate, saying a good soup treated better than medicines.

The landlady grinned and raced down to the kitchen.

They heard her ordering the servants to hurry up with dinner. After finishing the bowl of savory chicken soup, Ella reclined on the pillows. The hot meal warmed her whole body in a pleasant way. She did not want to think about what Dr. Miller's words meant just yet.

"Did you get any studying done?" she asked Oli, getting back to her study partner role.

"I did, but there is no point now. Dr. Miller wants to fail me spectacularly. You heard it in his tone. I will not go."

She sat up and glared. "Don't you dare back out. I will help you prepare. He can only fail you if you make a mistake. You will be in front of a committee of professors, and he will not act unfairly in front of his colleagues."

"I did some reading while you were ill and made notes on things I did not understand. If you feel well enough tomorrow, we could go over my questions, but not too long — you should be resting."

Her eyelids closed, and she cozied under her blanket. Before slumber had her, she heard Oli blowing out candles and felt him fixing her pillows. "Sleep well, my friend," he said with tenderness.

Ella's cheeks flushed with humiliation. She knew appeasing Dr. Miller would likely be impossible, but giving up on her dreams after two years of grueling work was heartbreaking. She owed herself this one last try, no matter how much the rejection would hurt. From what she gathered, Dr. Miller did not disclose her secret. When other students remarked on her absence, he told them Alan Parker had taken ill, and she even received some get well wishes through Oli. She hoped against hope that her beloved professor could forgive her and allow her to graduate. An hour before the exams, she donned Alan Parker's clothing and knocked at Dr. Miller's office. The tirade that followed dug a nail into her heart with every word.

"Please, doctor, I beg your forgiveness for my deception, but I am still the same person you came to know. I cannot see my future without medicine and being useful to suffering patients. Why should my sex matter when I am able to save lives?" She said her last argument in a trembling voice.

The professor balled his fists and glared at her with loathing. "It matters because you are breaking God's laws.

Surgery is unnatural for women, and a female pursuing this field is an abomination. The board of surgeons will never accredit you. I am losing my patience, and exams are about to start. Another word from you, and your friend Mr. Higgins may strongly regret coming here. Now, please leave both my office and this campus, as you were already asked."

She staggered out of the room with her shoulders slumped and head lowered. Oli, who paced the corridor, rushed to her.

"He did not budge. I am afraid I made him even more angry, and he may release his wrath on you," she said, shaking her head.

"You had to try. Now you know you did all you could. I am so sorry."

She gave Oli a quick embrace. "Good luck. Come see me after your final. I will pack to go home."

* * *

Baby Alan burped and spat some milk on Ella's shoulder. Jane rushed to clean her up.

"Nice parting gift for me, Alan," Ella said with a smile. She planned to change out of that shirt into one of her dresses anyway.

"I am so happy you've recovered," Jane said as she packed her few belongings into a sack. "Who was that nice young man who stopped by to inquire of your health?"

"Daniel Carter. He was one of my first patients, wounded in a duel. It was kind of him to visit, but I did not have the energy to make myself look presentable and come down to see him." She considered sending him a note, but he was likely gone after completing his law exams yesterday.

Jane took the baby into her arms and kissed his nose.

"Well, we are ready to go. Mrs. Bunting's sister will let me work in her house. I will still be able to see him."

Ella wondered what would be harder for Jane: to give Alan away and never see him again, or to see him each day but not be his mother. Either option seemed like a cruel torture.

As Jane stared into her boy's sparkling blue eyes, Ella slipped an envelope into the young woman's pocket. "Save that money for a rainy day. In case you will need to leave and start over."

Jane turned, wide-eyed. She put the baby down into his basket and swept Ella into an embrace. "God bless you, Miss Parker. I heard you are leaving too."

Ella nodded. "I am. Going back to my home to do whatever rich girls are supposed to be doing."

She did not want to cry in front of Jane. A wealthy woman's problems were negligible compared to those experienced by someone who could not keep her baby. They said their goodbyes, and Ella turned to go when the girl called her back.

"Did you take that letter that came for you while you were sick? It sat forever by the kitchen window."

"No. No one mentioned a letter."

Ella ventured to the kitchen and found a large, thick envelope with 'Eloise Parker' on it. The return address was her estate.

More reports from Mr. Smiley, except he forgot to put 'Alan Parker', she thought with frustration.

* * *

Her bag was bursting at the seams, but she still attempted to cram in more books. A knock on her door interrupted her

255

packing. She wiped her tears with her sleeve and opened the door. Oli staggered in and threw himself on the divan.

"My head is killing me," he moaned.

Ella put a pillow under his head and gave him a cup of water. "Did you pass?" she asked.

"I did. The professors hated my thesis, appalled at my suggestion that doctors could cause infections with dirty hands, but they agreed my paper was well written and supported with evidence. For the exam, they held me at least a half-hour longer than any other student, and Dr. Miller asked about topics we never covered in class. He became all red in the face and his veins bulged when I answered all his questions. Dr. Sanders stood up like a hunter ready for the kill, but the head of the university pointed out that I demonstrated my mastery over the subjects and other students were waiting their turn. Jeffers failed, by the way. He plagiarized his thesis from another student who graduated years ago. Dr. Miller recognized that paper almost immediately. He may be expelled for doing such a thing."

"I hope he is. Now let me see your diploma."

Oli grinned and took out the rolled paper stuffed into his shirt and passed it to her to read.

Ella suppressed a sigh while caressing the expensive paper and admiring the elegant writing. She would never receive such a diploma with her name on it. The thought hurt more than she cared to admit.

Oli sat up and embraced her. "I am sorry you will not have your degree. You deserved it more than anyone. And I would not have mine if not for you."

She let him hold her. "It's maddening that I am this upset," she answered. "The diploma would give me nothing. I became caught up in exam preparations and dreams of holding this piece of paper, but the name on it would be 'Alan

Parker'. I cannot be him for the rest of my life. I need to be Ella again."

He patted her shoulder. "You still won. You imbibed everything this school could give you. They can deny you your degree, but they cannot take away what you learned. The knowledge will stay in your head and in your hands. You can become a fantastic midwife or a healer. People will come from all around to consult with you."

"Midwifery never appealed to me and the whole medical community is on the attack against female healers. Best I go home and figure out what to do with myself," she said with a sigh.

"You should leave this university with pride in your accomplishments. You ranked at the top of the class, cared for patients, saved lives, delivered a baby…"

"And made a best friend," she gave Oli a smile.

They were quiet for a while. Oli pointed at the thick envelope that lay next to her bags. "What's this?"

"Oh, just some reports from my estate caretaker."

"His name is Ivy?"

"No, Ivy is my maid. Does it say Ivy? That's peculiar, she never written before."

Curious, Ella unsealed the letter. Inside she found a short note from her maid stating that when she put the last few things remaining in her mother's bedroom into the storage room, she had found a box of letters addressed to Eloise. Ivy thought that her mistress would want to see them right away, and after getting the address from Mr. Smiley, sent them all in this envelope.

Ella began reading her mother's letters one by one. The first letter was written shortly after Ella was born; it explained that her mother planned to write regularly and present the whole bundle on her daughter's sixteenth birthday. Mesmerized, Ella entered the world of these letters.

Oli went downstairs to chat with Mrs. Bunting, but it didn't matter what anyone was saying or doing. Her mind stayed on those letters until all were read. These were accounts of what she did as a baby and a little girl, birthday and holiday wishes, stories about her mother and grandparents, and family legends. One letter she read over and over.

My dear daughter,
You are only a baby now, and days ago took your first steps. You have no idea how much joy it gives me to see you reach that milestone. Everything you do makes me proud.
However, there is something else in my life that is making me proud these days, almost as much as you. Today, I managed to save the lives of over a hundred small children by inoculating them against smallpox. Smallpox is a terrible disease that's sweeping through the country. Terrified for you and other loved ones, I read anything I could about the disease and found the letters and publications of the amazing Lady Mary Wortley Montagu, who learned from the natives in Turkey and inoculated British people years ago, from prisoners to royalty.
My friends came together, and we searched for doctors to teach us her technique. Several physicians refused, calling our endeavor improper and dangerous, but my friends supported me, and we kept trying until we found mentors willing to teach us. After inoculating ourselves and members of our households, we visited orphanages, asylums, and poor houses, inoculating anyone who was willing. Today I inoculated you, so you would never know smallpox. I hope you will stop crying by suppertime.

I also submitted an article about our efforts to a medical journal. The editor wanted to publish it under a man's name to give it more credibility. I refused. The article will have my name on it, or not be published at all! Sure, it would be easy to hide under a male pen name, but what good would it do for women? Men often erase women's names from history. We cannot let them do that! If you ever do something great, let everyone know what a woman can do. And when that moment comes, I will be with you, wherever I happen to be.
With love forever,
Mother

She hugged the letter to her chest like the dearest treasure and sat with it, tears running down her cheeks. As she thought of her courageous and inspiring mother, those tears cleansed her very soul. She could feel her mother looking down at her, just as she promised she would. And Ella knew she had to try one more time. Replenished with energy, she ran downstairs, where Oli was finishing a plate of eggs Mrs. Bunting had served him. A couple of other tenants sat at the other end of the table, eating, and holding their heads with their hands.

Ella's voice rang. "Oli, I am going to try again to take the exams, and I will not leave until they let me."

One of the men eating looked at her with annoyance. "For heaven's sake, keep it down."

Oli lowered his fork. "They may call a constable and remove you by force."

"True, but they are less likely to use force if I'm not alone. Remember, you said you wanted me to throw our school board's hypocrisy back at them, like a modern-day Agnodice? How did Agnodice win?"

Oli frowned. "By the legend, she disguised herself as a male doctor in ancient Greece and was arrested for practicing medicine. The village women defended her in court, and supposedly overturned the ban on women doctors."

"Right, but it did not have to be only women who came to her aid. I want to come to the exams as Ella Parker, a female medical student, and ask to take the exam. The committee will ask me to leave, but I will not play into their hands and go quietly. And if I will come with friends, it will be easier to make some noise."

Mrs. Bunting came near. "Did you say you need friends to make some noise? I will be glad to help. Jane!" she called, "You can delay your leave by a few hours, can't you? Come with us. You can leave your baby with the girls."

"Alan can come with me. He is good at making noise too," Jane replied.

Oli chewed his lip. "Noise may not be enough. We need someone who can eloquently argue on Ella's behalf."

Ella frowned. "You mean a lawyer? But who?" Then it dawned on her. She and Oli answered simultaneously: "Daniel Carter!"

"Where do we find him?" Oli wondered.

She drummed her nails on the table, thinking. "The law school exams concluded yesterday. He's probably gone already."

Mrs. Bunting snorted. "If I know anything about young men finishing their education, the morning after their graduation they are stuffing themselves with greasy foods to absorb the spirits they drank the night before." She nodded towards the groggy patrons who mechanically chewed their eggs and black pudding. "Or they would be still in bed with a pounding headache. Either way, if Mr. Carter celebrated his graduation yesterday, I doubt that he has already left."

"That's brilliant, Mrs. Bunting. We will check the breakfast houses and cafes," Ella said with a smile.

"As well as lodging houses. And just in case, the library, and the law school," Oli added.

Jane beamed. "Mr. Carter left his address when he visited. I still have it." She took a note out of a drawer and handed it to Ella.

"It's best we split up to check as many places as possible. Then we should meet near the library in an hour," Oli suggested.

"Let's go," Ella cheered, but a knock came at the door. Mrs. Bunting answered, letting Matilda in. The midwife, carrying her trunks, first greeted Ella and then stared at her in disbelief.

"You are wearing a dress? What's happening?" the midwife asked, her eyes widening.

Ella beamed at her. "Matilda, please join me. We'll look for a friend of mine, Daniel Carter, and then I am going to take my exams."

An hour later, Ella and Matilda were catching their breath near the library doors.

Matilda fanned herself with vigor; her face showed displeasure. "I am quite weary after my journey. I wanted to see the campus, but not at such a mad pace!" she complained. "Are you sure you even need this Daniel Carter? A lawyer requires time to prepare his arguments. And this young man graduated only yesterday."

Ella sighed. They had visited a dozen dining establishments, searched through tables full of hungry or weary students, but Daniel was not among them. "I have this feeling that he would make a difference. But if the others didn't find him, we have no choice but proceed without him."

Oli came back, shaking his head. "I've checked his rooms, this library and the law school. He was not at his lodging, although he has not moved out. He's still at the campus."

"Then there's some hope that Jane or Mrs. Bunting has found him," Ella replied.

The landlady and the scullery maid with her baby

returned a few minutes later, unsuccessful in their quest of searching through coffee houses and taverns.

"We can't delay anymore. The exams will be over soon," Oli urged.

They started towards the medical building, with Oli and Ella speeding ahead, followed by Jane with her baby on her hip, and Mrs. Bunting and Matilda keeping the pace with difficulty. They walked in silence, and Ella could hear her pulse in her ears. When the outline of the medical school and the hospital became visible, Mrs. Bunting pointed towards a busy café. "Did anyone visit The Broken Egg? It's popular with the students."

No one responded, and Ella volunteered to check. Oli protested they had little time, but seeing that Ella was already sprinting towards the eatery, hurried after her. They scanned the dining room, panting. The room was full of students nursing their cups of steaming beverages.

One group seated at a long table seemed animated with conversation. A tall, young man walked up to them and spoke at full volume to overcome the noise from the other patrons. "Gentlemen, the Whig supporters are gathered at the town square for a rally. What do you say we treat them to some rotten eggs and tomatoes?"

"Hear hear!" an enthusiastic cheer went all around the table.

"He said 'Whig'. Did you say Daniel fought his duel over an argument about the Whigs and the Tories?" Ella asked Oli.

"Correct. I don't know which party he prefers but it sounds like these fellows may know."

Ella approached them and piped, "Pardon me, but would Daniel Carter be attending this rally you speak of?"

There was an annoyed groan from most of the people at the table. "Please don't say that name in front of me. My leg starts hurting whenever I hear it," one of them spoke, and Ella recognized Daniel's dueling opponent.

"Good. I mean, sorry to hear that. So do you believe he'd attend the event?"

"Attend? He likely organized it," the man who made the announcement replied and spat on the floor.

Ella and Oli glanced at each other and dashed back to the rest of their group.

"I propose Ella goes ahead to the exams while we head to the town square to find Daniel Carter," Oli said when they rejoined Jane, Matilda, and Mrs. Bunting.

"No. I already tried coming alone, and Dr. Miller dismissed me. This is my last shot, and I must get it right. I know we have little time, but we'll all go to the square together to find him. Luckily, it's not far." They proceeded, as Matilda muttered about her tight shoes, and Alan cried of hunger.

A large gathering of men, young and old, occupied the square. A tall fellow in his late twenties stood on top of two crates yelling his speech, at times interrupted by claps and cries of support. With all of the men wearing hats, it was difficult to find a face in the crowd. Ella and her friends went around asking about Daniel but received no helpful replies. The orator completed his fiery speech, and the crowd applauded with enthusiasm.

Oli caught Ella's hand. "Time to go. We'll never find him here."

"I have an idea," she replied and wedged among the attendants towards the front. An older gentleman, leaning on his cane, attempted to climb onto the makeshift platform. Ella curtsied and asked him to allow her to precede him. "Well, I always allow a lady to go first, but never in such a situation before," he said with amazement.

Ella ascended onto the platform. She believed her plan to be simple: yell for Daniel Carter to come to her and leave with him. But she had never been in a situation in which she had faced a large crowd of people, all staring at her. Her stomach lurched, and she felt nauseous. She tried to find a friendly face to focus on, but her eyes noticed Matilda and Mrs. Bunting; the midwife blanching and holding her hand to her heart, and the landlady fanning her. Ella's knees trembled. After drawing a deep breath, she tried to speak, but no sound came out.

"We can't hear you!" someone yelled when she stammered Daniel's name.

"Why don't you sing, darling! Or dance a jig!" a man in front bellowed, followed by the crowd's laugh.

Her cheeks flushed with embarrassment and anger. Those men listened to the male speaker before her. Shouldn't they give her the same respect? Her fury loosened her vocal cords, and she spoke in a clear and strong voice.

"I am looking for Daniel Carter. Mr. Carter, if you are here, please come to speak with me urgently."

"I am here." The young man raised his hand among the front rows.

"Your sweetheart missed you so much she came to find you," someone quipped loud enough for all to hear as Daniel pushed his way towards Ella.

Meanwhile, Ella felt much calmer standing on the platform. The faces in the crowd, warmed up by the incident, no longer scared her and even made her excited. She yelled with all her might, "Universities should accept women! Education for all!" and jumped off to the laughs and boos of the crowd.

Daniel gave her his hand and led her away. The young man looked amused and appalled at the same time.

"How may I be of help?" he asked when they stepped away from the rally. "Are you Alan Parker's sister? You look much like him."

"This *is* Alan Parker." Oli replied for her, approaching with Mrs. Bunting, Jane, and Matilda. "The bright medical student who saved your life was a young woman."

Daniel stared at Ella, then took her hand and kissed it. "I am at your service."

"I've been found out and prevented from taking medical school exams. I need your help as a lawyer to argue on my behalf in front of the committee of professors. Let's go, and I will explain more on the way."

Daniel shifted his feet. "I would love to help, but I am supposed to be the next speaker, and the topic means much to me. I don't know if you were listening, but we are rallying support for a fairer system of voting."

"Do you mean women voting?" Ella asked, wide-eyed.

"No. All adult male citizens. Currently only three percent of the population are allowed to vote," Daniel explained. "Women voting. What a peculiar idea," he muttered, frowning.

"Come on, you owe her. She saved your life," Oli argued, but a large group of men, yelling and whistling, drowned his voice out.

"Whig toadies, how would you like to taste some tomatoes?" someone bellowed, and a group of fellows began throwing rotten fruit and eggs at the crowd and the speaker.

"Confound it! The Tories are here," Daniel spat.

"Best we all leave now before we catch what those ruffians are throwing," Mrs. Bunting said, leading the women away from the panicked crowd where men pushed and shoved, hurrying to disperse.

"Or before we get entangled with the police," Oli added,

pulling the law student out of harm's way as an egg flew in his direction.

Constables' whistles and shouts became audible, and the mob forced its way out of the square. Ella and her friends struggled to extricate themselves from the pushing crowd, screaming for each other. Ella lost her footing and almost fell, but Daniel caught her by the shoulder and pulled her upright. Protected by his grip, she made her way back to the safety of the school campus, where she found the rest of her friends. Miraculously, no one was seriously harmed. Jane received a few shoves to her arms and back while protecting her baby; Ella tore the hem of her skirt, Oli lost a few buttons of his coat, Mrs. Bunting parted with her bonnet, and Daniel wiped the dripping egg mess from his hat. Matilda came out unscathed but pallid and shaken. After inspecting her troop, Ella, with the sureness of an army general, ordered them to follow her to the exams.

The strange procession trudged on the university's trimmed paths towards the medical building. As they walked, fatigued and winded, Ella related her story to Daniel, and he listened openmouthed. "I wish I had time to prepare. I could have researched the university rules for a loophole allowing you to receive a degree," he said.

"It will be a tough fight. The university does not allow women to enroll and therefore, graduate," Oli said.

"Of course not." Matilda snorted from the back. "Why would men hand women a stick they could use against them?"

"But if they won't give Ella her diploma, what's the point?" Jane asked.

"The point is to be heard and seen by the professors and prove my qualifications to them. I want them to acknowledge my accomplishments as a female student," Ella explained.

"Do you think it will make any difference?" Matilda challenged.

"I only know I must try. My mother, who never studied medicine, managed to inoculate people from smallpox and insisted on publishing an article under her own name. I would not be her daughter if I did not face these professors and give them my best shot."

"They will pick on you like vultures. Are you ready to show them, Ella?" Mrs. Bunting yelled.

Ella flashed a smile. "I am ready."

They all huffed and puffed when they reached the medical building. Oli led the group through the heavy doors and through the halls. As they approached the exam room, Ella leaned in to listen and shushed her friends' talk.

"Well, Dr. Miller, I have to say, apart from Mr. Higgins and a couple more fellows, the exams were disappointing. Certainly not the best group you taught. What a shame that Mr. Parker, of whom I heard so much, took ill."

"That was Professor Harris speaking, the head of the university," Oli whispered to Ella.

"Unfortunately, it is so." Dr. Miller's deep, melodic voice was unmistakable. "Medicine remains unpopular. Many parents object to their sons selecting this field. I was largely left with young men who coasted through classes without the work ethic required for the profession. I am at a loss as to who to choose as my intern."

With a deep breath, Ella decided to make her move. "I am here to take the exam," she announced, marching through the door.

The stunned committee stared back at her. Dr. Miller

flushed, Dr. Sanders blew cigar smoke, and the professors from other disciplines including chemistry and Greek, regarded her in dumbfounded silence. The small, grey-bearded man in the center, who she guessed to be Professor Harris, fixed his glasses, and raised his eyebrows.

Dr. Miller broke the heavy silence. "Young woman, you know perfectly well you are not welcome here. Will I have to send for the police to remove you?"

"They will have to remove all of us," Mrs. Bunting shouted as all of Ella's friends walked in. "And we are quite tired. Matilda, let us have a seat. And Jane needs to rest her legs and nurse her little one." The three women took empty chairs at the table, and Jane turned away to feed Alan. "Now we shall see how brave these gentlemen will be in trying to remove two women of respectable age and a young mother with her child," she added with smugness.

"This is an outrage!" the chemistry professor, Dr. Spears, exclaimed.

Daniel raised his hands in a peaceful manner. "Miss Parker is not asking for anything unreasonable. She wishes to take the exams like all other students."

Dr. Sanders blew another puff of smoke and said through his teeth. "We are finished with the exams. I have patients to treat." Other professors murmured in agreement.

Professor Harris cleared his throat. "What exactly is happening here? Did this woman take classes at the medical school?"

Dr. Miller scowled. "Yes, this lady took the name of Alan Parker and hoodwinked everyone into believing she was a man. I discovered her falsehood a week ago and requested her to leave before she embarrassed the university any further."

"It is a shame I had to go to such measures when men are granted admission freely," Ella remarked.

"The university does not accept women for a reason. Women dishonor their sex by seeking knowledge that is unnatural to them. Miss Parker, if that is her name, stole our time and the school's resources to satisfy her curiosity," Dr. Miller said.

"I paid my tuition like any other student," Ella rebutted. "And I worked harder than most."

Oli came forward. "Miss Parker's time was well spent here. Not only did she stand above the other students, but she also tutored me. Thanks to her, I caught up in my classes, passed my exams and received my degree."

"She saved my life," Daniel spoke up. "When the doctors were not around to help, she knew what to do. She was ready to risk expulsion to help me.

Jane turned to the committee with the baby on her breast. "She delivered my son. I went into labor with no midwife or doctor around, and she comforted me and caught the baby."

Alan gave a little whimper, as if on cue.

"She treated me and my servants when they were sick or hurt," added Mrs. Bunting.

"And I can attest to her knowledge of herbal remedies," Matilda piped up.

Professor Harris looked around. "This is most remarkable, but I am at a loss for what to do. The university's rules are clear on forbidding women from seeking degrees. The board would have to vote on changing the bylaws, and the motion would fail. Our board are men of tradition and will not look on such a change favorably. Look, this is all explained here," he took out a black leather-bound book of the university's rules.

"May I see this?" Daniel asked, and the professor passed the book to him.

The young man leafed through the pages, studying them.

"It says women cannot be accepted to the university and cannot be awarded degrees, but it does not say they cannot take the exams."

"Well, naturally, it is not necessary to say so, since they cannot study here in the first place."

"But it's not explicitly forbidden." Daniel pointed out.

"Did I see you yesterday at the law exams?"

"Yes, I've been a lawyer a whole day."

"It already shows." Professor Harris rolled his eyes and a few men chuckled.

"I understand I cannot receive a diploma, but please let me take my exams," Ella pleaded.

"Why do you wish to take them? What's the use?"

"I want to prove to myself, and to this esteemed committee, that I am qualified to practice medicine. And I want to set a precedent for future women. I am not the first woman to study medicine, and I won't be the last. Historians discovered accounts dating back to ancient Greece of women who broke rules to heal the sick. A statue of Anna Manzolini stands in the hall of this building, reminding us of her achievements in building medical models."

She takes another small step forward and straightens up, looking at each of them in turn. "My mother studied the inoculation techniques pioneered by Lady Mary Wortley Montagu and saved lives from smallpox. Women healers, like my friend Matilda, treat patients while the medical community scorns them. This is bigger than me. I want to take these exams to do my small part, so one day women can walk into this building, and any other medical school, welcomed at last."

Alan whined, and Jane rocked him in her arms. Ella scanned her audience. A couple of the professors looked back with warmth, but most showed emphasized indifference. Dr.

Sanders sneered with disdain, and Dr. Miller glared at the desk. Ella's chest was heavy with disappointment, not with herself, but with them. These were the brightest medical minds she admired, and they were rooted in their prejudice against women, despite having watched her progress.

Professor Harris, unlike the others, seemed intrigued. "I find such sentiment inspiring. For the last two years I have heard extraordinary accounts of Alan Parker and looked forward to his examination. Gentlemen, if you have another thirty minutes, I say we fulfill this young woman's request. Let us look at it as an experiment. Dr. Sanders, if you must go, please do. Midwifery is an optional subject, after all."

"I can spare thirty minutes," Dr. Sanders replied with a tight mouth.

"In that case, our visitors must step out, and Miss Parker, please stand over here by the chalkboard."

Matilda, Mrs. Bunting, and Jane, gave Ella quick embraces, Oli clapped her on the shoulder, and Daniel shook her hand. Then her friends shuffled out of the room, while Ella took her place in front of the examiners.

CHAPTER 22

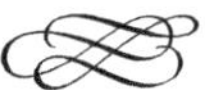

Ella stood before the committee, with Dr. Miller and Professor Harris facing her directly, and the other professors seated at the sides of the long table. Her hands trembled, so she hid them behind her back. She wished them to start, as the anticipation was torturing her.

Professor Harris spoke first. "Do we have her thesis?"

Dr. Miller took it out from the pile of papers and passed it over.

"While we examine it, please give us a summary," Professor Harris asked.

"Imagine you are strolling on the beach," Ella started, making eye contact with her audience, "and you see people rushing into the water and pulling a lifeless woman to shore. How would you attempt to revive the victim of drowning? Use your lancet to bleed her? Search for a barrel to roll her over one? Or my favorite, administer a tobacco enema? While rescuers have been known to apply all those methods, few can boast success. Doctors know that air is essential for life, and since she is not breathing, the aim should be to push air into her lungs."

She moved on to Dr. John Hunter's recommendation of blowing air into the victim's mouth or nose with a pair of double bellows. Oxygen would be even better than regular air, she argued, and described the experiment she conducted with mice. She then went on to discuss Hunter's suggestion of restarting the heart with electric shock by using a Leyden jar. When such a solution was not available, she proposed to perform a manual stimulation of the heart by pressing on the chest in regular repetitions. Two rescuers should work in tandem, with one concentrating on providing air to the lungs, and another on heart pumping, as described by Dr. Hunter.

She stopped after speaking for a good fifteen minutes, and no one interrupted or challenged her. Mr. Harris inquired if she had presented her experiment with mice in class. Ella confirmed she conducted it in front of Dr. Miller and his private students.

"Well, the thesis is well supported. We don't know if your recommendation would work in a real situation, but it is intriguing. I see Dr. Miller graded your work highly," Professor Harris said. *He must have graded it before he found me out and forgot to change my grade*, she thought. As confirmation, Dr. Miller glowered at the paper as if he wanted to burn it with his eyes.

With the thesis review out of the way, the oral exam began. Dr. Miller asked to describe steps of lithotomy operation. *Is he trying to embarrass me?* she wondered. In an unperturbed tone, she described how the bladder stone is probed by inserting a finger inside the patient's rectum and pushed till it bulges outward. Sometimes, in male patients, a curved metal tube would be pushed up the penis and into the bladder. Then the tube would be removed and replaced with a wooden staff, which acted as a guide when cutting towards the bladder. The surgeon would make an incision through the perineum, cutting until reaching the wooden staff, and use forceps to remove the stone. The fastest surgeons conducted such operations in under a minute.

Then Dr. Miller asked about treatments for syphilis. *He is trying to embarrass me.* It felt so childish, she wanted to laugh. Nonchalant, she described the symptoms, common locations of lesions, and the doses of mercury prescribed.

The chemistry professor, Mr. Spears, asked her to describe the method for Cadet's fuming liquid, which she answered with ease. The Greek and Latin professors gave her words and phrases to translate, and she had no trouble with their questions either.

Professor Harris looked at his watch. "We went well past the thirty minutes. Let's have one last question."

Dr. Sanders jumped in as though he was waiting for just that moment. "Describe how you would deliver a baby in a transverse lie."

First, she relaxed, thinking of Mrs. Bennett, the patient with this complication. Since she remembered the case, she trusted the answer would come to her. And then the ground sank beneath her feet. She recalled the day with stark clarity. They started the lesson when the midwife interrupted because of the dying patient, Anna Walters, whose twins were delivered by cesarian section. They never went back to study the transverse lie. Did Dr. Sanders realize this so that he could use it later as an opportunity to fail any student he wanted? She should have researched the method on her own, like she would for any other subject, but she avoided doing extra reading for midwifery. Thinking frantically to the day they examined Mrs. Bennett, she recollected one thing Dr. Sanders told them, and clutched at it like a drowning man to a straw.

"I would perform the podalic version," she answered.

"How is it done?" he fired.

She reddened, and his cold eyes and sneering mouth revealed that he knew he had her. *Midwifery is an optional subject*, she fumed inside. But all eyes were on her, and if she did not give an answer, she would be ridiculed. She forced herself to regain calmness and think. Her knowledge of Greek hinted that the word 'podalic' had to do with feet. Turn a baby by the foot? Deliver the baby feet first? Both made sense. She visualized the fetus lying across the womb, as she did when she touched Mrs. Bennett's belly. With aversion, she remembered the dissection, that same fetus revealed in that wrong position, which caused the hemorrhage and death. Oli said the baby would not fit through the birth canal. So how could the baby be turned by the feet? Again, she envisioned the procedure, her hand going inside the cervix, finding the baby's foot. It should help to put her other hand on the mother's belly while turning the infant inside.

"The version would be done with one hand assisting on the outside, and the other taking the fetus by the lower foot down and extracting the baby by that foot."

Dr. Sanders stared, saying nothing, his mouth twisting.

"Well, is she right?" Professor Harris asked.

Dr. Sanders nodded, gnawing on a nail.

Professor Harris looked around, then stated, "If this were a male student, we would be congratulating him and issuing his diploma. Miss Parker, we cannot do that for you today, but please be assured that you have given us much to think about. We don't know if you are a rule or an exception, but if your goal was to prepare the soil so that future flowers may bloom, I think you did your part beautifully."

There was no applause or compliments, but all eyes in the room, except for Dr. Sanders, looked with more kindness than before. Even Dr. Miller cocked his head, watching her with silent approval. After thanking them for the examination and the knowledge they shared with her through her schooling, Ella addressed Professor Harris. "I would like to contribute a large sum to the university if this institution would look more favorably on women's education."

Professor Harris leaned forward. "I can propose to the board that they organize a separate school for women. We would not start with medical studies, but something more traditional, perhaps, courses for teachers and librarians."

"And midwifery. Taught by midwives," Ella added. With that, she smiled and exited the room with her head held high.

Her friends waited in the foyer with the statues. When she approached with a triumphant grin, they gave a loud cheer and rushed to congratulate her. Ella was squeezed with hugs, patted on the back, and kissed on both cheeks. When they broke the embraces, Ella described the examination in detail, and they listened avidly, laughing at times. Caught up in the story, Ella did not notice that her listeners were staring somewhere else. When she realized their inattention, she found that Dr. Miller had joined in behind them. She stopped talking and gazed at him as well.

"Miss Parker," he said, "may we speak privately?"

Ella followed him to his classroom.

The familiar room felt like home. She grinned at the pair of skeletons. It was moving to realize she was standing inside those walls for the last time.

Dr. Miller cleared his throat, and she was surprised to notice that his hands trembled.

"Miss Parker," he spoke with gravity. "I was somewhat harsh with you. I much admired Alan Parker, and the deceit pained me. With your brilliant performance at the examination, I decided to put my hurt feelings aside. You were the best student in my class, and one of the best I've taught. Acknowledging that, I have a proposal for you."

Ella's breath caught.

The surgeon proceeded. "I will appoint you my apprentice if you continue playing the part of Alan Parker as convincingly as you have been these two years. If I am not mistaken, you want the position. You would first travel to hear some lectures in Edinburgh or Glasgow, or in other prominent medical schools, while the rumors die down. I would ensure your thesis gets published with my dedication. Then, in a year or so, you would return and work closely with me on all my surgeries and research. You may be called upon to treat patients, lecture to students and colleagues, and write cases to leading medical journals. The position would be a stepping-stone to a prominent career that could take you wherever you wish."

Ella's heart sang — he was offering her the position she desired. But then a thought hit her like a cold drizzle. The position was hers if she continued to play Alan Parker. To verify, she asked, "Do you mean I must continue to disguise my gender?"

Dr. Miller nodded. "That is an absolute condition. I will not be seen with a woman working by my side. Even if I allow such a thing, my colleagues, students, and patients would not. To be truthful, I don't see what you could be doing in medicine as a woman, outside of midwifery and herbal cures. You would not be able to open a practice, and no hospital would hire you. Alan Parker, on the other hand, could have a bright future."

She bit her lip. Change did not come easy or quick; Dr. Miller would not see beyond her gender. Part of her wanted to agree to his offer and see what happened. After all, she managed for two years. She could continue starting her days by binding her breasts till they hurt, practicing speaking in a deeper voice, and wearing men's clothing — the last part she even liked.

But lies, even made with the best intentions, would not stay hidden forever. And the bigger the lie was, the bigger the discovery, and the scandal would burn her and everyone around her.

"I am sorry, but I cannot accept your generous offer. I cannot pretend to be a man forever. I used to tell lies often because it was easier than telling the truth, or to keep people at arm's length, or for no reason at all. Playing Alan Parker involved enduring physical pain, distancing myself from friends, and living in constant fear of discovery. As a result, I was lonely and anxious, and my friendlessness almost killed me. I must forge my own path in medicine as a woman."

His lips curved into a tight line. "As you wish. Good luck in your endeavors, whatever they may be."

He was a man she greatly admired as a surgeon and an innovator, and she wanted them to part on good terms. "I will be forever grateful for the learning opportunities you provided for me. I hope to use all I learned to benefit patients."

He extended his hand to shake. Before taking it, Ella added. "If you want a loyal, inquisitive, and diligent apprentice, I recommend Dr. Higgins. He showed mastery of all subjects, original thinking, and genuine empathy towards his patients. And when I became ill, he stayed by my bedside for days and saved my life."

The doctor withdrew his hand as if a snake bit it. "I will not have that Jew as my apprentice! Bad enough I had to stand him for two years because of you. He hid behind a Christian name and your backing, but I smell his kind a mile away. He received his degree today and good riddance to him."

Ella crossed her arms. "My friend will not be insulted in front of me. I am disappointed in you, Dr. Miller. I worshipped you, but now my eyes are open to your short-sightedness and meanness. Farewell."

She turned on her heel and swept out from the classroom.

* * *

"But Ella, such an outing is not proper for a young woman. I will go with you as a chaperone," Matilda reasoned with Ella as they stood in Mrs. Bunting's dining room, waiting for Oli.

Many of the tenants had departed; Jane and baby Alan left, and the house became strangely quiet.

Ella smoothed her peach colored dress and fixed a bonnet that covered her short hair. "Sorry, Matilda, but this celebration is well overdue. I will show you more of the campus tomorrow, and we will have dinner somewhere nice. This night is for Oli and me."

Mrs. Bunting removed her apron and approached them. "Let the young people go, Matilda. We can trust Dr. Higgins with Ella. Let's have a fun evening of our own with some cherry liquor and apple tarts. You will tell me about your life in London." After fixing Ella's dress collar affectionately, Mrs. Bunting whispered into her ear. "If he steals a kiss from you, it's not a bad thing."

Ella's cheeks flushed like pink apples, and her heart raced.

Oli came through the door. Under Matilda's scrutinizing gaze, he assured, "I will take Ella to an appropriate place and bring her back at a decent time."

"Otherwise, she may turn into a pumpkin," Mrs. Bunting

said with a laugh. "Matilda and I will wait up for her, so keep your promise."

He took her to a tavern with cozy booths and a cheerful atmosphere. The patrons were loud, and the fiddlers were even louder. Servers hustled from table to table, carrying pints of beer and ale and large plates of meat. The diners included students, groups of workers, and older couples. Ella tensed when she noticed familiar faces from school, but then relaxed. It did not matter if they recognized her; university days were over.

"Should we have champagne to celebrate?" she offered.

"I am afraid this place does not serve anything that fine. Do you prefer wine or beer?"

"I had wine only once and never had beer," Ella confessed.

"Then you should taste both."

He ordered dark beer, red wine, and steaks. Ella found the wine too tart but enjoyed the beer and the scrumptious meat. They toasted Oli's graduation, Ella's seventeenth birthday, and her remarkable final. Ella told Oli of Dr. Miller's offer and his disgusting behavior when she recommended him in her place. He rolled his eyes, unperturbed . "After two years, I expect nothing else from Dr. Miller but I appreciate you endorsing me… Ella. I wish I had your courage to stand up to him, and to reveal my secret. In these two years, I all but forgot my birth name and the religious practices I grew up with. I hope that soon enough there will be non-church-based institutions open to men of all religions. Likely that will happen before women are accepted into universities."

Ella agreed. She wanted to make an impact, but she was not naïve. It would take many years and many more courageous women and receptive men to change the status quo.

"What are you planning to do?" she asked.

"My parents expect me to set up a practice in my community, but I would prefer to do that sometime later. I want to start at a military or naval hospital."

"It's not what I thought you would choose, but you should find plenty of opportunities," Ella reasoned. "Hippocrates said 'He who wishes to be a surgeon should go to war.'"

"Right. Even though I hid behind an English name, I felt like an outsider. I hope that if I contribute to the war effort, my patriotism would count for something. And I will learn to treat wounds and illnesses I am unlikely to see in a quiet little town. What about you? Are you going to London with Matilda to help her with midwifery and herbs?"

"I will pay a surprise visit home and check how my estate caretaker and lawyer are handling things. Afterwards, I will stay with Matilda, but not too long. I've decided what I want. Sometime this summer, I will commit my last act as Alan Parker and stand the naval board examination. It does not require a medical degree. My plan is to persuade Dr. Pesce and his captain to take me on as assistant ships' surgeon. I will not hide my gender anymore. When we are out at sea, the seamen would have to accept my help. It's not like they could go to anyone else. And I would treat injuries and diseases without anyone telling me what a woman can or cannot do."

Oli's eyebrows rose. "That sounds like quite an adventure. You, on a warship, among rough seamen, battles, and storms."

"I know, it's madness, but exciting as well."

After taking a long sip of beer, she took out a small, wrapped box and handed it to Oli. "Here is one last thing, your graduation present. I am sorry, your watch was sold, so I bought you this one instead."

Oli unwrapped the package and found a gold pocket-watch with tiny diamonds by the Roman numerals. He turned it over and read the engraved lettering: "*To Doctor Oliver Higgins for the fondest memories of medical school from his friends Alan and Ella Parker.*"

His cheeks flushed pink, and he beamed. "It's gorgeous, Ella. Thank you."

He leaned over and swept her into a hug. Ella, tipsy from her drinks, entertained the thought of kissing him. Many great firsts had already happened for her today, and she wondered if such an experience should be added to the list. Yet she decided against it. They were terrific friends, and she did not want things to become awkward between them. Her first kiss would go to someone else.

"We will write often and see each other again," Ella promised. "We should go before Matilda and Mrs. Bunting get worried. This has been a fantastic day, but I am quite tired."

Oli agreed. "Yes, we better get a good night's sleep. Tomorrow, we start our next chapter."

WRITE A REVIEW

I would love to know what you thought of
A Girl with a Knife!
You can write a review with your thoughts at:
• Amazon
• Goodreads

Connect with the author:
Instagram: Alina.Rubin.Author
Facebook: Alina Rubin Author

Website: alinarubinauthor.com
Email: alina@alinarubinauthor.com

AFTERTHOUGHTS FROM THE AUTHOR

Like Ella, who thought she was going to become a governess but became a medical student instead, I began one book and ended up with a different one. I had zero intention of becoming a writer until February 2021, when a story came into my head about a brave female ship surgeon and her friend midshipman who she rescued. I stayed up so many nights thinking about these characters, and I started writing the story just so I could sleep again. And guess what, I found that I love writing! It was quite a challenge, because I knew little of ships, battles, and nineteenth century medicine. So, I read and researched, visited museums, and enjoyed the new world opening to me.

When I finished my manuscript, however, I realized the journey won't be that easy. Smart readers made me see a serious plot hole. How did Ella become a doctor at the time when there were no women doctors? I had a couple paragraphs in the beginning, explaining that after she met Dr. Pesce, he sent her to medical school (without a disguise), and she did well there, but people pointed out that was too unbelievable, even if he wrote her the nicest recommendation letter. So I went back to work, thinking I will write a book that will combine the medical school years as Alan Parker and Ella's first voyage, but then the medical story took on a life of its own and became A Girl with a Knife.

Writing this book made me appreciate the safety, efficacy, and comfort of modern medicine. Many monumental medical discoveries were made in the 19th century, but not in the very beginning, where I have set the story. It was a bit of a shock to me that even the simple stethoscope or medical thermometer did not exist yet. I did my best with research about what instruments and procedures were available, used my imagination at times to fill the gaps or enhance the stories, and I apologize for any inaccuracies.

Here are some historical facts about 19th century medicine that pertained to the story:

In this book, I did not make a distinction between surgeons and physicians, allowing Ella to treat all kinds of patients, with surgery and other means. Surgeons were towards the bottom of the medical career ladder, and looked upon as manual practitioners, just above barbers. Physicians were on the top of the same ladder, and many of them did not touch patients during exams, relying on listening to patients' complaints. The field of medicine was not prestigious or well-paid for most, and medical students had a wild reputation. The universities accepted boys as young as ten, and thus it was possible for Ella to begin medical school at fifteen.

Before the germ theory, which came in the 1850s and is credited to Louis Pasteur, doctors rarely washed their hands and instruments. Several doctors, however, advocated for hand washing before the discovery of germs; one was Alexander Gordon, who wrote in 1795 that puerperal (childbed) fever was caused by infection transmitted by midwives themselves instead of miasmas. I resisted the urge to make Ella smarter than everyone else and wash hands often, but I made Oli inspired by Gordon's work.

Inflammation of the appendix and treatment by emergency surgery was described by Dr. Reginald Fitz in 1886, but one appendectomy had been successfully done in the 18th century, as Dr. Miller mentioned. If Dr. Miller would've done such surgery, he would become famous, but he's a fictional character.

The ovarian cyst surgeries were first done in 1807, and the first surgeons to attempt them were nicknamed "belly rippers".

The stomach pump was invented by Dr. Philip Physick and used by him in 1812 to save three-months old twins who were given laudanum and went into coma; one survived and fully recovered. Dr. Jukes in 1822 took ten ounces of laudanum and used the pump on himself as an experiment, which he survived.

I was hugely impressed by the story of Lady Mary Wortley Montagu, which I came across when I was looking for something inspiring that Ella's mother could have done. During her visit to Turkey in 1717, Lady Montagu witnessed the local women performing smallpox inoculations. She was a survivor of the disease, and after learning the procedure, had her children inoculated by a surgeon. (The term 'vaccination' came later, with Dr. Edward Jenner.) Then she approached Caroline, the Princess of Wales, to try the treatment, but the princess wanted it done on prisoners first. When the prisoners did not become ill, the Princess and her children agreed to receive inoculations. Mary Wortley Montagu published about her work under a pen name, and many people took her advice, including Catherine the Great of Russia.

Ella wrote her thesis on reviving drowned victims, and the methods she described were eventually adopted in 1959. With no crystal ball, she researched the work of Dr. John Hunter, who recommended mouth-to-mouth resuscitation and heart stimulation by electricity back in 1776. Otherwise, there was a society of rescuers in London ready to save people by tobacco enemas. Good luck! The same Dr. Hunter was also first to successfully treat popliteal aneurysm, avoiding amputation.

The first women doctors to receive medical degrees were Elizabeth Blackwell in 1847, first to graduate from a medical school in the United States, and Elizabeth Garrett Anderson, who in 1865 was qualified as the first female to gain medical qualifications in England. There was also Dr. James Barry, born Margaret Ann Bulkley, who completed medical school in 1813 and made a prominent career as a male doctor, her gender discovered only after her death. Barry's best known accomplishment was the first successful cesarean section in the English-speaking world, saving the mother and the baby.

Ella's schedule of classes, including midwifery as an optional subject, came from James Barry's biography, The Perfect Gentleman, by June Rose. I wanted to make sure Ella does not steal any credit from these amazing historical figures; yet there were many great people who've been erased from history, and maybe there were women who attended medical schools or performed successful surgeries but never received credit. It's possible their work eased the path for others, as Ella hoped she would by taking her exams.

Reading is my lifelong passion, and my favorite books that helped me write this story were: The Butchering Art: Joseph Lister's Quest to Transform the Grisly World of Victorian Medicine by Lindsey Fitzharris, and The Knife Man: Blood, Body Snatching, and the Birth of Modern

Surgery by Wendy Moore, as well as a wonderful novel A Girl in His Shadow by Audrey Blake. My favorite books that made a huge difference in my writing were: Save the Cat! Writes a Novel by Jessica Brody and Polish Your Prose: Essential Editing Tips for Authors by Harmony Kent and Nonnie Jules.

ACKNOWLEDGEMENTS

When I began writing, I wondered, who are all those people that authors thank in the end of their books, besides their family? Don't they sit at their desks alone and type their stories? As I progressed in my writing journey, I learned I can only take my stories so far. A writer needs feedback from trusted friends, and the best feedback comes from other writers. And thus, I thank my editor Kirsten Rees, especially for how she handled feedback with my first manuscript, telling me that my book deserved better, and that I had much to learn and fix before coming back to her for a professional edit.

Thank you to my wonderful beta readers, Becky Paroz, for teaching me that good fiction must be believable, Jane Charney, for her encouragement, Becky Smalley, for ensuring nothing comes too easy to Ella, and Christy K Lee, for dissecting the medical scenes and adding a sprinkle of romance to the story. Thank you to my first readers, Inessa Levin and Olga Goldenberg, for believing in me. A special thank you to the Niles Library Writing Club and its wonderful members.

In the end of the story, Ella succeeds not only thanks to those friends who were by her side, but those who knew her before she went to medical school. Her medical journey started with her mother. As I was writing, I felt the love and guidance of my mom and dad, Yelena and Joseph Frumkin, both gone too soon, as well as my grandparents, Oktyabrina and Leonid Fridman, and my father-in-law, John Leach. Their memory is a blessing I carry with me.

I did not name Ella's science tutor, but he had an important role in steering Ella on her journey to become a doctor. My teachers in Prospect High School, Mr. Kevin Hickey, Mrs. Barbara Fryzel-Marquette, and Mrs. Barbara Schuman had a great impact on me as an avid reader and a writer.

Huge thank you to my husband Vitaly, for his patience, and for designing the experiments with mercury oxide, inspired by the work of Joseph Priestley, who invented seltzer. No live mice were hurt in the process, only fictitious ones. Thank you to our daughter Elanna for all she teaches me, and just for coming into our lives.

Most of the names in this book are random, but a couple have a special meaning to me. Dr. Catherine Pesce is a talented and a compassionate surgeon. Oliver Higgins's real name is David Fridman, as revealed in the story; he was named after my grandfather Leonid Fridman, who had to change his birthname (Israel) to enter law school and pursue career in law enforcement in USSR.

Lastly, my huge respect and thanks to medical workers everywhere. What you do is incredible and inspiring.

ABOUT THE AUTHOR

Alina Rubin is an IT professional and a mom, who, during the pandemic, used the time and energy saved on the commute to write an adventure story about a nineteenth century woman surgeon. Writing became her passion, and her characters took her on a journey beyond her wildest dreams.

Alina obtained a B.S. and M.S. in Business and Information Technology from DePaul University. She lives in Chicago with her husband and daughter. When not working or writing, she enjoys yoga, hiking, and traveling. A Girl with a Knife is her debut novel, the first book of the Hearts and Sails series.

NO JOB FOR A WOMAN

HEARTS AND SAILS, BOOK 2

Will Ella secure a job on a ship, survive the perils of the sea, and win the respect of seamen and officers?

Find out in No Job for a Woman: Hearts And Sails, Book 2.

www.ingramcontent.com/pod-product-compliance
Lightning Source LLC
Chambersburg PA
CBHW071242300726
48975CB00002B/524